When Love Takes Over

JACOB Z. FLORES

Dreamspinner Press

Published by
Dreamspinner Press
5032 Capital Circle SW
Ste 2, PMB# 279
Tallahassee, FL 32305-7886
USA
http://www.dreamspinnerpress.com/

When Love Takes Over
Copyright © 2013 by Jacob Z. Flores

Cover art by Michael Breyette
http://www.breyette.com
Cover design by Paul Richmond

Cover content is being used for illustrative purposes only
and any person depicted on the cover is a model.

ISBN: 978-1-62798-022-7
Digital ISBN: 978-1-62798-023-4

Printed in the United States of America
First Edition
August 2013

For Bruce,

The day I met you, love took over.

$$Chapter\ One$$

ZACH KELLY collapsed onto his bed. Had he heard Ben right? Did the man he'd spent the last three years with just dump him? No, that couldn't have been what he'd heard. Sometimes he didn't pay attention. Drifted off in midconversation when an idea for a story hit as it often did. Perhaps that's what happened.

Yeah, he'd been thinking about his latest plot bunny that just so happened to start with a bad breakup scene. That wasn't Ben. He'd simply been confused.

"What did you say?" he asked. His constricted throat muffled his words into a whisper.

Ben sighed. He ran his fingers through his blond hair and rolled his eyes. "Why do you want me to repeat myself? Isn't it enough that I said it once? Why does *everything* with you have to be *so* difficult?"

"I just don't understand." Zach didn't know what else to say.

Ben sighed again. If he sighed one more time, Zach might have to toss him out the bedroom window. He could do it too. He was stronger and taller than Ben. He wouldn't even break a sweat.

But Zach also knew he'd never do something like that. It just wasn't who he was.

"I just want to understand," Zach muttered. He was being pitiful, and he hated that. Why could he never man up and deal with life's crap? Why did he always bend over and ask for seconds instead?

"What do you want to understand?" Ben asked. The sweet voice that had greeted him every day turned lemon sour and stone hard. "I can't do this anymore, Zach. It's over."

Zach couldn't process the information. He'd gone out to buy some bread for dinner, anticipating a quiet evening at home and maybe a movie. He never saw this coming. Sure, there had been some distance between him and Ben but not this much. At least, he didn't think so, but he'd often gotten *many* things wrong before.

Apparently, this was just one more to add to the list.

"It's time for us to cut our losses," Ben said. "This isn't going anywhere. Not anymore."

If he could have found the energy to laugh, Zach would have. When they first met three years ago, Ben had thought they had a lot of potential. Ben had introduced himself to Zach at their gym's boot camp class. Ben had asked him to be his workout partner. He'd always been terribly shy, so he had only answered with a head nod and then barely spoken to Ben for the remainder of the class. That had apparently appealed to Ben because afterward, Ben had asked him out.

Their date had been a disaster. He spilled his wine all over Ben's almond-crusted chicken and then almost knocked over the table when he stood to help Ben clean up the mess. He had secretly hoped his persistent clumsiness might take a break for the evening, but Zach stayed true to form and closed out the night by falling down in the parking lot after tripping over the curb.

Ben had thought his clumsiness endearing, especially since Ben fancied himself a perfectionist. Ben had thought they complimented each other well. That they had the potential to last a lifetime.

From Ben's now distant, cool gaze, however, that was evidently no longer the case.

"What happened?" he finally asked when the shock surrendered its control of his vocal cords. "What changed?"

Ben stood before him, scanning the ground for some unseen answer. After a few moments, he shrugged and then stared blankly at Zach.

"That's it?" he asked. A raging fire coursed through his blood. "*That's* my answer? A *shrug*?"

"What do you want, Zach?"

"How about the truth? You owe me that much."

"Alright, how's this for truth? I'm tired, Zach."

"Of what?"

"Of you." Ben's answer shot through him like an arrow. "You're too much work. Like a big, redheaded, hairy baby. I've tried to make you better. Into the man I knew you could be. But you're never going to be him. You're happy with yourself. And that's good. I guess. But I'm not happy with it. I deserve better." He paused and then absently added, "So do you."

If he weren't sitting on the bed already, he'd have collapsed to the floor. Ben had never spoken to him so callously before. Sure, Ben wasn't the easiest person to live with. He liked things done a certain way. He had a procedure and a process for everything. The mail had to be stacked on the small table by the front door. The toilet paper had to hang down toward the back, not drape toward the front. Dates had to be scheduled in advance, and surprises weren't exactly welcome. If anything in life didn't follow Ben's rules, there was hell to pay.

That was what he didn't understand. He'd spent the last three years making sure Ben got what he wanted. He'd done a lot of work to make Ben happy.

Maybe that was part of the problem. Maybe Ben was tired of Zach being a wuss.

"Can we fix this?" he asked Ben. God, he hated how pathetic he sounded. He needed to find where he'd put his balls.

Ben's blank expression answered his question. He used to look at Zach with love, at least when he wasn't pissy or annoyed at Zach's clumsy nature. Even in the height of a particularly bad mood, there had always been some affection reflected in Ben's green eyes. Now, Ben looked at him as if he were a stranger.

The arrow in his heart dug deeper and twisted.

"So, that's it, then?" Zach asked, unsure what else there was to say. For a writer, he sure was at a loss for words a lot. Maybe that was why his book sales sucked worse than a two-bit man whore.

Ben gave no answer. Just more silence and a sigh. Ben then glanced over at the clock on the nightstand. He evidently had somewhere more important to be.

Zach blinked back his tears and swallowed the lump in his throat.

"I'm sorry," Ben said after a few moments. His voice broke the silence like an exploding cannon. "I truly am."

Although the words were apologetic, the tone expressed no such emotion. Ben sounded irritated, like he often did when Zach proved too dense for Ben's liking.

He had to get the hell out of there. Now.

Zach stood up from the bed and crossed to the closet. He reached inside, grabbing his suitcase from the floor and his backpack from the chair that sat to the left. He placed both on the carpet just outside the closet door.

Ben said nothing. He simply watched in silence, but the arch to Ben's eyebrow told Zach Ben was interested in what he planned on taking with him. What he wanted to take was the big screen television or the expensive leather couch they had bought a few months ago, but none of those things would fit in his luggage. Ben's head would. If he could stuff the oversized melon filled with Ben's own high opinion of himself into his backpack.

But instead of acting out or saying the awful things that crossed his mind, Zach kept mum like the lame-ass loser he was. He also only reached for the items that were his, not anything they'd purchased together.

He shoved a couple pair of jeans in his duffel bag. He lifted out his suit jacket, the one Ben had bought for him to wear on their last trip to New York. The trip that Ben had planned because Zach sucked at making travel arrangements and packing appropriate attire. The one trip Ben had allowed him to be cruise director for hadn't gone over well. He had booked accommodations not to Ben's liking and then didn't bring clothes worthy of dining or clubbing. Ben had been mortified and shanghaied all future travel plans after that debacle.

That was why Ben purchased the suit. He wanted Zach to look the way Ben expected him to.

Before he could stop himself, he turned around, suit jacket in hand, and asked, "Should I?" Then, realizing what he'd done, he put the jacket back. Even now, after Ben had kicked him to the curb, he fell back on asking Ben if he should or shouldn't do something. He needed help. Or a lobotomy. Yeah, an ice pick shoved into his eye just *might* do the trick.

"Just take the jacket," Ben blurted. "It's yours!"

Zach didn't answer. He tore some of his favorite shirts off the hangers and tossed them into the open suitcase. He then yanked open his assigned drawer in their dresser and emptied the contents on top of the balled up shirts.

While he tossed his underwear into the disorganized mess, he watched Ben's blank expression change. He was no longer indifferent. The absolute mess he was making of his belongings and the fact that he wasn't taking any of the nice clothes Ben had purchased over the years evidently pissed him off. Ben's face burned red, and his hands clenched into fists.

"You're making a mess!" Ben shouted as he crossed over to the closet. "And you're not even taking the good stuff." He carefully removed the button-down shirts from some Italian designer Zach couldn't remember. Ben then began folding them and placing them into a nice, even pile on top of the chest of drawers. "You might as well take them," he told Zach. "Lord knows, I can't fit into them. I'm far too lithe for your clothes."

If Zach had a bat in his hand, Ben's head would be a bloody red spot on the wall.

"I don't want them," Zach told Ben.

Ben didn't listen. He continued folding the shirts into perfect little squares. When he was done, he headed for the open suitcase. He stood over it, eying its contents. No doubt trying to decide how best to reorganize the clothes until it met Ben's approval.

When he bent down to begin the process, Zach snapped. He yanked the suitcase out of Ben's reach, spilling his clothes onto the bedroom carpet. "Don't touch my shit."

"I agree," Ben replied with a crooked smile. "Your clothes *are* shit. That's why I want you to take the *nice* ones."

Zach couldn't respond. His throat once again closed shut. He swept the pile of tumbled clothes back into his open suitcase and zipped it shut. He headed for his desk. On it rested his laptop, which sat next to the *Out* magazine he had been reading that morning, the one that had all those entrancing pictures of a place called Provincetown at the back of the magazine. He'd wanted to discuss possibly vacationing there with Ben. In fact, daydreaming about it kept him from writing, but now, the sight of the magazine and the vacation they would never have together punched him in the stomach.

He scooped up his laptop and placed it in his backpack. He turned to leave, but he just couldn't leave the magazine behind. So he rolled it up, stuck it in the back pocket of his shorts, and headed for his suitcase.

With it in hand, he exited the bedroom, the one where he and Ben had planned the future they would no longer have. He left the apartment without a word and with a shattered heart.

He had no idea where he would live, but right now that didn't matter. He had a plan.

He was going to Provincetown.

ZACH sat in the Starbuck's just a few blocks from his apartment. He hadn't made it very far, but if he had his way, he'd be jetting across the country to Massachusetts and landing on the Cape. That was if he could actually find a room.

Right now, he was on hold with Sebastian, one of the owners of the Carpe Diem, one of the swankier places to stay in Provincetown. He couldn't really afford it, but he couldn't pass up the opportunity to stay at such a high-end bed-and-breakfast. It would serve as a *fuck you* to Ben. To show him that he damn well could choose a nice place to stay.

But that wouldn't work if he couldn't get a room. He'd tried searching online, but most places had already been booked for the past few months. Provincetown was evidently more popular than the ad at the back of his magazine led him to believe. Making no progress over the Internet, Zach hoped blind phone calls might provide better luck.

So far, nothing had turned up during his first three attempts. Zach hoped Sebastian would come back with good news.

"You there, Mr. Kelly," Sebastian said on the other end of the phone. The man's German accent was thick.

"I'm here," he answered far too quickly. He needed to calm down. He didn't want to appear desperate and then be price gouged.

"I'm afraid that we have nothing here. We haven't had anything available for months. It's very hard to find spur-of-the-moment accommodations in P-town."

Zach squeezed his cell phone until he heard the plastic casing pop. Why had Sebastian put him on hold if they had been booked solid for weeks? Did the man get his jollies from raising people's hopes and then chastising them for not planning properly? He'd gotten enough of that from Ben.

"However," Sebastian said, "I do have a friend who's had a last-minute cancellation at the property he manages. It's a condo, though. Not a bed-and-breakfast. I called him to see if it was still available, which is why I had to put you on hold."

If it were possible, he would leap through the phone and kiss Sebastian on the lips. With lots of tongue. "I'll take it," he answered.

Sebastian laughed. "Let me give you the information, so you can make the arrangements."

"Thank you," Zach said as he fished a pen out of his backpack and wrote the information on his hand. "I really appreciate it. I'll call Mr. Travers now."

"Don't call him Mr. Travers," Sebastian warned. "He doesn't like that. Everyone calls him Gary."

"Gary," Zach said with a nod. "Got it."

Zach ended the call and then quickly dialed the number he had scrawled across his palm. As he hit send, he scanned the coffee shop, which was filled with couples talking to each other and laughing. Sitting there with his packed bags, he no doubt looked like someone who'd been dumped on his ass. How many people were talking about him and pitying him right now?

If he had the balls, he'd tell them to suck his cock, but that was far too vulgar and hostile for Zach. So he plastered on a fake smile, pretending to be someone on vacation in Houston instead of trying to get as far away from this fucking place as possible.

"Hello," the voice on the other end answered. "You've got me. Now what do you want to do with me?"

Zach held the phone away from his ear and stared at the caller ID. He checked the displayed phone number with the one Sebastian had given him. He had to have dialed the wrong number. The man who picked up had answered with far more familiarity than he was accustomed to. One quick check of the numbers, though, told him he had not.

"Don't be shy," the voice in the phone said. "I won't bite. Unless you want me to."

"Mr. Tra—" He stopped himself, remembering Sebastian's warning. "Gary, this is Zach Kelly. Sebastian from Carpe Diem said you might have a condo I could rent for the week."

Gary squealed in delight over the phone. He imagined from Gary's reaction that the man was most likely jumping up and down as if he had just won the showcase showdown on *The Price is Right*.

"I'm so happy you called, Zachary. When Sebastian said he was sending someone my way, I about pissed my panties. We had our fourth unit booked solid for months. A dear friend of mine from Boston, who was supposed to be staying this week, had a death in the family. Naturally, he had to cancel, and I just couldn't in good conscience charge him for the week. Even though I could have."

Gary rambled on, telling Zach how awful it was to lose even a week's worth of a rental. Evidently, the Townies, or the year-round residents of Provincetown as Gary explained, made eighty percent of their income for the year during the summers. Losing just one week on a rental could prove disastrous.

"You, my dear, sweet Zachary, have helped us avert financial disaster."

What was he supposed to say? He wasn't accustomed to someone who emoted as much as Gary. After three years with Ben, he'd grown used to silence and scowls. "I'm glad I could help," he finally said, feeling the need to say something.

"Help?" Gary asked. His voice rose an octave, not in distress but in incredulity. "You're a godsend, I tell you."

"Well, I wouldn't go that far," he hedged. "I'm just a man in search of a port in the storm."

"Hmm," Gary said into the phone. "I can tell there's a story there."

Zach didn't answer.

"I *love* a good story, so when you get here, you'll tell me *all* about it. And I don't take no for an answer. Just a little FYI."

A smile inched its way across Zach's face even though he tried to stop it. "We'll see about that."

"You've never been to P-town before. Have you?"

"How can you tell?" Had he come across as inept at travel as Ben seemed to think he was?

"Well, besides the fact that you're looking for a place to stay this late in the season?" Before Zach could open his mouth to explain, Gary rolled on with the conversation. "It's just something I sense in your voice. You don't have that rabid determination I typically hear in the horny bastards who come here. You sound so sweet. Innocent. And I gotta tell you, I just love popping the cherry of a P-town virgin. In fact, I'll even be your date to Tea Dance."

What the hell was a tea dance? And why would *anyone* dance while drinking tea? He couldn't. That was for fucking sure. He was too much of a klutz to be able to carry a beat and a cup full of tea at the same time.

He'd likely spill the tea, slip in the mess, and then sprawl onto the middle of the dance floor. At least, that was the way things always seemed to work for him.

He also wasn't so sure he wanted to attend this tea dance with someone who wanted to pop his cherry. Although he definitely liked the idea of chomping down on some fresh produce, he planned to choose who sampled his goods.

He might be single now, but that didn't mean his samples were free.

"Alright, Zachary. I think I have everything I need," Gary said. "Just get yourself to P-town, and you'll be in good hands."

"Will do, Gary. See you soon." Zach ended the call and stared around at the busy Starbucks. The impact of what he'd just done dawned on him for the first time. He was going to Provincetown. On a spur-of-the-moment trip. This wasn't like him. At least not the man he'd become.

Years ago, in a childhood he preferred not to remember, he'd once been impulsive. He just wasn't that person anymore.

Maybe that was what he needed. To find the person he once was. And maybe he'd find him in Provincetown.

Chapter Two

ZACH leaned his head against the thrumming interior of the small puddle jumper that flew him to Provincetown, Massachusetts. Gazing out into the azure sky, he looked down upon the many sail and motor boats which spotted the cobalt ocean down below.

I should just go home.

He couldn't believe the thought to return to Ben still persisted. It ate away at him as he drove to the airport and stepped into the security line. He'd never traveled alone, and he immediately wanted Ben by his side. Ben had become his security blanket, the person he used to shield him from the unpleasant aspects of life. The need for Ben had grown so powerful, he had almost bolted out of the airport. Thankfully, he had moved to the front of the line before he could make an ass of himself.

He really *was* a loser.

To free his mind from the nagging call to head home, he focused on the ships below. Their passing cut the ocean into white, foamy ribbons that skimmed across the top before once again being consumed by the sea that surrounded them. Sprinkled around the boats and their passengers, who were enjoying a warm summer day in the harbor, small patches of land dotted the water. Like bright oases, the lush greenery of the islands staked their claim in defiance to the expansive waters that sought dominion.

A kinship formed between Zach and those islands, especially now that he'd been stranded by the man he loved in the middle of life's ocean. He briefly entertained the idea of pulling out his laptop and composing a few lines for a new novel. But that required too much effort. Besides, according to the reviews of his books, he apparently sucked at writing.

Among other things. Like relationships.

His desire to write died as quickly as it was born.

What he wanted to write, if he had the energy or the determination, was that he, too, was alone in a merciless sea with nothing but his own rocky foundation to support him. But there was a difference, and Zach saw it plainly. There were no boaters frolicking in the waters about him. No one navigated their ship to dock where he lived. In fact, all boats had raised anchors, unfastened their moorings, and bid him bon voyage as they departed for oceans unknown that no longer included him.

Yeah, he definitely had no desire to write that. It made him sound more pathetic than he already felt, and this trip was supposed to help make him feel better. Not worse.

I should just go home.

He had never heard of Provincetown, which sat at the outermost part of Massachusetts, before he saw it in his magazine. Since then, and especially since Ben dumped him, the pictures of dozens of men, embracing each other and having the time of their lives, called to him like a siren song. He longed to lose himself as one among the droves of gay men who, like the ad explained, converged upon the Cape every summer, to indulge both spoken and unspoken fantasies that could only be found on its sandy shores.

And after the repressed way he'd lived his life over the past twenty-odd years, he had more than a few inhibitions clogging up his pipes. Hell, it had been so long since his pipe had been properly handled that he feared a stiff breeze might be all he required.

Zach needed an escape. That much was certain. If he hadn't fled what had once been his home, he was uncertain what might have become of him, even though he hated going places by himself. His shy nature practically dictated that someone accompany him everywhere he went.

No matter how much the prospect of vacationing by himself on the other side of the country frightened him, it was something he had to do. He couldn't go on living as an outsider in his own life.

He needed to change how other people saw him and how he saw himself.

Then maybe he'd understand the pain that wrenched his insides and why thoughts of returning home followed him through the security lines, across the skies from Houston to Boston, and into the propeller plane that now carried him to his destination. No matter how hard he tried to banish the notion from his mind, the idea of heading home coiled about him like a python intent on consuming him whole.

Even though he wanted to go home, there was no home to go back to.

The realization made him lash out. He slammed his elbow against the wall of the plane and though it felt good, it also drew what he hated the most—unwanted attention. The man who sat in front of him looked over his shoulder disapprovingly. Zach fought his desire to tell the man dressed in a tight black muscle T-shirt that his fauxhawk was meant to be on the head of a man twenty years younger. If he'd been the same person he once was in his youth, he would have.

Zach kept mum instead.

These days, he cared more about vanishing within the crowd than standing out in it, so he apologized for his disturbance and returned his gaze to the world outside, just like the lame-ass loser he'd allowed himself to become.

God, not only was he a mass of pent-up frustration and a certified klutz, but he'd traded his cock for a pussy.

Maybe that was why he'd lost everything that had been important to him.

Ben, his ability to write, and the future he'd once thought carved out in stone.

Besides Ben, writing had been the one thing he could count on. He had yet to become successful at it, but being an author was his dream. He wanted to quit his daytime teaching job, write full time, and live happily ever after.

That happy ending was supposed to have been with Ben, and when he thought about how that dream had been killed for him, by the very same man he once shared the dream with, his breath caught in his throat.

He needed to understand *why* it had happened and *why* he had changed so much from the person he once was.

I should just go home.

If he could have punched himself in the head, he would have. It was obvious that Ben no longer cared for him, that he had stopped loving him some time ago. He needed to let the notion of returning home go.

"There she is," said the man with the fauxhawk in front of him. "The Pilgrim Monument. We're almost there, boys!"

The announcement caused an eagerness to spread through the cabin. Where before everyone had sat in quiet contemplation, the mood within the plane changed. A renewed sense of vigor permeated all those around him.

Their eyes flickered with life as they each gazed admiringly at the impressive gray-bricked structure that heralded their descent into Provincetown.

The tower, which proudly stood upon its swath of land, didn't elicit the same reaction from Zach as it did from the others in the cabin. They murmured excitedly to one another like children on a school bus.

He didn't see what all the fuss was about.

The monument was architecturally beautiful. It even reminded him of a giant rook on a chessboard, but the mere sight of the structure and the peninsula didn't bring forth a wave of celebration as it had for the others.

This wasn't a no-holds-barred vacation for him like it was for them. Zach had serious work to do on himself. *For* himself. He had to find his way again and figure out why he'd allowed himself to be turned into a doormat. He refused to let anyone treat him like Ben did. Ever again.

So while the other passengers came to life like blossoming buds before the sun, Zach took a deep breath, signaling to himself that he was ready.

Even though he still longed for home. And for Ben.

IT DIDN'T take Zach long to collect his luggage and find a cab to take him from the airport to the condo. Unlike the other guys on his flight, who arrived with two huge suitcases *and* two carry-on bags each, he only brought his small travel bag, containing a portion of his clothes from his apartment, and a backpack, which carried his laptop.

Evidently, part of the Provincetown experience required constant wardrobe changes, and since he'd only brought about three or four days' worth of clothes, he'd come underprepared for this adventure.

That was par for the course in Zach's world, though.

He rarely took the requisite time to plan or research a trip. Not that he actually had time to plan this one. Still, he was quite content with packing light and bringing along only the essentials. That used to drive Ben crazy.

Ben enjoyed planning trips as much as the vacation itself. It was part of the experience, or so he used to say. Ever since New York, Ben had booked the flights and hotels. It was Ben's way of making sure they stayed in quality accommodations instead of the cheap deals Zach preferred. Ben even made a packing list for each trip that Zach was expected to follow to the letter.

Since Ben drew up a detailed itinerary for each hour of their vacation, he made certain Zach's wardrobe reflected the plans.

At first, Zach thought the behavior a bit much, but it made Ben happy. Besides, he relished the way Ben took care of him. It made him feel special.

Now that he thought about it, maybe he had relied on Ben too much over the years. Perhaps Ben tired of taking care of all the little details that always seemed to slip Zach's notice.

Maybe that was why they were no longer together.

"This must be your first time here?" the taxi driver asked from the front seat.

The voice startled Zach out of his thoughts. He'd completely ignored her since he had entered the cab and given her the condo's address. He hadn't even realized that they had pulled away from the terminal or that they had been driving in silence for a few minutes.

"It is," he replied, staring into the rearview mirror at the driver's kind face. Her long silver hair was tied back in a ponytail, and the breeze from the open windows whipped it back and forth as if she were riding horseback instead of driving a car. "How could you tell?"

"You packed way too lightly for someone who's ever been here before. Most guys bring more clothes than they'll ever wear. Especially since most of them walk around half-naked down Commercial Street anyway."

Zach attempted a smile, but he wasn't happy enough to pull it off. She either didn't notice or was kind enough to let it slip.

"Where's home?" she asked.

While it was a simple enough question, Zach had no answer. He no longer knew where home was. Ben had moved on. He hadn't spoken to his father since Zach's hometown found out Gil Kelly enjoyed cock as much as Zach did. That little revelation shattered Zach's core. He'd spent so much of his life trying to be perfect for his father that when he realized how imperfect a man his father was, Zach could no longer deal with him.

He and his sister Sami were close, but she had her own family to take care of, and Zach had no close friends to stay with for the interim.

He wasn't just alone. He was completely isolated.

"You okay?"

He shifted his attention back to the rearview mirror and found genuine concern reflected in his driver's kind, wise eyes.

"No," he admitted. It was the first time he acknowledged the fact out loud. Doing so didn't make him feel any better.

"Want to talk about it?"

"Not really."

She nodded in understanding and drove on in silence.

Zach closed his eyes and focused on the wind rushing through the cab. He expected a heavy brine scent to engulf his senses, especially in a town that practically existed in the middle of the ocean. Instead, the breeze smelled sweet, as if the wind carried a bouquet of flowers in its invisible arms.

He inhaled deeply, drawing the refreshing fragrance into his body. He hoped the candied fragrance would chase away the fear and sadness that resided deep within. Although he scented promise in the air, it seemed incapable of breaking through the doldrums that held him fast.

As they continued through town, the landscape passed him by. Cape Cod-style houses lined the street. He found their steep, pitched roofs and large central chimneys enchanting. Though petite, their solid, squat frames bespoke a sturdiness of foundation, as if they openly defied Mother Nature and taunted her to bring whatever stark weather she could summon to challenge their fortitude.

The simplicity of their designs also fascinated him. He'd grown accustomed to the overzealous, grandiose nature of south Texas living, where bigger always seemed better. These houses held none of that bravado. No embellishments marred the structures, and no ostentatious decorations hung from the doors or windowpanes.

These homes didn't boast or try to be more than what they were. They simply existed.

Zach envied that characteristic.

He found it almost impossible to simply be who he was. He always felt the need to apologize for himself and change whatever people didn't like about him until he'd become whatever they might need.

That had started long ago, when Zach was a kid trying to live up to a potential he could never reach.

Of course, now that Zach gave it serious thought, his promise shouldn't look as far away as it once did. After all, his father had been pretending to be straight when he wasn't. His father wasn't perfect. He couldn't be perfect.

He could only be Zach Kelly. Nothing more. Nothing less.

Still, some habits didn't just die. They came back from the dead like flesh-eating zombies.

"We're here."

Zach turned his attention to the long, gravel driveway. The road beneath them crunched loudly as they approached the row of condominiums that would be his home for the next week.

They were nothing spectacular. A gray and weathered wood shingle frame topped with a gray asphalt roof. A stained wooden deck wrapped around the front of the structure with the condos at either end claiming the larger share of the patio.

Ben would have hated it immediately.

The taxi driver pulled in front of the condo on the far left, and as she got out of the car, he found himself incapable of exiting the vehicle. Once he stepped out, his arrival would be complete.

That meant everything that had driven him to flee Texas had won.

"You didn't pay all this money to come here and sit in my cab, did you?" the taxi driver asked as she pulled open the left rear door. In her aged hands that possessed a quiet strength he couldn't understand, she held his small suitcase and his backpack.

"Maybe" was all he replied.

She chuckled and reached out to him. Zach stared at her offered assistance, and the genuineness of the gesture made him feel less alone. Even though she knew nothing of his circumstances, it made him feel safe.

He hadn't felt that way in a long time. Far longer than he cared to admit.

"Thanks," he told her as he took her warm hand in his and left the vehicle behind.

She handed over Zach's belongings and nodded to the condo on the far right. "Gary and Quinn live there," she told him. "They own this place. They're great guys and can give you the lowdown of this crazy town. Gary's usually home at this time, so just go on over. He'll take good care of you."

Not knowing what else to say, Zach simply nodded in response and then paid the woman for the ride. He pointed his feet toward the condo she gestured to, but before he made it halfway across the pebbled drive, she called out to him.

"You look like a man with a heavy heart."

"What makes you say that?" he asked as he turned to face her.

"Honey, it's all over your face, and I've lived here long enough to have seen it a hundred times. In about twice that many young men and women who I've shuttled back and forth around town."

He nodded. "And did they get better?"

A smile stretched wide across her wise face. "It's P-town."

"What does that mean?"

She chuckled as if he'd been the punch line to some untold joke.

"You'll find out," she told him as she got into her car and drove away.

"COMING!" A cheery voice from inside the condo yelled in response to Zach's light rap on the sliding front patio door. A few minutes later what sounded like a stampede bounded down the steps leading to the second floor.

Zach stepped back. From the ruckus, he expected an entire football team to file out of the hallway and come crashing out the front as if the threshold were a paper banner stretched across a field by cheerleaders.

He was surprised when a squadron of jocks didn't turn the corner. Instead it was just one man, whose face beamed so brightly he had to squint to look at it. Zach had never seen such pure joy reflected in an adult before.

In a child, yes. In a full-grown man, no.

The man then practically leaped from the stairway to the front door. He slid open the patio and was embracing Zach before he had time to react.

"It's so good to meet you, Zachary!" the man effused in his ear. "I've been wondering what time you'd arrive."

"My plane landed about twenty minutes ago."

The man he assumed was Gary finally released him from the extended embrace. Who else could it be? The only other person besides his grandmother to address him as Zachary had been Gary. Now that he had stepped back, Zach got his first good look at him. All he had been before this moment was a blur of motion.

Gary was attractive, but not in that picture-perfect model fashion. He didn't have a finely chiseled body, and the slight swell of Gary's shirt told him that no flat belly existed underneath.

Zach didn't care. Like most gay men, he enjoyed a nice body, but Zach had always been more attracted to the person than the physique. From what he could tell from Gary's enthusiastic greeting, Gary *definitely* had a personality.

Gary's wire-rimmed glasses didn't quite fit his face. He continuously had to push them back up his nose. The glasses and the repeated gesture made the man more endearing.

"I'm Gary, by the way," he said as he took Zach's bags from his hands. "In case you hadn't figured that out."

Zach nodded. "It's nice to meet you."

"Oh, honey, it's nice to meet *you*," Gary said as he gestured Zach inside.

He dragged his big toe while crossing the border and stumbled rather ungracefully inside Gary's condo.

"Are you okay?" Gary asked as he inspected the threshold for the stray object that tripped Zach.

"I'm fine. Just a natural klutz is all. You'll likely see me fall down at least three times this week."

"I'll alert the insurance adjustor," Gary teased before closing the patio door. "I know I told you this on the phone, but you seriously pulled my rather large, white ass from the fire. I was telling Bobby Quinn that we might have to sell blowjobs down at the dick dock to make ends meet."

What the hell was a dick dock and why did he find the name oddly intriguing? It awakened a part of himself he thought he'd snuffed out years ago, the sexual explorer with an insatiable appetite.

But as he'd done for years, Zach shoved that more carefree side of his personality down beneath the control he'd learn to cultivate.

After placing Zach's luggage on the floor next to the patio door, Gary continued. "I figured that even if we sold them at twenty dollars a pop, we'd probably still be in the hole."

"What's this about blowjobs and holes?" a voice from behind Zach asked. "And why do I always seem to walk in at the ass end of these conversations?"

Zach turned around as another man exited the stairwell, dressed in blue shorts and a white T-shirt. A small purple boat sat in the middle of the shirt with the word BOATSLIP stamped in fuchsia across the design. His face, which sported a closely trimmed dark beard, was both rugged and welcoming.

"And here's the Captain to my Tennille," Gary announced as he walked over and kissed the newcomer. "Zachary Kelly, this is my husband, Bobby Quinn. Bobby Quinn, this is the fabulous man who rescued us from the sex industry."

"So I have you to blame for that," he said as he offered Zach his hand and a friendly grin. "I always wanted to see how much I could get someone to pay me for sex, but alas, I will never find out now. And if you expect us to be friends, you must call me Quinn, not this Bobby Quinn nonsense."

"Quinn it is," Zach responded as he shook Quinn's hand.

"What's wrong with Bobby Quinn?" Gary asked, pretending to be deeply offended. "It's the name of the man I love!"

"Yes, dear," Quinn replied after delivering a peck to Gary's cheek.

"I use the full names of all those I love dearly. It's how I show affection."

"Perhaps a little less affection might be good."

Gary tossed a fake sneer at Quinn, who winked in response. Feigning exasperation, Gary turned his attention back to Zach, who stood there watching the spectacle that was Gary and Quinn. "What you don't know about my Bobby Quinn is that he loves to tease me. I, however, always have the last laugh."

Quinn groaned in response as if he knew what was coming next.

Zach found himself intrigued. "Why's that?"

"I have Penny."

"Penny?" Zach asked while Quinn practically doubled over in faux pain. "Is that like your best friend that Quinn can't stand or something?"

Gary let out a devilish laugh. He appeared to relish in his lover's misery. "Kinda. But not really."

"I don't get it," he told them.

"And you don't want to," Quinn replied from the couch, where he plopped himself in resignation.

"Ah, but he will," Gary added. "All experience Penny. In all her grandeur."

"You and I have different definitions for grandeur," Quinn told Gary.

How else was he supposed to reply than with a shrug?

"Don't you worry your pretty little red head about Penny, Zachary. You'll know her when you meet her."

To this, Quinn moaned even louder than ever. He sounded like a man who wanted to die.

"Quit your complaining, Bobby Quinn. It does you no good anyway."

Quinn snuffed in reply.

"Now that we've been so rudely interrupted by Bobby Quinn, let's get you settled in your condo. I'm sure you have tons of friends to meet up with."

"I don't actually," Zach admitted. "I'm here by myself."

Gary and Quinn exchanged glances, and Zach could tell that a private conversation had just been exchanged. He hated it when couples did that in front of him. He had never experienced that type of intimate connection with anyone before. Not even with Ben. And when he saw how close some couples were, it made him feel as romantically inept as he was clumsy.

"Well, you're in luck," Gary told him. "Bobby Quinn and I have lived here for almost fifteen years. Not only do we know everything there is to know about this place, but we also know the best people in town. We'll introduce you. Show you around."

"That's very sweet, but I doubt I'll be going out much. I'm here to think. And to write."

"An author!" Quinn exclaimed. "Published anything I might've read?"

"Doubtful. But I'm hoping to change that."

"Well, even shut-in authors need to eat, and there's plenty of great restaurants here. You have a standing dinner date with us. Even at a moment's notice."

"That's very kind, but…."

"I don't do 'no' very well. I already told you that," Gary reminded him.

"He doesn't." Quinn nodded in support. "It's easier just to give in. Believe me."

Zach grinned, and he realized how being in Gary and Quinn's presence brought it out of him quite naturally. He didn't stage the smile for their benefit as he typically did whenever he met new people to whom he didn't know how to relate.

That had been his status quo for years. Meet new people, feign interest, and then retreat as quickly as possible.

Where had his typical anxiety gone? He found the abrupt change a bit disconcerting, even though he also enjoyed it. In just a few short moments, they managed to make him feel slightly better. Even the sting of losing Ben had been lost in the face of the freely shared camaraderie.

How might a few more days in their company further affect his mood?

"Okay, I give in," Zach announced. Gary clapped merrily in reply.

"Now that that's settled, let me take you to your condo."

Zach nodded and followed Gary out the front door.

As they walked across the deck that led to the last condo on the left, Gary offered advice on the upcoming Tea Dance. But his words faded away. Zach, instead, focused on something else that had been foreign to him.

Gary and Quinn were a genuinely happy couple. Sure, they were a bit over-the-top, but they were completely at ease with each other.

Never in his thirty-something years had Zach experienced that with another person. In fact, he'd never seen that in his parents.

He had never realized that until now.

Chapter Three

THIS is fucking great!

Van Pierce rested on all fours as the muscled, hung top behind him drove his cock relentlessly inside Van's guts. The force of each thrust massaged his prostate at just the right rhythmic intervals. His cock leaked precum onto the black-leather play sheets their director, Johnny Tripp, had purchased for the shoot they were filming in Provincetown.

Slick with both men's sweat from forty minutes of hardcore fucking since their last break, Van's knees slid farther apart. His costar, who went by the name Ram Steele, took full advantage of the extra room. Ram balanced himself on one knee while his left leg jutted out at a right angle. He grabbed Van by his shoulders and impaled him backward on his nine-inch cock.

Van loved the feel of a man inside his butt. Opening himself up, taking another guy's hard, throbbing prick all the way to the hilt, somehow made him feel more alive, more like the man he always knew he was.

When the cameras were rolling and the clothes came off, he turned into his alter ego, Hart Throb. Horny men pulled their puds while watching him power-bottom. They wanted him. They desired him. More than anything else, they longed to possess him and make Hart their own, but Hart wasn't someone who could be possessed.

At least not for long.

Sure, he fulfilled their fantasies. Whatever his randy followers wanted, he became. It was his job to embody sex, to transform into its living, panting, slutty representative. It was what sold the movies and kept him fed.

And it was certainly a far cry from being regular Van Pierce, the guy men loved taking advantage of, and dumb fuck that Van was, he let them.

Something Hart would never do.

Even though Hart played the bottom, he remained in complete control. The men in his videos were there to please him, not the other way around. Van had never been able to draw that line. He'd let the men in his past use him. He was their toy to be played with, to be put on display at a sex club and fucked by strangers. To be loaned out to good friends and then to be discarded when the toy had lost its shiny, new appeal.

What he'd thought had been about pleasure and trust had turned out to be tools for degradation and deceit.

After having his heart broken and stomped on far too many times, his good nature snapped like the waistband of a worn-out jockstrap, and Hart Throb was born.

Now, he could have his sex and eat it too without the ridicule and humiliation that usually accompanied a relationship. Hart Throb didn't have to worry about love, not in this industry. That kept Van safe and his ass plugged by whatever hot top the production studio cast in a scene with him.

He was free to give his body without handing over his heart. It was his job, after all, and one he did quite well.

Oh, God! This is fucking *great!*

Ram flipped Van onto his back. The move made the man's throbbing hard-on corkscrew inside Van's ass. Van's eyes rolled inside his head. Waves of pleasure rippled outward from Van's well-lubed butt and spread to his endlessly leaking cock.

He so wanted to jack himself off and come while Ram continued to abuse his ass. That was his favorite way to get off, to make himself cream while his butt grew numb and the magic button inside his body was overstimulated. He typically shot ropes of cum across his body, even jettisoning some over his head, if he timed it just right.

But it wasn't time for that yet.

His director, Tripp, had yet to say the word that would grant Van his needed release. Tripp was too busy massaging his dick through his jeans to give the command. His dreamy, faraway eyes told all that right now he was more interested in his own pleasure than his directorial duties.

Until he quit playing with himself, he and Ram were expected to hold back.

"Damn, your ass feels so fucking good," Ram grunted as he hovered above Van. Sweat ran down his costar's bronzed, angular face and collected in large drops at the base of his square jaw. His face burned red from the frenzied pace with which he continued to assault Van's body.

Van moaned in response. "You feel so fucking good. Stretch me open, you big fuck!"

His dirty talk resulted in Ram slamming into him harder. He had to wrap his arms around the bigger man's neck to prevent being fucked right off the bed from Ram's uncontrollable thrusts. At just over six feet and just under two hundred pounds, Van wasn't exactly a dainty flower; he'd definitely held his own against an overeager top in the past, but Ram's muscled-out mass dwarfed him by comparison. Ram's size also made it almost impossible to avoid being knocked off the bed.

Since Ram was lost in his fuck frenzy and Tripp now had his hands full in the corner, it was up to Van to make sure they both stayed within the camera shot. If they had to start all over now that they were coming to the end of a six-hour day, Tripp would blow a gasket instead of the load he was milking from within his worn denim. Reshoots cost money and turned Tripp from the offensive asshole he typically was to a whining bitch.

"*Fuck!*" Ram bellowed as his pace quickened. Van could tell the big guy was on the verge of nutting.

"Not yet," he whispered in caution. Busting a nut without Tripp's explicit direction pissed him off more than a reshoot. A premature explosion meant that the money shot, which was basically the whole point of the shoot, might not be caught on film.

"I can't stop it," Ram said through gritted teeth. "Your ass is so fucking tight." He then threw himself back on his haunches and yanked his throbbing dick from inside Van. Two quick strokes after tearing off the condom and Ram's spunk flew from his cock and splattered all over Van's balls, cock, and stomach.

Van wanted to lube up his dick with Ram's come and finish himself off, but he knew what was coming next.

"*Cut!*" Tripp yelled from the corner. He angrily fumbled his hands out of his jeans. "God *damn* it! Cut! Cut! Cut!" The balding, overweight, bearish director marched over to the bed and got in Ram's face. "What the *fuck* is wrong with you? You're not supposed to come until I say so. What's so *fucking* hard about that? It's not rocket science, you dipshit. It's just *fucking*!" The anger in Tripp's voice cracked louder than a feedback loop in the production speakers.

"I'm sorry," Ram replied, casting his eyes downward. To Van, Ram looked more like a little kid being reprimanded by his father. Never mind that Ram stood well over six feet and had shoulders wider than Tripp's thirty-eight-inch waist. It was clear that in this instance, size meant nothing.

Poor Ram. He really was just a big, oversized boy, who was too dumb to know he could squash Tripp like a grape. Like most of his other costars, Ram struggled with personal demons that kept the large man quite docile. He typically only came to life when his dick got hard.

While Van had his own problems, he certainly never cowered before anyone, much less a man like Tripp.

He owed Tripp for taking a chance on him and casting Van in his first movie last year, but he felt nothing for Tripp beyond gratitude. Tripp, however, had wanted to make Van his full-time boy toy. Ever since Tripp fucked Van during his interview, which was a disgusting industry standard, Tripp wanted more and had become smitten.

Van recognized Tripp's attraction for what it was. He was new to Tripp. That was the only reason his director wanted him, not because he cared about the person Van was but because Van had become something he couldn't have.

That alone drove Tripp crazy.

If Van's first movie hadn't become so popular, he doubted he'd be here with Tripp today. Instead of handling rejection like a man, Tripp became an insufferable ass. He likely would have lorded his status over Van and not hired him again. But Van's rising star power robbed Tripp of some authority.

"Give the guy a break," Van finally said as he hopped off the sweat-drenched bed. He snatched a white towel out of one of the production assistant's hands and patted his privates dry of Ram's sticky goodness. "He was pounding me for over half an hour. It's not his fault you were too busy playing with yourself to call the cum shot."

Tripp wheeled around and glared at him. "Watch your mouth, Pierce!" For some reason, no one at his photo shoots called him by his stage name *or* his first name. They all addressed him by his last name. How aggravating was that? He went through the agonizing process of choosing the name Hart Throb. He expected people besides his admirers to address him by it.

"You forget that I'm the fucking director here," Tripp continued. The red flame in his cheeks spread outward to the bald spot on his fat head. He resembled a hairy tomato. "You're just the fucking meat."

Van crossed the remainder of the distance between them. He was more than just the meat, the term his studio gave to its actors. With just a few movies under his belt, he had blossomed into quite the attraction for Nasty Boy Studios. His videos constantly sold out at the adult stores, and orders for more were always pending. In just a few short months, he had outsold the likes of Jim Wilder, Tim Topper, and Buck Wylde.

Hart Throb was a commercial force to be reckoned with, and Tripp damn well knew it.

"If that's the way you see it, that's fine," Van said. His trademark smirk inched across his face. It was the same one he used on film, when he was just about to come. "I'm sure there are other studios out there that might be interested in my meat." He paused, letting the silence engulf his overt threat.

Tripp's eyes grew wide for a minute, when he apparently realized that if he lost Van for the studio, it would mean his head. But the man was too much of a prick to let anyone win an argument. His crafty eyes darted left to right as if he were scanning his brain for a response that would allow him to save face but still backpedal like the coward he was.

"Everyone knows the rules, Pierce," Tripp grumbled through his gritted, jacked-up teeth that were most likely a result of too much crystal meth in his younger days. "No one comes unless the director calls it."

Van strode over to Ram's side. The big man's shoulders slumped and his head lolled to the right. Ram looked completely defeated and miserable because he hated disappointing anyone. Van could relate.

He'd been there before. That was why it was his duty to defend someone who seemed incapable of standing up for himself.

"What are the rules about a director not doing his job?" Van asked as he placed a reassuring hand on Ram's meaty shoulder. Like an often-abused animal, Ram's skin flinched at the contact before his body leaned into Van's touch. "It's your job to give direction, and you've been jerking yourself off for a good half hour. What does the studio say about that?"

"Are you kidding me right now, Pierce? Half the guys here play pocket pool while shooting these scenes! But they all manage to do their jobs."

Van couldn't argue with that. Still, it infuriated him how Tripp spoke to the models, and even though most studios considered their actors expendable, Van was on the verge of being hired as a Nasty Boy exclusive. The company desperately wanted him, and he planned on using that to his advantage. "True, but Ram's not entirely to blame. If he gets punished for making a mistake, then someone might find out about *you* slacking on the job. How do you want this to play out? Should we just call it a day and shoot this scene later or should I ask for a new director for this shoot? I've been dying to work with Randy, you know."

Tripp's gray teeth chewed on his bottom lip as he obviously considered the prospect of Randy replacing him on this film. A new director to the studio, Randy made a huge splash with his debut movie *A Hole to Remember* last month. Rumors already abounded that Randy was being primed to take Tripp's spot as executive director.

There was no way Tripp was going to allow that to happen or add any more kindling to the studio rumors. He had been backed into a corner, and they both knew it. While Tripp had the authority here, Van had truth and Tripp's paranoia on his side.

Together, they were a persuasive combination.

"Fine," the director added with a wave of his hand. "We'll call it a wrap for today." He switched his glare from Van to Ram. "But if you so much as squeeze out one drop of cum that I haven't asked for next time, there'll be hell to pay."

After Ram silently nodded, Tripp stormed out of the room and loudly stomped down the hallway.

"Thanks," Ram uttered after the front door slammed shut. "I owe ya."

Van shook his head. No one owed him a thing. He owed it to himself to do what no one had ever done for him. "Don't worry about it," he finally said after heading over to the chair where he disrobed before the shoot. "The guy's a prick."

Stan and T.J., who made up the camera and lighting crew for the shoot, silently nodded in agreement as they packed up their equipment.

"See," Van said as he pointed at the two men.

A huge, childish grin lit up Ram's face. He obviously felt absolved. Before Van could react, he was lifted off the floor and crushed within the steely grip of his costar.

"Aren't you two done fucking yet?" a voice at the door asked.

Although Ram's constricting embrace prevented Van from seeing the newcomer, he recognized the voice of his best friend Nino. He sounded impatient and ready for some fun of his own.

"All done!" Ram announced as he released Van from his unintentional stranglehold. Van dropped back to the floor and almost fell into the chair holding his shorts and muscle shirt. Ram chuckled as he padded across the room to find his clothes.

"Hurry up and get dressed," Nino ordered. "I just heard the ferry horn from the bay. You know what *that* means."

As if Nino ever let him forget. The incoming ferry meant fresh meat was arriving in Provincetown from Boston, and as usual, Nino called dibs on the tastiest of the new arrivals.

"Isn't your cock sore yet?" Van asked as he slid into his red briefs. "You've been fucking nonstop since the start of the season."

"That would be funny if it didn't just come out of the man whose ass has been ridden more times than a mechanical bull at a country-and-western bar."

"Are you calling me a slut?"

"Slut? Hell, no!" Nino responded. "Sluts do it for free. You, *meu amigo*, get paid. You're a bona fide *puta*."

Van rolled his eyes as he slid his shirt over his head. It wasn't the first time Nino had teasingly called him a whore in Portuguese, and

Van didn't really care who called him what. He'd long moved past caring what others thought of him.

Doing so had been a necessity.

"Let's go!" he told Nino after sliding his feet into his flip-flops. "It's time to go shopping for cock and ass."

Nino hooted in excitement. As they walked down the hall and toward the endless opportunities for sex that awaited them in town, Van couldn't wait to see what new adventure Provincetown had in store for him.

Chapter
Four

HE AND Nino hadn't gone a couple of steps down Commercial Street before Van was recognized for his movies. In mere seconds, a dozen men broke away from the steady stream of tourists flooding the street. They immediately schooled around him, wanting his signature on their shirts or their asses.

He'd even been asked to sign a cock before.

Van didn't care what he was signing. He simply enjoyed being asked. What other job came with these kinds of perks? He sure as hell couldn't think of any.

After signing his third exposed ass, which was quite fuckable if he were in any way a top, he glanced over to where Nino leaned against the wall of Adams Pharmacy. Nino rolled his eyes and threw up his hands in surrender.

Van understood the gesture. Nino was giving up on his quest for fresh ass off the ferry so that his best friend could enjoy his notoriety.

He loved Nino for that selfless gesture. In a completely platonic way, of course.

The two of them were best friends—well, brothers, really—and the thought of having sex with Nino, the guy whose farts were dubbed "canary killers," made Van's flesh crawl.

It wasn't that he didn't find Nino attractive. He was a hot guy. Like smoking hot. Curly, dark brown hair that made him appear deceptively innocent. Coffee-colored eyes that matched his sandy-brown skin, and a wicked smile that typically enchanted anyone on its receiving end. To top it off, Nino had a rocking hard body, but despite all the characteristics that typically caused Van to present himself on all fours, they were best friends. Nothing more.

Besides, fucking always seemed to ruin his relationships.

"You almost done being the Susan Lucci of gay porn?"

"I think so," he told Nino after taking a picture with a group of guys in their mid to late twenties, who squealed like little girls whenever they looked at him. He always found those kinds of reactions from men his age a little silly.

He was their peer, nothing more. Well, a peer who fucked other men for a popular gay porn studio, but that was beside the point. It wasn't as though he was an older, established actor like Jeff Palmer or Michael Lucas.

Then, he'd understand the panty pudding they seemed to be churning.

"You're so fucking hawt," one of the guys swooned. He had a round baby face and short-cropped hair. "That scene with you, Rod Major, and Mark Iron in *Ass Pussy* made me come buckets. How the hell did you take both their thick cocks up your ass at the same time? It's like trying to shove two beer cans up your butt."

"Tricks of the trade," Van commented with a wink. "I can't divulge industry secrets."

"Aww, come on," another of the guys pouted. He jutted out his lower lip in an attempt to induce sympathy. This guy was leaner with nicely sculpted arms. "I've always wanted to be double penetrated, but my ass just can't handle it."

In response to that particular mating call, Nino sidled up to the young buck and draped his arm around the guy's neck while flashing his trademark grin. "You know, I can help you with that."

The guy bristled at first in response to the unwanted contact, but when he got a good look at Nino with his model-perfect body and flawless skin, he quickly changed his tune. His initially icy response thawed as a fire evidently started to smolder in his groin. "Can you?" the guy asked as he pretended to be shy and demure.

"Most definitely. I've got mad skills."

"Really? Like porn skills?"

Nino nodded.

"So you've done porn?"

"Have I done porn?" Nino asked, pretending to be outraged. "Let me tell you…."

Van rolled his eyes at the blatantly slutty display and tuned out the rest of Nino's seduction. He'd seen the scene unfold far too many times, and he already knew the drill. Nino would tell the guy whatever he wanted to hear. As long as Nino got what he wanted in the end—his cock buried deep up someone's butt—he would say whatever was necessary to secure the deal.

Watching Nino work a potential trick was like watching a politician work a town hall meeting. He pandered and complimented just like any elected official did. After all, the goal of both was to get a lever pulled in some fashion.

Nino's lever might not decide any national election, but he wanted it pulled nonetheless. And like any good politician, he did whatever was necessary to get his ballot in someone else's box.

While he loved Nino dearly, he didn't care for the big, fat lies Nino told. His friend was better than that, but Nino didn't seem to mind telling lies.

All he cared about was securing the prey. Everything else could take a flying fuck.

Eventually, Van's crowd of admirers thinned until only Nino and the guy he was working remained. He found it ironic that though he had many fans, none of them ever tried to pick him up. They enjoyed watching him have sex on screen, but the thought of actually having sex with him never seemed to cross their minds.

What was up with that shit?

Maybe they were intimidated by the fact that he was paid to have sex on film. That was what Nino thought anyway.

Van wasn't so sure. Was there some other problem? One he just didn't see and Nino wouldn't point out to him?

It wasn't that he was looking for a relationship. He *definitely* didn't want another one of those. But like Nino, he also enjoyed getting down and dirty off screen. With men who hadn't been paid to sleep with him and who he didn't find in a bathhouse or at the dick dock.

Van scored more than his share of cock up his butt. Probably more than any one man had a right to, but it always seemed to be a result of Van being the pursuer and not the pursued. Was there something inherently wrong with him, some vibe that he put out that caused men to only want to admire him from afar?

Kind of like Tom Cruise, who still looked pretty but who'd turned into one crazy motherfucker.

Crazy was one thing Van wasn't.

When Nino and the college guy started making out against the wall of the pharmacy, Van turned around and headed in the opposite direction. The deal had been secured, and Nino would need some time alone in their apartment with his newfound toy. That meant Van had to occupy himself for an hour or so.

Unless Nino was really horny. Then, he'd only need about fifteen minutes.

Since Van was uncertain of Nino's sexual needs, a fact he was glad to be ignorant of, he entertained seeing a movie, but he hated sitting in a theater by himself. Nothing screamed loser quite so loudly as that, so instead he continued past Water's Edge Cinema and headed toward the west end of town.

Being outside amid the crowds of people shuffling up and down Commercial Street seemed much more attractive than an empty theater.

Besides, out here, he ran into people who knew him as Van and not just as his porn alter ego. Although he enjoyed his second identity, he was sometimes swallowed up by it. He'd created Hart to escape the pain of last year, but he found it sometimes difficult to return to who he truly was.

After all, it was far easier to be Hart than Van.

What he needed right now were the friends he'd made since settling in Provincetown almost two years ago. The friends who loved Van, not Hart.

There was Connie, who worked security at one of the local bars. She was an absolute riot and always went out of her way to say hello, even if she was tits-deep in work. The Carpe Diem innkeepers, Sebastian and Jonas, invited him to dinner at least once a month. The two didn't particularly care for Nino, since they had a three-way that went awry. Van never got the details, but from what he did know, someone apparently had Mexican food just before the tryst. Van shuddered at the implications. Still, Sebastian and Jonas always made sure to include Nino in the invites. They understood how much Van cared for his best friend.

There was also Tara Tebow, the most sought after bartender at the Boatslip. The gay boys clamored for her affection, and she deserved every ounce of their love. She greeted everyone with a big, genuine smile that sparkled beneath her thick, wavy, and often unkempt hair. She was one of the first to offer Van a shoulder to cry on when he needed it the most. He'd forever be grateful to her for that.

As he made a mental note of all the people who had become like family to him, Ken and Sean, Gary and Quinn, and the battalion of drag queens who had taken him under their wings, he felt truly loved.

Yet, he still couldn't shake the loneliness that sometimes descended upon him like it did now or when he watched Nino with that college guy. People no longer saw *him* anymore. The only person they saw was the fantasy he'd created.

Van inhaled deeply and tried to shake the emotion from himself like unwanted dust motes.

After all, he'd created Hart out of necessity. He didn't understand why pangs of regret thrummed within him now.

After a few moments, when he was more centered, he continued down the crowded street, at least until the next group of guys recognized him and his admiring fans once again surrounded him.

Yes, being Hart Throb was tough, but Van was happy to do it.

If he didn't, he might think too much. Right now, that was a bad thing.

Chapter Five

ZACH immediately regretted leaving the condo as he fought his way through Commercial Street. The major thoroughfare resembled a disturbed ant pile as people scurried along the sidewalks and down the street where cars mostly sat idle on the asphalt, only able to move a few inches down the congested road.

Every few steps, his progress was halted by some thoughtless tourist coming to a dead stop to take a picture of a building or of their friends. He found the whole ordeal aggravating, especially when their unexpected stops meant that he crashed into them.

He was awkward enough as it was. He sure didn't need any help being less graceful.

Now that he was here, though, he longed for the quiet solitude of his condo.

Zach had wanted to write, a fact he made quite clear to Gary during his tour of the condo he had rented, but Gary insisted that Zach head into town and see what Provincetown was all about. Apparently, heading to Commercial Street upon arrival was part of the ritual, one of many according to Gary.

Against his better judgment, Zach had done as Gary suggested, especially when thoughts of Ben constantly bombarded him. He tried to write before he left, to use his words and his imagination to work through the pain. If he could do that, it might somehow fill the gaping hole in the pit of his stomach.

Instead, the blank, empty document upset him.

He had nothing to say, no words to share about the loss of a three-year relationship. He didn't understand what that meant, so instead of dredging up emotions he preferred to suppress, he left the condo and headed down the hill to Commercial Street.

Now that he was here, he wished he'd stayed put and battled his creative constipation and emotional catatonia. Anything had to be better than dealing with this crowd.

Then Zach took note of the people around him for the first time.

Men in various states of undress paraded up and down the street. Most had their shirts off, tucked in the back pockets of their short shorts or much too tight jeans. Those men, however, proved the most conservative of the bunch. Their more liberal brothers flaunted about in Speedos with their packages bulging against the see-through fabric. Zach could practically make out the head of one guy's cock with the way his junk was smashed inside the material.

That *had* to be uncomfortable.

The few guys who actually wore their clothes looked dressed for the clubs. Whether in button-downs, polos, or muscle shirts, they all had one aspect in common. The clothes were formfitting and stylish.

No one wore loose T-shirts or baggy shorts. They all looked well put together and ready to impress.

His blue-and-white T-shirt, which was two sizes too big, and the out-of-date camouflage cargo shorts, which hung past his knees, made him stand out from the crowd. Others were starting to notice it as well.

Some of the guys who passed stared at him out of the corners of their eyes.

They obviously thought he was out of place, and now so did he.

Zach needed to get out of there immediately.

All he had to do was cross the street and head back the way he came, and he could exit the madness.

Two lesbians with a clutch of children of assorted races cut in front of him as he tried to make his way across. He allowed them to go first, and after he waved off one mother's apology, a lumbering, red trolley made its way to where he stood and proceeded to stop and block his escape.

Zach turned to his left to go around the trolley, but a group of excited college-aged kids congregated behind him. They fawned over some picture they had taken with a porn star he'd never heard of. Unlike Ben, who amassed quite the collection over the years, he had never been a fan of porn. The actors typically looked bored or the sex was horribly scripted.

Sex wasn't supposed to be either.

Even so, those young guys obviously were enthralled by their find, and he could tell they had no intention of moving for quite some time. They huddled about their phones, no doubt uploading their photographs to Facebook in order to commemorate the chance encounter.

How did getting paid to have sex in front of cameras make anyone a possible celebrity? It only made them notorious in his book.

Still, who was he to judge?

All he cared about was getting out of this clusterfuck.

The only avenue of escape remaining was to continue to his right, where a couple had decided to make out and further impede pedestrian traffic. They created a bottleneck of people in front of a white building with the words ADAMS PHARMACY etched across the sign above the door.

He was just about to march up and push past them when the trolley started its engine and moved forward a few feet. That gave Zach all the space he needed to squeeze between it and the cars lined up behind.

Unfortunately, the other side of the street proved just as packed, so he walked as quickly as possible for a few blocks until, by some miracle, a part in the crowd formed, connecting where he stood to a small basement store. He jogged down the slowly narrowing path as it began to fill with people and bounded down the four steps that led to the front door.

He turned around and watched as his escape route closed, swallowed up by the tourists.

Claustrophobia immediately claimed Zach.

Having no desire to continue the losing battle against the onslaught of people, Zach decided to spend a few moments, if not hours, stocking up on whatever this store sold.

The sign on the door read FK LEATHER.

Zach sighed in relief. Perhaps he could find some appropriate clothes here. He did need a new belt and probably a nice pair of shoes, especially since he doubted he'd packed either of those before leaving his apartment in Texas.

Without further thought, he opened the door and dashed inside.

V AN stood against the back wall of the leather shop, thankful for the brief break from his adoring fans. Although he enjoyed the attention, it sometimes overwhelmed him.

Did Susan Lucci go through the same thing with her adoring soap fans?

Like La Lucci, he enjoyed the spotlight and the notoriety, but sometimes he wanted to go all Erica Kane on their asses and slap the shit out of them, especially the ones who thought it was okay to grab his cock.

Van was obviously not a prude, but he didn't enjoy people thinking being a porn star meant it was okay to get all handsy. Had Susan Lucci ever had a fan honk her boobs?

He seriously doubted that.

Most days, Van could deal with the celebrity his role provided, even the guys who saw with their hands instead of their eyes, but today, he just didn't have the strength.

The loneliness that had come over him earlier persisted, and he needed to shake it off.

When he made it to FK Leather, after being stopped three more times since leaving Nino sucking face in front of Adams Pharmacy, he quickly ducked inside. The gear shop didn't get as many customers as some of the other stores. Those who came in usually gawked at the merchandise, manhandling the giant-sized butt plugs or poking fun at the assless chaps.

Few, if any, made it all the way to the back of the store where the currently occupied fitting room was located. That suited Van's needs.

He was safely hidden from overeager fans.

The front door to the store swung open, and Van cursed under his breath at the thought of being followed in here. He moved behind the display case, which held the more expensive cock rings, nipple clamps, ball weights, and sounding devices. Behind him sat the racks where the deprivation suits and catsuits hung.

Unless the new customer was a real pig, he'd be safe.

The door to the dressing room opened, and Andrew, the store manager, poked his head out into the store. "I'll be right with you," he told the customer.

The man on the other side of the store mumbled an incoherent reply. Andrew glanced over at Van and rolled his eyes.

"Another Looky Lou?" Van asked in a whisper.

"Most likely. It's twink week, after all," Andrew replied in disgust. "I don't know why those fairies even come in this store. It's not like they buy anything that isn't brightly colored or bedazzled."

Van took stock of the predominantly black garments mostly comprised of leather, rubber, or neoprene. "None of that here," he commented.

"Damn straight! If they start making gear for twinks, I think I'll kill myself."

Van laughed.

Twinks weren't the most celebrated visitors to Provincetown. The younger and more finicky of the gay groups to descend upon the town, they were all in their early twenties and rarely ate since they all had to be skinny. They dressed only in designer clothes and therefore visited the high-end retail shops along Commercial Street. Most wouldn't be caught dead in a full-body rubber suit since it would likely mess up their hair.

They also didn't tip well and were downright bitchy.

To say they weren't celebrated tended to be an understatement.

Van gestured to the other side of the store, where the unseen customer still shopped. "Will that twink recognize me?"

Andrew snorted so hard he almost blew the diamond stud out of his nose. He looked back over at the customer and smiled politely at him before returning his gaze to Van. When he spoke, his voice was barely audible. "First of all, that guy's *not* a twink. He's got to be somewhere in his thirties. At least. Secondly, this guy doesn't look like he's got himself together enough to know about anybody else's business. I mean, really? Baggy-ass camouflage cargo shorts paired with a blue-and-white-striped shirt. He has zero fashion sense and looks lost in here, so I doubt he's a porn connoisseur. I think you're safe." Andrew glanced back at the customer to flash another smile. "Besides, he looks straight."

"Really?" Van asked as he slowly inched his way around the display case.

"Look for yourself." Andrew motioned. "Those twinks out there will eat him alive. And not in a good way, either."

When Van finally moved enough past the case to get a peek, he couldn't believe his eyes. Although the guy's back was turned to him, Van could see that not only did his clothes clash worse than most professional golfers', but they were also far too big on him. Not only was his shirt blousy, but his shorts hung far too low on his legs, looking more like Capri pants, which they obviously were not.

Although he couldn't tell much about the guy's body, he could *definitely* tell the man in no way filled out the oversized clothes.

To top it off, his full head of ginger hair had no product. That wasn't necessarily a bad thing. Some guys successfully pulled off the disheveled look. This guy didn't. His hair stood up like flames dancing around a campfire.

Quite simply, the man looked like a hot mess. Van couldn't fathom why anyone visiting Provincetown would present himself so sloppily, especially during a week devoted to prissy, judgmental queens.

Didn't he understand he would be judged harshly? Didn't he realize he cut his tricking potential down to zero?

This guy needed to buy a vowel and get clued in to how things worked around here.

"I told you," Andrew sung behind him.

Van nodded in agreement and chuckled. "Yeah, it's bad. *Real* bad."

Then, something unexpected happened.

When the guy turned around, Van forgot how to breathe.

SHOULD he continue to fake interest in the leather harness or dash out of what was obviously not the sort of leather store he commonly frequented? Judging from the amused expressions of the two men on the opposite side of the store, Zach was leaning more toward a speedy exit.

But he couldn't move as he silently berated himself for not realizing what type of store this was. It wasn't as though he'd never been inside a leather shop before. Ben had taken him to one in Houston a couple of years ago, and it made him uncomfortable.

The raw sexual depravity on display had called to the part of him he'd spent years getting under control, and the fact Ben had been trying to school him on the uses of harnesses and masks only hastened the awakening.

He'd exited the store and promised never to return for fear of releasing a part of himself that needed to remain checked. Ben hadn't understood. In fact, they'd argued about Zach's continual need to remain in control of aspects of his life that Ben saw no need to rein in, but there was no way Zach could make Ben understand.

Within him existed something so primal it defied comprehension, and Zach repressed anything he couldn't figure out, a trick he picked up from his father.

And as Zach stood there, battling the rising swell of lust created by the smell of leather, he spotted a man so beautiful that the sight of him almost made Zach cast all his previous inhibitions aside and rush toward him like a wave crashing toward the shore.

It wasn't the guy who obviously worked here with the diamond stud in his nose. It was the guy next to him. The one with short brown hair that also cut a manly swath down from his sideburns across the rugged cut of his jaw and around a pair of perfectly symmetrical lips. He also had a perfect pair of steely eyes.

He looked intimidating but gentle at the same time, especially in the way the strong angle of his nose was softened by the plush indention of flesh at the cleft of his chin.

Well-muscled arms extended out of a brown tank top. On the shirt was a picture of a cupcake with the words EAT ME written across the top. Zach wanted to do just that.

He'd never seen someone so beautiful. Whenever he ran across some perfect model type, their flawlessness would usually piss him off, especially since Zach only ever saw flaws in himself.

But this guy didn't stir up his usual feelings of self-loathing.

This one made the snake in his shorts uncoil as he fantasized about licking the icing off the man's cupcake.

The response worried Zach. Just a few hours ago, all he could think about was Ben. Now, as he stared into the silvery-blue eyes that peeked at him from around the corner, he had difficulty recalling what Ben even looked like. Shouldn't he be feeling more gun-shy right about now instead of wanting to crawl on top of some random stranger?

Still, the only thought that sped through his mind as quickly as his cock stiffened was to take the man in his arms and caress his sun-kissed skin.

But there was no way a guy like that would be interested in Zach, who'd had his flaws catalogued by others for most of his life.

Not only was he a bumbling, insecure fool, but Zach's glaringly white skin and red hair made him unpopular in a gay world where tanned bodies were all the rage. All the sun did for him was scorch his flesh a cherry red.

Besides, from the look of his six-foot, well-toned frame, the guy was most likely a top and probably enjoyed wrecking someone else's ass more than having his own ass plundered. Zach had bottomed before, on special occasions like birthdays and anniversaries, but he didn't enjoy it.

He preferred to fuck rather than be fucked. There existed within him a need to dominate.

He doubted Mr. Tanned Body offered up his ass to anyone.

"Looking for anything special?" the guy with the diamond stud asked. An impish grin played across his face. It told Zach that he was obviously the butt of a joke between the two.

That wasn't something new. People often laughed at his tentative nature, but today, he wouldn't surrender to it as he typically did. He needed to prove to himself, and to the hottest man he'd ever laid eyes on, that he wasn't a joke.

"Just browsing."

The employee's polite smile immediately told Zach that his lie hadn't worked. He didn't care. He planned on doing one lap around the store, perhaps study an article or two of clothing, if rubber suits and assless pants counted as clothing, and then depart as quickly as he'd dashed inside.

He'd rather deal with the mobs of people on the street than stay in here a second longer and risk unleashing a part of himself that howled to be set free.

"Just let me know if you need anything," the guy said before disappearing back into the dressing room he'd previously stepped out of.

Zach nodded and then realized he'd been left alone in the store with Mr. Tanned Body, who still stood silently staring at him. The realization urged his feet to move toward the back part of the store.

As he worked his way around the gas masks, he tried to forget about the fact that he was being watched. Maybe the guy worked security and had somehow pegged Zach as a potential shoplifter.

There couldn't be any other reason that Zach could fathom, so he gave the guy his back and inspected the leather harnesses along the far left wall. They were obviously different styles, but he had no clue what the smaller ones that looked like holsters were called. He entertained the idea of trying one on just for show, but that would mean taking off his shirt. He definitely didn't want to do that.

People typically poked fun at how white he was.

Instead, he worked his way past the harnesses and approached the back wall, where the dressing room was located. There, he found a cardboard display spotlighting a tub jam-packed with lube of assorted varieties he'd never even heard of—Boy Butter, Elbow Grease, Spunk, and FIST Powder.

The last brand name made him shudder. The thought of someone shoving an entire fist up his ass caused Zach's hole to clench tightly shut. No matter how much being here excited him sexually, fisting had never turned him on, and the unpleasant image of some guy elbow-deep up another man's ass calmed the raging waters that had churned so vigorously inside.

In fact, he was certain his asshole wouldn't relax until he left this place that sold objects whose sole purpose seemed to be destroying the elasticity of a part of the body he preferred to remain tight.

He made his way around the tub of lube and stood studying the latex wrestling suits and leather aprons that covered the far wall. He could understand the fascination with the wrestling singlets. Muscled guys rolling around in skimpy gear turned him on too.

However, why would anyone purchase a leather apron?

It resembled something a sadistic butcher might wear in a horror movie.

As he pondered what the aprons were used for sexually, the door to the dressing room fell open, and Zach gasped.

The store employee struggled to help a rather obese man shove himself inside a full-body rubber suit. Talcum powder spotted the interior of the room and the outside of the outfit. It had also gotten on their faces. There was so much powder everywhere that Zach figured this must be what a coke den looked like. At least one that had imploded.

Turning around seemed the politest response, but the spectacle proved too much of a train wreck.

The large man, who resembled Jabba the Hutt trying to squeeze inside a Hefty bag, cursed as he attempted to force every roll of fat inside. His constant struggle caused sweat to drench his body, turning the powder that caked his pregnant, hairy belly into paste.

The poor employee, who knelt before the sweating crotch from which hung a tiny Vienna sausage, attempted to hike the suit farther up the man's meaty thighs. When that failed, he stood and yanked with all his might as the rotund fellow lifted his left leg in a vain attempt at assistance. The slick material, made even slicker by the man's perspiration, caused the employee to lose his grip.

The rubber snapped back quite unexpectedly for the big guy who already teetered precariously on one bulky limb. Unbalanced, he toppled backward onto the dressing room floor, causing the layer of powder to explode upward and resulting in a momentary whiteout in the small room.

Before he could help himself, Zach broke out into laughter.

The customer didn't appreciate Zach's sense of humor and called him a fuckwad.

"I'm sorry," he said as he backed up.

Zach needed to get out of there before he embarrassed himself further, so he turned around and bolted forward, completely forgetting about the display behind him. He struck the lube bin, which began a rather horrifying chain of events.

The display fell over, causing bottles of lube to roll throughout the store, some of which he squashed open with his large, blundering feet. When Zach backed up in surprise, he collided with the wall, which contained the aprons and rubber wrestling suits. The force of the impact caused the top row of hanging garments to fall from their perch and rain upon his head.

"Need some help?"

Zach looked up from amongst the aprons and crushed bottles of lube to find Mr. Tanned Body standing before him with a humorous twinkle in his steely eyes.

The roiling passion within Zach reluctantly surged forward once again.

WHY did Van find this guy so freaking adorable?

When he first laid eyes on him, his breath caught in his lungs.

That had never happened to Van before. Not even when he was being fucked stupid by his favorite porn star, Slake. He'd first seen Slake in the now classic *Fucking in the Rain*. The muscled Adonis with a fat ten-incher had been an icon for Van since that movie, and he used to fantasize about having his ass stuffed full with Slake's meat. And even when his dream became a reality for his third movie *All You Can Eat*, he'd remembered how to breathe.

But for some reason, this redheaded, mismatched klutz made him feel loopy.

What the hell was *that* about?

Was it the flaming red hair that set his head and jaw on fire? It certainly sparked a raging boner in Van's shorts. Or was it the milky tone of his skin that made Van want to curl about the man's body and lap it up like a mewling kitten? Or even worse was it the way his beautiful brown eyes darted about like a child surveying the mess he'd made?

Van never thought he would be attracted to someone who looked so innocent, especially since he'd spent the last year having the shit fucked out of him by the sexually depraved.

"I'm fine," the guy finally responded quite testily. He then knelt down to pick up the wrestling singlets and aprons.

Van squatted beside him and scooped up the bottles of lube that had squirted their contents upon the gray painted floor. "Not to be rude, but 'fine' isn't exactly the word I'd use."

"What the hell is going on out here?" Andrew asked as he exited the dressing room and surveyed the disaster. Van had to stifle a laugh since Andrew was covered head to toe in powder.

"Just a little accident," Van replied.

"Accident? This place is a fucking disaster! First Mama Cass in there insists on squeezing his big fat ass into a size small catsuit, and now I've got leather apparel on the floor and tubes of lube jizzing all over the place. This place looks like the morning after a blackout party."

"That could be good for business."

"Don't try and sweet-talk me," Andrew told Van. "I like a good fuck party too, but this is my livelihood, man."

"I'm sorry," the redhead offered. "I'll pay for whatever I've ruined."

Andrew opened his mouth to no doubt say something shitty, but when he saw the evident remorse and embarrassment reflected in those sweet brown eyes, his cattiness abruptly died. Apparently, this guy affected everyone in a strange way. Van had never known Andrew to dial it down so quickly.

"No worries. Just help clean it up and all will be forgiven."

"Are you sure?"

Andrew nodded reluctantly before turning around to see the fat guy in the dressing room floundering on his back like a giant dung beetle. He sighed and turned back to them. "You two clean up. I'll try and solve my recent bug problem."

Van laughed at that, and he was surprised when the redhead chuckled too. It was the first time he'd seen any emotion besides uncomfortable embarrassment since the guy walked into the store.

"Sorry about being such a dick to you," he said. "I'm just more clumsy than graceful, and it typically pisses me off."

"No apologies necessary."

"I'm Zach," he announced and extended his hand out to Van. "And you are?"

What? Zach didn't know who he was? *Everyone* knew him as Hart Throb. Zach's ignorance of his daytime job made him somehow want this man even more.

How fucking stupid was that?

When he realized he hadn't introduced himself or shaken the man's outstretched hand, he finally replied, "Name's Van." Then he took Zach's warm hand in his own. Zach's touch was comfortable and reassuring. Whenever he typically shook a stranger's hand, Van found their flesh cold and foreign.

What the hell was the deal with this guy?

"Van?" Zach asked. "Like I drive a van?"

Van laughed. He'd definitely like this guy to take him out for a spin.

"It's my nickname. Short for Evan."

"Never met a Van before. At least not one that didn't have four wheels."

"Even those are pretty rare these days," Van admitted.

Zach nodded as he bent down to continue the cleanup on aisle four. "Is there a mop or anything around here?"

"It's in the closet behind the counter," Van answered as he went to retrieve it. By the time he returned, Zach had picked up the remaining bottles of lube and placed them back in the case.

"Thanks," he said as he reached out for the mop.

"I'll do it."

Zach shook his head. "It's my mess. I'll clean it up. Believe me, I'm used to it."

He took the mop from Van's hands and began to wipe up the spilled lube. As he worked, Van decided to place the fallen clothes back on their hangers. When they were both done, the back of the store looked like it did before Zach made his mess.

"I think Andrew will approve," Van told Zach.

"And I do," announced Andrew as he came out of the dressing room with his customer, who was now fully clothed. Covered in more powder than Andrew, the man cast his eyes downward and skulked silently out of the store. When the door closed, Andrew turned to them and sighed. "And after all that, that big bitch didn't even buy the fucking suit! I'm gonna have to hose it down to get the smell of his stanky ass out of the latex."

Zach laughed heartily, and his laughter quickly infected Van and Andrew. The three of them snickered and giggled like kids.

Van needed that. He was feeling crappy about himself and his life before this, and from the look on Zach's face, Van could tell the laughter was good for his soul as well.

"Well, I think I've caused enough damage here for today," Zach announced. "I should probably get going. I'm supposed to meet a friend at Joe's Coffee."

Although Van didn't want him to go, he simply nodded in reply.

"Once again, I'm sorry for the mess."

Andrew patted Zach on the back, and Van found the friendly gesture made him jealous for some reason. He wanted to be the one who touched Zach.

"Don't worry about it," Andrew told him. "No harm. No foul."

Zach nodded in appreciation.

"It was good to meet you too, Van. Perhaps I'll see you both around."

"It's Provincetown," Van told him.

"You know, that's the second time I've heard that phrase today," Zach said. "Maybe I'll find out what that actually means."

Zach waved good-bye and headed for the front door.

Van wanted to stop him, to tell him not to go. He even entertained the idea of asking Zach out on a date, but the problem was that Van didn't date. He fucked.

He and dating didn't have a great track record, so instead of doing what he most wanted to do, Van simply watched Zach exit the store and turn right on Commercial Street.

Chapter Six

SINCE leaving FK Leather, Zach had been at ease with himself. Which wasn't typical. The last time he visited such a store with Ben, he'd been uncomfortable, as if the shop mocked the urges that existed within but that he could never enjoy. This time had been different. Sure, he'd made a mess and a jackass of himself and those suppressed desires reared their ugly heads, but somehow cleaning up the mess up and laughing about it made him feel better. About everything.

As he walked down Commercial Street toward Joe's Coffee, where he had promised to meet up with Gary, his change in attitude prompted him to take the time to appreciate the crowds of people instead of being annoyed by their presence.

People smiled all around him. No, that wasn't quite right. They beamed.

Pure, unadulterated joy reflected in their faces. Couples kissed and held hands, and these weren't just the straight people, who were definitely in the minority.

The public displays of affection came from the same-sex couples who freely showed the world how much they were in love with their chosen partners. They didn't have to hide their feelings or affections. They embraced them and proudly put them on display.

Maybe he could do the same thing. Embrace the parts of himself he'd rejected for far too long. Was he even capable of that?

He couldn't go there. Not now at least.

He hadn't felt this good in a long time, much longer than his recent troubles with Ben.

Although he wasn't certain what that meant, he wasn't going to linger. Instead, his mind turned to a far more attractive subject—Van, the sexy tanned man. God, he had been striking. So much so that he questioned that strong, immediate attraction. He also didn't get why he felt the need to prove he could be more than a fuckup. Was that really important, though?

All that really mattered was that he seemed to take a step in a direction that wasn't his usual path. He didn't continue to fumble like an idiot in his actions or his words. Sure, he'd been embarrassed—mortified even—but he'd laughed it off.

No, *they'd* laughed it off.

His buffoon-like quality hadn't pissed either Van or Andrew off as it typically did Ben. They hadn't called him an idiot or suffered in silent disapproval like his father.

Was that Provincetown's doing? Did this town somehow cause people to be friendlier and nicer to each other? Did being here somehow connect everyone and make everyone feel less alone and more a part of some thriving community?

That had to be the answer.

After all, the kind taxi driver had tried to help even though he hadn't let her. Most people back home wouldn't have given a fuck, much less taken the time to find out what was bothering him. And they said Texas was the friendliest state! Apparently, those people had never been here.

And then there were Gary and Quinn. He hadn't known them longer than a few minutes before Gary was embracing him like a long-lost relative. Quinn, too, warmed up to him rather quickly, and there didn't seem any hidden motive in their offered friendship.

It simply was.

"There's Zachary Kelly now!"

The unmistakable sound of Gary's cheery voice up ahead signaled he was close to the coffee shop. He spotted Gary outside sipping a beverage while sitting next to a woman whose face beamed upon seeing Zach.

Who was she and why was she so excited to see him? Even though he didn't have any answers, Zach couldn't stop the smile that involuntarily stretched itself across his face in reply.

"Hey, Gary," he said as the man stood up and held his arms open. He obviously wanted another embrace. It seemed hugging and kissing were standard greetings in Provincetown.

Zach preferred to shake hands, but it seemed his way wouldn't work here.

Once he'd properly greeted Gary, Gary turned to the woman who sat to his right sipping on an iced tea. Her curly, untamed hair sprouted around her face. On anyone else, it might make them look frumpy and unattractive. This woman looked radiant, not despite the crazy mass of curls but because of them. Her beauty rested in its simplicity and its chaos.

"My sexy, fiery-haired Zachary, I must introduce you to the always fabulous and extremely luscious Tara Tebow."

Tara rose to embrace him, and Zach couldn't believe how tiny she was. She stood no more than five feet tall, but her smile and personality seemed bigger than both he and Gary combined. She also had a pair of the biggest ta-tas he'd ever seen. How did she manage to stand up straight? "I'm happy to meet you," she told Zach after hugging him tight and kissing his cheek. "Gary's told me so much about you."

"Really?" he asked, looking at Gary. "But he doesn't know anything about me."

Tara laughed. "Oh, he will."

Gary nodded in agreement. "It's a fact, Zachary. All know Gary Travers, and Gary Travers knows all. I'm a veritable fountain of information."

Zach took the seat next to Gary and opposite Tara. "So, tell me, then. What have you been saying about me?"

"Well, besides the fact that you're as cute as a button? I told our dear Tara how you rescued Bobby Quinn and me from turning tricks."

"It's not like I set out to save you or anything. It was a happy coincidence."

Gary wagged his finger at him. "There's no such thing as coincidence in P-town. You don't know that yet, but you will."

If there were no coincidences in Provincetown, then what did that mean about his experiences here so far after only a few short hours? Was he meant to meet Gary and Quinn? What role was Andrew going to play in his P-town experience? Or Van?

Well, the role he'd like Van to play was obvious enough, but he shook that thought immediately from his mind. Van was simply being friendly. Nothing more. Besides, he still needed to work through his crap with Ben.

It wasn't right for Zach to be lusting after some strange man when he'd just been dumped. Wasn't there a grace period of enforced celibacy he had to follow?

"Hello!" Gary said, waving his hands in front of Zach's face.

Zach blinked and stared at Gary and Tara. He'd zoned out so completely he forgot where he was. "I'm sorry. That was rude."

"Yes," Gary agreed. "But saving our financial asses gives you a permanent Get Out of Jail Free card. So, what's going on? You looked a million miles away."

"I was just thinking about what you said. There being no coincidences in P-town. I was trying to figure out what that meant for me."

"That's easy," Gary told him. "And Tara Tebow here can back me up. What happens in P-town is supposed to happen. This is a special place. It changes people's lives. The problems and worries that you bring with you don't mean as much. Once you realize that, once you really let P-town take over, you'll know where you're supposed to be."

He looked at Tara, who nodded in agreement.

"But how can you put so much stock in that? How can you just leave your life and your future up to fate? Aren't we responsible for how our lives turn out?"

"Of course we are," Tara replied. "But when you're here, you're able to be freer than you are anywhere else. Before I came to P-town, I was divorced with a seven-year-old. I had no money. No job. No place to live. I only came because my best friend said I needed a vacation, so we packed up the car and drove from Manhattan. I met some fabulous people who offered me a job and a place to stay until I found my footing. That was twelve years ago this past June."

"You just up and moved after one vacation?"

Tara nodded. "That's not uncommon. Talk to any of the Townies. You'll find similar stories."

"What about you, Gary?"

"Bobby Quinn and I lived in Boston, so we always knew about P-town. We wanted to find a way to live here permanently, but our jobs sucked and we couldn't afford to buy a place. Over the years, we became good friends with Arthur Mackenzie, who used to own our row of condos with his partner, who died many years before. The condos were run-down and needed some fixing up. Bobby Quinn and I offered to do just that in exchange for a place to stay. Arthur, being the dear that he was, agreed. Shortly after we fixed them up, he passed away. That was a sad, sad day, but the funny thing about sadness in P-town is that it doesn't last long. Arthur willed the condos to us. He had no living family members, and he said we were the sons he never had. He knew we would be happy, and he was right. We've lived there ever since."

Zach found it difficult to believe that anyone would up and leave their lives after spending a few days anywhere. He'd been on fantastic vacations before in Hawaii and London, but even though he enjoyed himself, he never really entertained the idea of picking up roots and transplanting himself somewhere else.

That seemed ridiculous and irresponsible, but considering he just up and flew halfway across the country to escape a painful breakup, Zach admitted that the notion was at least plausible.

"So, tell us something, Zachary," Gary said as he looked at Tara, who nodded.

"Okay."

"What brings you to P-town?"

Zach opened his mouth, prepared to lie his butt off. He didn't open up to strangers. He rarely confided in anyone, except Ben, and look where that got him. But when he started speaking, Zach surprised himself by revealing everything.

By the time he was done, Gary and Tara were each holding one of his hands in comfort.

"That's just awful," Tara told him.

Gary simply shook his head. "Men can be filthy, stinking pigs. And this Ben guy sounds like the worst of them all!"

"He's not a pig," Zach said. "He's probably the cleanest guy I know."

"You're taking me far too literally," Gary explained. "He's a pig because he broke your heart and has probably moved on to someone new."

Moved on? Zach almost fell out of his chair. "I hadn't even thought about that." Gary and Tara's pitying stares told him he'd been a tad naïve. *That* was why he hadn't gotten an explanation. Ben had already found someone else. How much more of an idiot could he be?

"What's funny about all this is that I feel like I'm partly to blame." Now he sounded like a loser instead of an idiot. Big improvement.

"How so?" Gary asked incredulously. "You didn't shove Ben's cock into some random slut's ass!" He paused and then stared at Zach suspiciously. "Did you?"

"Of course not!" Zach responded. "Jeez! Besides, Ben's a total bottom."

He blushed a bit at that admission, but neither Gary nor Tara batted an eye.

"Hey, I'm not judging," Gary told him. "Playing with a third isn't exactly uncommon in our community."

Zach shook his head in disgust. "I've never done that. Never will."

"Never say never in P-town," Tara advised.

Zach was about to ask what that meant when Gary interrupted him. "It doesn't matter. The simple fact is that you didn't do anything wrong. You can't be held responsible for someone else's actions."

"No," he agreed. "But I feel like I'm missing something. Like there's something I did or didn't do that started Ben and I on this path."

"What could that possibly be?"

"I don't know," he told Tara. "That's one of the reasons I'm here. To find out."

As Gary launched into another tirade about Zach not blaming himself, Zach tuned the man out. Zach was on to something. Just beyond his grasp lay the answer he looked for, the reason he lost Ben and the source of his inability to write worth a damn.

They had to be one and the same.

ZACH hadn't wanted to go shopping, but Gary and Tara insisted as they dragged him into a store named Bravo for Men, which was fortuitously for them located next to the coffee shop. If it hadn't been, Zach doubted he would have been so easily convinced.

Once inside the store, however, he couldn't have been more out of place if he tried.

Muscle shirts of assorted colors hung throughout the store. There were also jockstraps and underwear that were definitely not the Fruit of the Loom briefs he typically wore, and skimpy bathing suits he doubted would adequately corral his junk.

"Um, guys," he told them as he turned around. "This place isn't exactly me."

"Nonsense," Gary told him as he hooked Zach's left arm and dragged him farther inside. "You're a gay man and this is a clothing store for gay men. Of course this place is for you."

"In case you haven't noticed, I don't exactly wear these kinds of clothes."

Gary nodded. "Believe me, I've noticed." He frowned as he gave Zach the once-over. "Now, Zachary Kelly, I say this with only love, but you scream for a makeover. Your clothes are *way* too big and outdated by at least three years. I mean, no one wears baggy camo shorts unless you're a bear or a muff diver."

"Gary!" Zach scolded. His face grew warm from embarrassment. He never spoke so crudely in front of a woman.

Tara laughed as she apparently intuited the reason for his humiliation. "Relax," she told him. "You can't be easily offended here. It's Provincetown."

"Besides," Gary chimed in as he started picking clothes from the rack. "She dove for muffs a time or two, but she's back to eating meat again. Thank God!"

Tara winked at Zach as she crossed over to inspect the jockstraps. Was Tara picking some of those out for him? He couldn't wear them.

Walking around with a bare ass, even if shorts or jeans covered it, went against the reserved nature he'd fostered for so long.

When Zach heard Gary speaking to an employee about getting a dressing room started, he sighed in resignation. He figured he better start choosing some clothing of his own before Gary and Tara dressed him up in Daisy Dukes and a belly shirt. Perhaps he could find something in his style amid the sizes that ran much too small for Zach's liking.

Along the right wall, Zach found some board shorts. He could wear those to the beach or the pool, so he picked out one with yellow-and-black stripes.

Immediately, Gary snatched the garment out of his hand and placed it back on the display.

"Hey! I liked that one."

"I'm sorry," Gary told him. "Were you going for bumblebee chic?"

Zach sulked as Gary led him to a table with folded muscle shirts.

"This is what you should be wearing. Although it's difficult to tell with all that material draped over you, I'm pretty certain there's a fit body under there."

"How do you know? I could just be fluffy."

Gary glared at him. "Nice try, but I'm an expert in all things regarding the manly physique. Your adorable face is strong and angular, not round or full. Your forearms and your calves aren't meaty. This means that you're hiding your awesomeness underneath a mountain of clothing, and it's time to let that light shine free."

"I like to hide," he told Gary. "It makes me feel safe."

Tara came over with her hands full of shorts that weren't denim, camo, or khaki, his usual style of choice. She carried clothes in brightly colored fabrics that he'd never in a million years wear. Not only were they the wrong color, but they looked short. Way too short. As though they only went past the midthigh, if he were lucky.

"What are the two of you trying to turn me into?"

"We're not trying to turn you into anything, sweetie," Tara told him. "We're only trying to free you."

"Free me? From what?"

"From yourself."

Tara had just exposed a cruel truth he thought he'd hidden from the world and himself.

He *was* holding himself back because he'd learned he had to live cautiously.

He had tried to be more carefree in his youth, but his father hated that. Gil Kelly didn't want a rebel without a cause. He wanted a man with a plan, and Zach saw that quite plainly when his father always seemed to prefer Zach's best friend Tommy to him.

Tommy had been a kid with ambition. He knew what he wanted and was going to make it happen. Tommy had even embraced the fact that he was gay far sooner than Zach did. Zach hadn't wanted to admit that looking at boys naked during gym class gave him a woody. It would just be another failure added to the tally of disappointments that his father tracked.

Why couldn't Tommy ever do wrong? Why didn't his father see him the way Zach saw himself?

But did that really matter anymore?

His father sure as hell wasn't perfect, and even though Zach seemed incapable of writing and had lost Ben, he realized Tara and Gary were right.

It was time to be the Zach Kelly he'd once tried to be.

"Fine," he said, snatching the clothes from Tara. "Let's do this."

Gary and Tara grinned triumphantly at him as he disappeared behind the white curtain of the dressing room.

Once inside, he tugged his shirt from his body and pulled down the cargo shorts.

He stood there in his saggy white briefs and sighed at his glaring white skin. It was so bright it made him squint. Ben had always said that he sometimes needed to wear sunglasses to bed. Ever since that comment, he'd taken to sleeping in a T-shirt and even wearing one when they fucked.

Ben hadn't complained. He didn't like the coppery body hair that spread across Zach's chest and belly. He preferred smoother bodies. Hair got everywhere, on the sheets, stuck in Ben's teeth, and it was an overall big mess for Ben. He'd wanted Zach to wax it off, but Zach hadn't given in to that request.

It had been the one thing that Ben had wanted that Zach refused to give. His one act of defiance against a man who had basically dictated his life to him for the past three years.

That tyrant, however, was now gone. He'd moved on, and Zach needed to move past what he used to be too.

He slipped the first shirt on. It was a green muscle shirt, which scooped really low in the front. His bright red chest hair was now predominantly on display. Was this how a woman felt when her titties busted out of her top?

Zach worried that Gary and Tara would laugh. But he didn't think they would. They seemed to think he would look good in these clothes. Maybe they were right.

Rummaging through the salmon-colored and powder-blue shorts that Tara picked out made Zach cringe. They were far too loud, and even though he wanted to change, he just couldn't bring himself to change *that* much. Then, he found a pair of dark brown cotton shorts. They weren't khaki, but they were close. He pulled the shorts on and studied himself in the mirror.

He didn't look silly at all. He looked plain ridiculous.

His white body had never been so revealed.

"What's taking so long?" Gary called from outside the curtain. "The best part of trying on new clothes is the fashion show. Now haul those buns of yours out here and let's have a gander."

Zach shrugged at his reflection. It was now or never.

He pulled back the curtain and stepped out of the dressing room.

"Good God, Zachary," Gary said. He clutched his throat. "Why the *hell* do you wear such ill-fitting clothes?"

"I like them," he told Gary, feeling the need to defend himself. "They make me feel good about myself."

"How is that possible? Your body is stunning."

Zach looked at Gary as if he were on crack. "Oh, please. You're just being nice."

"No, he's not," Tara interjected. "Believe me, if you looked awful, we'd tell you. The two of us are honest to a fault." She walked circles around Zach, looking him up and down. "You look fabulous!"

"I'm not buying it," he told them as he crossed his arms over his chest.

"Dylan, would you come here please?" Gary asked, calling out to the store employee who had helped start the dressing room for Zach.

"Gary, stop," Zach replied, trying his best to shush him, but it was too late.

Dylan, who looked no more than twenty-three, with tattoos up and down his arms, strutted over to where they stood. When Dylan looked at Zach, the younger man's green eyes sparkled with emerald fire. "Now what do we have here?"

"My friend here thinks we're lying to him. Please tell him he looks great."

Dylan stared at Zach in astonishment. "You've got to be shitting me. You don't look great; you're smoking hot!"

Zach rolled his eyes. "Naturally, a store employee would say nothing else."

"Nah, man, I tell it like it is. If you looked like a train wreck, I'd say so. This is where I work, and if you look bad, I look bad. But you," he said as he made Zach turn around, "look like something I'd wake up next to tomorrow morning."

Gary and Tara winked at Zach as they stepped back and let Dylan take charge.

"The shorts fit your ass perfectly," Dylan said as he smacked Zach on his butt. Zach hopped in surprise, causing Dylan to laugh. He then spun Zach around so he could once again look at the front. "And they show off your package rather nicely too. That's *very* important."

A warmth spread across his face. He was certain he looked like a ripened cherry.

"And the shirt shows off your nice guns," Dylan continued as he ran his surprisingly soft hands down Zach's right arm. All the blood in his body rushed to his dick. "And the fabric is nice and tight around the chest."

Then, to Zach's surprise, Dylan lifted the shirt to sneak a peek.

"Better watch it," Zach told him. "I'm so white I'll blind you."

Dylan let the shirt drop back down. "Maybe I wanted to be blinded."

Zach laughed nervously, but Dylan only stood there, staring at him as if he were a piece of meat waiting to be devoured. It turned Zach on, but it also made him a little nervous. He wasn't accustomed to being stared at like that.

No one had ever looked at him with such want before. Not even Ben.

And Zach liked it.

"Show me what else you got," Zach told Dylan, to which the man raised an eyebrow. "In clothing I mean."

"All right," Dylan told him. "Just more clothes. For now at least."

When Dylan left to gather more clothes for Zach to try on, Zach couldn't help but notice how pleased Gary and Tara looked. While his new friends practically gloated in silence, Zach turned around and stared at himself again in the dressing room mirror.

Just what did Gary, Tara, and Dylan see? Were they right, and had he been the one who'd been wrong all this time?

Chapter Seven

ZACH wanted to go back to the condo.

Gary and Tara wore his ass out shopping, and he spent far too much money on his new clothes. He needed time to recover. They had other plans, which didn't include allowing him to rest.

They wanted Zach to go to tea at the Boatslip instead.

When Zach informed them he wasn't craving a cup of tea, they had a good laugh at his expense.

Apparently, tea, which was more accurately called the Tea Dance, was a daily party that occurred from four until seven every afternoon on the pool deck at the Boatslip, which also happened to be a hotel. Mostly everyone, both visitor and Townie, went. They danced, drank, socialized, cruised, and generally had a great time.

It was the best party of the day, according to Gary and Tara.

It sounded fun, but Zach had no intention of carting around his shopping bags at a party. Gary, the good guy that he was, graciously offered to take the clothes back to the condo. He had to pick up Penny anyway and bring her to tea.

When Tara heard Penny was coming, she jumped up and down like a little girl. Considering Tara and Quinn's very different reactions to Penny, Zach relented. He just had to see who this woman was who could inspire such elation in Tara and such fear and loathing in Quinn.

So Gary made off with Zach's purchases, and Zach and Tara headed for the Boatslip.

As soon as they got there and Tara's evident popularity allowed them to bypass the long line of men clamoring to get in, Zach's inherent shyness almost got the better of him. He just about turned tail and ran.

Luckily, Tara grabbed a hold of his hand.

Her reassuring touch made him feel better, so he allowed her to guide him past the lines to where the music blared almost as loudly as the roar of the crowd inside.

There was no way he would've gone in if he'd come alone.

Behind a wall of windows to the left, people crowded the dance floor. Straight ahead of them and to the right, countless men spilled out onto the pool deck, which extended about fifty yards back and to the right. Every spare inch of space was covered with well-dressed or barely dressed men.

For the first time since buying his new clothes, Zach was grateful to Gary and Tara for taking him shopping. Being dressed in his new brown shorts and green muscle shirt made him less of an outsider. Tara had even used some gel in her purse to style his tousled hair.

Once they broke through the initial wall of men who stood at the perimeter, scores of shirtless men, gyrating on the dance floor, came into view. Sweat poured off their bodies as they twisted around each other while practically fucking to the beat of the music. It resembled a writhing orgy more than the dance area of a club. He doubted he'd ever feel comfortable enough about himself to wade into that crowd.

Others stood around the dancing, half-naked hot bodies who chatted while large groups paraded up and down the length of the deck. They wove in and out of the mass of people, either looking for friends or potential tricks.

The place looked like a circuit party on steroids. Not that he'd ever been to a circuit party before, but he was certain the analogy worked.

"This place is crazy."

"I know," Tara hollered in reply, struggling to be heard over the music. "Isn't it great?"

Just as Zach was about to disagree with her, Tara pulled him into the mess. They zigzagged their way through the horde until they arrived at the outside bar, which sat under a huge white tent, on the far right and just beyond the dance floor. Even outside and away from the music, the thumping bass beat thrummed inside his chest.

The sensation reminded him of a bad case of heartburn.

"What's your poison?" she asked as she walked straight up to the bar.

"I'm not much of a drinker," he admitted as he glanced back at the string of angry gays, who pointed at them for cutting in line.

"Planter's Punch it is," she said. Tara greeted the bartender whose nametag identified him as John. After she placed the order, she turned back to him and smiled. "You're gonna love it."

"These guys look pretty pissed off," he told her while nodding to the men behind them.

She shrugged in reply. "Not my problem. I'm a Townie. Plus, I work here at the Boatslip."

"You do?"

She nodded. "I tend bar. Today's just my day off."

"And you come in to work on your day off?"

"Look around you," she told him. "I wouldn't be anywhere else. Yeah, it's crazy busy, but it's the one day of the week I get to have fun instead of slinging cocktails."

Not knowing how to respond, Zach turned his attention to the angry men behind them. Should he apologize to the guys in line? He didn't dare go up to them. Some of them bristled with pissiness, and he didn't want to deal with it. Besides, he liked receiving the VIP treatment. He'd never experienced that before.

"Here you go," she said as she handed him the burnt-orange-colored drink.

He thanked her as he took the offered beverage. "How much do I owe you?"

She waved off his offer. "Not a thing. Hang with me, kiddo, and you'll never pay for a drink in P-town."

"That's good to know," he told her before he sniffed the contents. "What's in this?"

"151, pineapple juice, sweet and sour, and a splash of grenadine."

"Sounds toxic."

Tara smiled like a child introducing her new best friend to something naughty. "Give it a try."

Zach held the straw to his lips and took a big sip. Immediately, his throat burned as pure rum ran down his insides. When he fell into a coughing fit, she laughed.

"I guess I should've warned you that they pour a shot of rum into the straw, huh?"

"Um, yeah," he said as he tried to catch his breath.

She grinned mischievously as she dumped the rum out of her straw and mixed it into the drink. "I wanted you to get the full tea experience," she told him. "Choking down your first shot of rum from a Planter's Punch is tradition. All newbies find out the hard way, so you weren't going to be any different."

"Gee, thanks."

"Anytime," she said as she grabbed his hand and worked him back through the crowd.

Zach was amazed at how the tiny Tara managed to part the boys in front of her. Most moved of their own accord after they stopped to kiss and chat with her. Gary hadn't been lying; the guys here loved her, and since he now knew she was also a bartender, he understood why. Well, besides the fact that she was a terrific person. She held the power of alcohol in her hands. It was always a wise idea to cozy up to the bartender.

No matter how many admirers stopped her, Tara returned each greeting in kind and even introduced Zach at every stop. Most of the guys glared at him, obviously jealous that he was treated to a personal relationship with Tara while theirs was mostly consumer based.

It made Zach feel special to have such a close relationship with a P-town celebrity.

After a long battle through the revelers, they finally settled along the railing that looked out over Cape Cod Bay. The view proved spectacular. Countless white boats dotted the water in front of the hotel and extended all the way to MacMillan Pier. The bright sun reflected off their hulls, making each one sparkle like a precious gem amid the sky-blue ocean.

"It's beautiful."

"I know," she told him.

"Are you talking about me again?"

They turned around to find Quinn standing behind them in the same outfit Zach saw him wearing this morning.

"Naturally," Tara told him after she kissed his bearded cheek.

Quinn crossed over to Zach and gave him a substantial hug. "You enjoying yourself?"

"I am," he admitted, and it wasn't a lie. Zach liked that.

"Good," he said while scanning the immediate area. "Where's Gary?"

"He went to get Penny."

Quinn snapped back around to Tara. "Please tell me you're kidding."

"I will. If you want me to lie to you."

Quinn massaged the bridge of his nose with the thumb and forefinger of his right hand.

"Is Penny that bad?" he asked them.

"Yes!" Quinn answered emphatically.

"Don't listen to him," Tara told Zach. "He and Penny have a love-hate relationship."

Quinn shook his head in disagreement. "Not true. I have a hate-hate relationship with that goofy bitch."

Tara was evidently about to come to Penny's defense, when Zach decided to change the topic. "So you work here too?" he asked Quinn.

"Yeah, I'm in charge of security. You know, keep the drunken gays from drowning in the pool, and the minors from getting their paws on alcohol. I'm supposed to put a stop to lewd behavior too, but I only do that if the boss is watching," he added with a wink and a grin.

Zach surveyed the mass of people swirling about the deck. He didn't envy Quinn his job. Corralling all these people had to be a real pain in the ass.

After letting out a huge sigh, Quinn said, "I best get back to work. And do me a favor?"

"What?"

"When Penny gets here, let me know so I can leave."

"Behave!" Tara scolded as Quinn dove back into the ocean of people. If he heard her, he didn't respond. He had already been caught in a current of men and was carried quickly out of sight.

"I'll be back," she told Zach before she chased Quinn through the flowing stream of men.

What kind of insane sitcom had he landed in? Quirky characters populated this place. He was uncertain how to cope. Normally, he'd just fade into the background and let Ben, or whoever, deal with the crazy, but he had no one to disappear behind. It was only him, and he had to learn how to cope with new people in his life and new situations.

Right now, he couldn't be doing better. At least in his more than humble opinion.

He made new friends, bought a brand new wardrobe, and even met a smoking hot guy in a leather shop of all places. What did life have in store for him next here in Provincetown?

A flash of bronze at the corner of his eyes caught his attention. It was Van, the perfectly tanned man. Immediately, Zach's breath caught in his throat. Earlier that day, he'd sensed some interest on Van's part. It had been the way he stared at Zach. At first, he wasn't quite sure if he had read the signs right. He'd never been good at that. Ben had always said he needed to be smacked upside the head with a two-by-four before he could see the obvious. But he didn't need to be hit with a piece of wood to get that there was *some* interest on Van's part. He did find the idea of *Van's* wood hitting him upside the head rather intriguing, though.

He couldn't think about Van's hard cock right now. Well, he could. But that would only distract him. He had to focus.

He'd been too shy to do anything about Van's attraction at FK Leather. He made enough of a jerk of himself at the time. But now, dressed in his brand new clothes, he might just have a shot. If he could stop the teenage girl who now jumped up and down inside him. How lame would that be to walk over to Van, scream like a fangirl, and then run away? Yeah, that would get him nothing but a restraining order.

What he needed to do was breathe. He looked about a thousand times better than when he arrived. At least that's what Gary and Tara had said. They weren't being mean. Just truthful. Even Dylan had gone on and on about how great he'd looked. He probably could've even fucked Dylan right there in the store. Maybe in the changing area.

But who he really wanted was Van. The realization surprised him a bit. When did that happen? Shouldn't he still be pining over Ben?

Zach shook the questions from his mind. He had to stop thinking and start acting. This was P-town after all, and it was time for him to find out what the hell that meant.

He crossed the distance separating him and Van, who still hadn't seen him. As he drew closer, he imagined turning Van around and planting a huge kiss on his lips. Stealing the very breath from his body. That would be hot. And romantic. But hey, why couldn't he have both?

When he was a few feet from Van and planning on how he would deliver the kiss that would stop time, a tall, raven-haired motherfucker strolled past Zach, wrapped his arm around Van's waist, and strolled off down the deck.

Zach stopped in his tracks. Van and what looked like a perfect specimen of a man sauntered away. Arm in arm and laughing. They were the picture of perfection together. How could he ever think that *he* had a chance with someone like Van?

Who was he kidding? He'd never be good enough for someone like Van.

Hell, he wasn't even good enough for someone like Ben.

"I'm back!" Tara announced at his side. Her eyes turned to slits of worry. "What's wrong?"

He smiled, forcing the pain and a lifetime of insecurity down into the pit of his stomach where it hardened and solidified. "Nothing," he replied, painting on a smile. "So, what now?"

A smile stretched across her face. She obviously didn't believe his lie, but she seemed to have a plan to make him feel better. "That's easy," she told him. "Now, we dance!"

Zach stared reluctantly at the dance floor that Tara led him toward. The mass of sweaty, bare-chested men had grown exponentially since they arrived a short while ago. He didn't want to go in there. Especially now.

He hadn't been dancing in years, and he didn't want to make an even bigger fool of himself than he had almost done by coming on to

Van in front of his boyfriend. Besides, Ben had always told him his dancing looked like an epileptic seizure.

Tara, however, didn't give Zach time to argue. She pulled him onto the dance floor where the sea of men quickly swallowed them up.

AFTER only a few songs on the tightly packed floor, Zach's body was covered in sweat. It poured down his face and back and crept uncomfortably down his ass crack. He didn't particularly enjoy the feeling of swamp butt. Not only that but his cup was empty, and he needed another drink.

It helped him forget about Van.

"Ready for another?" Tara asked him. Her once wild curls now lay matted against her perspiring face.

"Yeah," he shouted. "I'll get it. It's my turn."

She shook her head and grabbed the cup from his hand. "Oh, please. There's no way I'm letting you stand in that long line. I've got it. Besides, it's free for me." She kissed his cheek and told him, "You stay here and enjoy. I'll be right back."

She couldn't go. What would he do if he saw Van and that guy again? He couldn't be alone *and* face that again, but Tara turned around too quickly for him to protest. She had slipped by the sweaty dancers and was already on the other side of the bar before he even registered that she was gone.

He looked around, unsure what to do. And surveying the crowd for Van. If he saw Van, he'd bolt. But he was nowhere to be seen. Thankfully. They'd probably already left tea. To go home and have hot, hunky sex together. Now why did he have to go and put *that* image in his head? He needed to focus on something else. Like dancing. He had never danced by himself. Hell, he'd never done anything by himself. Someone had always been by his side, taking the edge off his usual social anxiety.

For the past three years, that someone had been Ben.

The smiling faces that surrounded him were obviously lost in the beat. Why couldn't he do the same thing? So he closed his eyes and let the waves of the music wash away his typical unease. In response, his body involuntarily moved on its own. In just a few seconds, epileptic seizure or not, he was dancing among a group of strangers.

He couldn't believe the difference a few hours made.

When he had gotten there that afternoon, he had been heartbroken and lost. He didn't know if it was the music, the people, or Provincetown itself, but he was almost a new man. Who almost made a complete idiot of himself by coming on to Van. Still, he at least had made an attempt instead of just sitting idly by doing nothing. Like he usually did.

The music of the current song ended and as the first few notes of the next began, the crowd immediately cheered. People who had been lined up along the wall jammed onto the already packed floor, where everyone began to hop up and down.

Zach had no clue what the song was, but the tune sounded familiar. Then, a pair of women's voices broke through the speakers, claiming they were the Weather Girls. How dumb was he? He needed to turn in his gay card.

By the time "It's Raining Men" was in full swing, even more people had crowded onto the dance floor, and Zach worried Tara wouldn't be able to find him in the crowd.

But his concern didn't last very long.

The continual rush of people shoved him forward unexpectedly, and he slammed into a pair of men, who mistook his stumble for a come-on. They opened their arms to include him while simultaneously ripping his sopping shirt from his body.

In mere moments, he stood half-naked before them, and their hungry hands traveled up and down his body, consuming every part they touched or groped. He tried not to tense up, but he couldn't help it. Zach wasn't accustomed to strange men fondling him in public.

And liking it.

He tried to extricate himself from their greedy limbs before he lost control, but they sandwiched Zach in the middle, using their sweat-slick bodies to lock him in place and trapping him in the hottest prison imaginable.

They ground against him slowly, timing their thrusts to the initial leisurely beat of the song. As the music increased in tempo so did they.

The blond behind him rubbed his semi-hard cock against his butt while his dark-skinned partner ground his boner against Zach's pelvis.

The scent of moist, hot skin mixed with the heavy stench of sex hung on the humid air around them, pressing against him like a third body. He inhaled the sexual bouquet, and with every breath, he released his previous reserved nature until his body matched their yearning beat.

Dirty dancing with these hot studs was much better than pining over Van.

His cock throbbed painfully in his shorts, and the shame or embarrassment that typically descended upon him whenever the barn doors of his sexuality opened never occurred. He enjoyed how their hands surfed the sheen of sweat covering his body. When the guy behind him grabbed his ass, he backed up into it. When the one in front slipped his hand down Zach's shorts and jacked his thickening cock, he draped his arms around the man's neck and drew him into a greedy kiss.

Could this be happening? Was he actually living instead of watching others do what he had always been too afraid to do? And did guys actually find him desirable?

These two certainly did. They didn't shun him for his pale skin, bright red hair, and socially awkward ways. These men didn't care about any of his shortcomings. In fact, they didn't know a damn thing about him except what they saw, and they liked it. They wanted whatever Zach was willing to give.

And right now, he was happy to offer up a prize. Van and Ben's loss was these guys' gain.

The guy behind him undid the button of Zach's shorts. His reserved nature briefly returned, screaming for the man to stop, but the primal instinct that had been set free by the debauchery beat his rational side into submission. So when the man behind him pushed his shorts and his new stylish briefs down to his midthighs, Zach's only response was to back up even harder against the man's hard cock, which he had pulled out of his shorts and now pressed against Zach's sweat-moistened ass.

The man in front of him shoved his tongue down Zach's throat as he furiously beat Zach's dick to the rhythm of the music. Zach shoved his hand down the darker man's shorts and returned the favor.

He opened his eyes, expecting to find people staring at them in horror. Instead, no one paid them any attention. Each person around them was either lost in the music, their own passionate embraces, or completely immune to what was going on. It was as if such shameless public displays were common practice in Provincetown.

Accepting that no one cared made Zach even more sexually ravenous as his body burned with a passion completely unknown to him. The desire in the fingers gripping his erection and the pulsing cock sliding up and down his crack validated his existence. They unknowingly transformed him from the socially awkward and shy person he had previously been into someone who had started to realize he was more than the bumbling fool everyone thought he was.

"You're so fucking sexy," the guy behind him whispered in his ear as he chewed on Zach's neck. In reply, Zach turned his head to the right and pushed his tongue past the man's lips.

Suddenly, a warm, wet sensation enclosed around his cock. When he glanced downward, the top of the dark-skinned guy's head bobbed up and down on his prick. The combination of his dark features wrapped around Zach's pink dick as the crowd undulated about them drove him crazy. He'd never been sucked off in public before, especially not by some stranger in the middle of a dance floor.

This wasn't like the man he'd made himself be. He was far too conservative for such behavior. Ben had often wanted him to be more adventurous, to take more chances not just sexually but in life.

Zach had refused. Boundaries made him feel safe.

But as he cast all restrictions aside by shoving his cock farther down the throat of the guy on his knees, Zach felt liberated from his own daily and often fretted self.

"Do you like that?" the blond man whispered in his ear. "Do you like my man's mouth on your cock?"

Zach grunted in reply as the cocksucker's tongue darted around the head of his prick before the man once again swallowed it whole.

"Tell me how much you like it," the guy demanded as he slipped one of his fingers inside Zach's ass.

Zach had never been a fan of anal play in the bedroom, at least not when it was his ass being invaded, but in the middle of the dance floor with men bouncing all around him as the Weather Girls belted out their tune, he couldn't think of anything he wanted more. Zach bucked backward on the guy's finger as he wiggled it around inside Zach.

"I fucking love it," he uttered breathlessly.

"He loves sucking cock, and he loves guzzling some random guy's load. Feed it to him," the man urged. "Shoot your fucking jizz down his throat."

His words set Zach's skin on fire and caused his already hard cock to stiffen even further. The sucking, slick mouth wrapped around him combined with the finger-fucking and dirty talk took him quickly over the edge.

While the Weather Girls screamed about raining men during the song's crescendo, Zach unleashed a torrent of spunk inside the crouching man's mouth. He came so hard he almost blacked out, but his willing partner dutifully swallowed each spurt. He squeezed the base of Zach's sensitive dick, milking out the last drop before once again rising to his feet.

"Thanks." The man smirked as he licked his lips.

The world swam around Zach as he realized what he'd just done. The guy behind him pulled up his shorts and patted him on the ass in thanks. When did he become such a dirty little pig? The song ended and the couple walked away holding hands, leaving him behind like a discarded piece of trash.

He should be insulted. Revolted. Ashamed of himself.

Instead of liking it so damn much.

VAN violently shoved open the door leading out to the patio. Why did he always delude himself? When he met Zach earlier today, he'd imagined he was different from all the other sluts who came to P-town looking to get their rocks off.

Apparently, he'd been mistaken. Either that or Zach had an identical twin who just got sucked off in the middle of tea.

Who was he to judge, though? It wasn't like he was exactly innocent and pure. He got fucked on camera for heaven's sake. He had about as much of a leg to stand on as a peg-leg pirate.

Still, he couldn't help but be disappointed.

He'd been attracted to the innocent mess he met at FK. That guy either never existed or had been gobbled up by the depravity that stole the souls of so many who came to Provincetown.

Why did that bother him so much? So what if Zach wanted to drill every hole in town while he was here for the week? That was his prerogative. Just like it was his to get screwed on film by big-dicked muscled studs.

Whether it should bother him or not, it did, and Van spiraled into a vortex of pissy. He needed to get the hell out of here and go home. Perhaps in the comfortable surroundings of home, he'd be able to understand just what the hell was going on with him. If not, at least he wouldn't have to watch as Zach stumbled off the dance floor and into the waiting arms of his next trick.

Yeah, he definitely didn't want to see that.

Chapter Eight

AFTER stumbling off the dance floor in a daze, Zach wandered aimlessly around the pool deck. He told himself he was searching for Tara, but he really wasn't.

He was searching for himself instead.

He'd never behaved so recklessly. He prided himself on being able to rein in his baser instincts and always remain in control, but the fact he just allowed himself to be sucked off and diddled on a dance floor packed with other sweaty men told Zach that he most certainly wasn't.

What the hell was happening? He pulled his green shirt from his rear left pocket where one of the dance floor guys had safely tucked it.

With the shirt once again over his skin, control found its comfortable foothold. The simple act of covering up centered him, even though the sexual beast that had been awakened had resumed clawing its way up from inside.

As he passed one hot man after another, he entertained how each one of them might look sucking his cock or facedown and ass up on his mattress. His already spent dick even came to life again at the mere thought of another sexual encounter.

He needed help. Fast.

"Hello, dahling."

The voice behind him sounded familiar, but Zach couldn't place it. When he turned around, he was even more confused.

A six-foot-tall drag queen with neon-green hair met his gaze.

"I'm sorry," he told her as she drew Zach into an embrace, smashing her fake breasts against his still sweat-soaked chest. "Do I know you?"

"Do you know me?" she asked. Her voice cackled with incredulity. She tossed her long, fake green locks to the side and raised a comically enormous goblet, which looked as if it stood about a foot tall. It also currently held at least a half gallon of what looked like Planter's Punch. "Do you know me?" she repeated. "Look closely, dahling."

Zach did as instructed.

A black leather bustier wrapped tightly around her manly chest, and a shiny green mini skirt barely covered up her family jewels. Long legs, draped in fishnet stockings, descended like trunks from beneath the skirt and ended in a pair of thigh-high, green go-go boots with two-inch heels.

He had no clue who this woman was until he looked into her powder-blue eyes.

"Gary?" he asked, unable to believe the transformation from the attractive man into his scantily clad, brash persona. "Is that you?"

"Maybe at one time," she told him with a wink. "But for now call me Penny Poison."

"Penny Poison?"

She nodded as she took a long sip out of her straw, draining a quarter of the liquid. "That's me, dahling. In the flesh."

Immediately, Zach understood Quinn's distaste for Penny. While Zach loved the costume, he could see why Quinn wouldn't be amused that his attractive partner occasionally squeezed into such garish clothing.

"You look amazing," he told her.

"Of course I do," she replied with a flourish of her left hand. "I'm practically perfect in every way."

"I thought that was Mary Poppins."

Penny rolled her eyes. "That English biddy can't hold a candle to me."

Zach chuckled at the thought of Julie Andrews and Gary Travers going at it for the title of Miss Practically Perfect. Although he loved

Gary's Penny, he'd still give the title to Julie Andrews, hands down. "I had no idea you did drag."

"It's a hobby of mine. I haul Penny out occasionally. The girl needs to cut loose every now and then. You know, get her drink on and such. Besides," she told him, drawing nearer as if to let Zach in on a secret, "the boys just love me. I get to do things to them I couldn't normally do as Gary."

"And Quinn doesn't mind?"

"Mind? He hates it!" she told him. "But he's not exactly Mister Innocent. That boy's cute bearded face and otterish body get some serious cuddle time with others sans *moi*. I deserve some slap and tickle on the side too, don't you think?"

How was he supposed to respond to that revelation? He'd naturally assumed that Gary and Quinn were a monogamous couple, but apparently they played well with others. While he'd heard of such arrangements before, Zach had never actually met couples whose bedroom activities weren't limited to each other, at least no one who spoke about it so openly.

Apparently, Gary didn't care who knew, and he seemed almost shocked that Zach thought they were exclusive. Relationships appeared to be far more inclusive on the tip of the Cape.

"There you are!" Tara said as she suddenly stood at his side. Zach was thankful for the intrusion. He'd been having difficulty processing the loose constraints of Gary and Quinn's relationship.

It bothered and intrigued him at the same time.

"I didn't think I'd find you again once they started playing 'It's Raining Men.' I've lost more friends here at tea when those boys cram onto the dance floor. I thought for sure you'd have hightailed it out of here."

"I didn't," he told her as he took the drink she had gone to retrieve. He drank half its contents in one gulp, and when his head started to get fuzzy, he realized he needed to slow down. He already lost control once today. He was going to try not to let that happen again.

"Did you have fun?"

"You bet he did," Penny answered for him with a wry smile.

A slow flame worked its way across Zach's cheeks. Penny's response told him he'd been spotted getting naughty on the dance floor, but the kiss she blew him also communicated it would be their secret.

"I feel like I'm missing something," Tara admitted as she looked back and forth between them.

"Oh, dahling. It's just boys being boys."

Tara nodded. "Yup. I definitely missed something."

"You didn't miss a thing," Zach lied. "Besides me making a fool of myself on the dance floor."

"Never a fool," Penny told him. "It's Provincetown. There are no fools or rules."

"Amen," Tara added as she held her drink up for a toast. "To Provincetown."

"To Provincetown," he and Penny replied in unison.

When they clinked their plastic cups together, Penny's words as well as Tara's toast echoed through his memory.

Were there no rules here? Could he function without them?

While Zach didn't have the answers, the animal within howled in reply.

AFTER they finished their fourth Planter's Punch, Zach's head spun. He'd never drunk so much, and he worried his excessive intake and his rather recent loose sexual morals indicated that there was a problem he wasn't addressing.

He'd come here to get away from Ben and the pain of being dumped by his lover of three years. Who *might* have cheated on him. He also had every intention of using that pain to fuel his writing and create a good book, one that would get him published.

Instead, he'd turned to impulse shopping, binge drinking, and anonymous fucking.

He needed to get his head on straight. But even more importantly right now, he needed to sit down.

"Take it easy," Tara told him as she leaned him up against the wall next to the outside restrooms. "You're not looking so good."

"I feel good," he told her. "In fact, I don't feel a damn thing. Which for me is pretty damn good."

He was slurring his speech, but Zach didn't care. There were no rules in Provincetown, so he'd decided to embrace hedonism and abandon his long life of self-denial. Everyone else did it. Why couldn't he?

At least when he indulged himself he got sucked off. That had to count for something.

"I'm gonna go get you some water," Tara told him. "You stay here."

"Wh-where's Penny? I just love her!"

"Penny went to say hi to some friends. She'll be right back."

"I just love Penny," he told Tara. "Penny Poison."

He loved the alliteration of her name. In fact, he loved it so much he decided to sing it.

"We all love Penny."

"Not Quinn," Zach reminded her. "He hates Penny."

"He doesn't really," Tara replied. "He just thinks she's a bit much. Now stay put, I'll be right back."

He gave Tara a huge hug before she finally untangled herself from his wild limbs and disappeared into the crowd in search of the water that would bring him back to his senses. Did he want that, though? Did he really want to return to his rational ways?

He'd been sensible too long as it was. It was time for him to just have fun.

Why did he have to be so serious all the fucking time?

He surveyed the crowd around him and contemplated diving into it, to find someone new to sink his cock into, but a huge wave of nausea washed all over him. He leaned back against the wall and bent over, certain he would blow chunks right there in front of everyone.

Zach didn't enjoy vomiting, especially in public, but he'd done a lot of things today he didn't like doing before. Why the hell not add public regurgitation to the list?

"Fancy meeting you here."

When Zach looked up, he gazed into the sparkling green eyes of Dylan, the hot tattooed employee from Bravo. The younger man shoved his hands inside the pockets of his red shorts, and although it was difficult for Zach to tell through the haze of inebriation, Dylan looked to be preening for him.

His inked arms looked flexed, not relaxed, which meant Dylan obviously wanted him to check out his goods.

Who was Zach to turn down such an invitation?

His gaze traveled up from Dylan's lean, toned legs and past the nice bulge in his shorts. The fabric of his white shirt clung tightly to his flat abs, stretching tautly across his lean, trim chest, which although smaller than Zach's, still looked quite impressive. When Zach gazed into Dylan's face, an alluring twinkle reflected in Dylan's eyes and on the upturn of his crooked smile.

Although he typically was clueless when a guy was interested in him, Zach needed no one to tell him Dylan was ready to be drilled.

"It's me," the younger man said, breaking the silence. "Dylan. From Bravo."

Zach couldn't help the smile that inched its way across his face. He found it adorable that not only did Dylan think Zach had forgotten him but that he also looked disappointed.

How cute was that?

"I know who you are," he finally replied, trying not to sound sick. "How could I forget the man who took most of my money?"

Dylan chuckled. "You *did* spend a lot, but hey, looking good requires a lot of green."

"Apparently so."

"Speaking of green," Dylan began as he drew closer, "how are you?"

"Regretting that last Planter's Punch."

Dylan leaned with him against the wall. "I can't tell you how many times I've heard that one."

Zach turned to his right, staring into Dylan's flirty green eyes. Was it the alcohol, Provincetown, or the fact that he really wanted to nail Dylan that sexually empowered him? He'd become a lion stalking a gazelle and just waiting to take it down. "Know of any home remedies?"

Dylan shrugged. "A couple."

"Maybe you could, I don't know, share them with me."

As a naughty smile slowly slid across Dylan's face, Zach couldn't believe how forward he was being. Well, he had planned on sweeping Van into a passionate kiss earlier, but that had been an epic fail. Why was he so willing to throw caution to the wind again so quickly? Whenever he had sex with someone, it just sort of happened. No other man had ever really pursued him, except for Ben, and he'd certainly never been the pursuer. Yet here he was. Trying to charm this sweet young thing into his bed when he'd just dumped a load down some random guy's gullet a few moments ago.

What the *hell* was going on?

Maybe his breakup with Ben had somehow turned him into a manslut.

"Come on," Dylan said as he grabbed Zach's hand.

"Where we going?"

"Your place," Dylan told him. "I've got a cure for what ails ya."

Without another word, Zach followed Dylan out of the Tea Dance. His previous concerns about the person he was becoming lingered within the back of his mind, but his slowly hardening cock shooed those pesky thoughts away.

He'd listened to the head on his shoulders for too long. For now, he relinquished all control to the head that swung between his legs.

Chapter Nine

"HERE we are," Zach told Dylan as he slid the patio door to his condo open. "Home sweet home. At least for the week, anyway."

Dylan walked around the living room. His gaze swept past the small sectional couch before eying the staircase that led upstairs to the second floor, where his big, empty bed waited for them. "You feeling any better?"

He nodded. "The fresh air on the walk over here did me some good." Zach closed the door and then clicked the lock shut. He threw the keys on the small dining room table to the right and closed the distance between him and Dylan. Now that the prey stood in his den, it wouldn't be allowed out until he was done. "But I'm still in need of that home remedy."

"Let me check out the kitchen," Dylan told him. Before Dylan had time to move, Zach wrapped his arms around Dylan's smaller waist and pulled him close.

"I haven't gone shopping yet."

Dylan relaxed quite comfortably in his arms. "I thought you wanted my home remedy."

"I do. Can't you think of *anything* else that might make me feel better?"

"I can think of a few actually."

Zach bent over Dylan and inhaled his cologne-scented neck. He wasn't a fan of artificial fragrance—the odor made his nose twitch—but Zach didn't care. He would just avoid the areas where too much had been applied. So he trailed his tongue from Dylan's smooth jawline toward his chin and up to his lips.

When Zach pressed his lips against Dylan's, Dylan opened wide like a baby bird about to be fed by his parent. How could he open his mouth that wide? Did his jaws somehow unhinge themselves?

Zach took a step back to get a better view. He'd never seen anything like it. Dylan resembled someone about to scream in fright instead of a guy about to be kissed.

How much more bizarre could this get?

Dylan then licked his lips and closed the remainder of the gap. That was when Zach was treated to a generous helping of spit. Dylan's tongue went wild in his mouth, writhing out of control as it slid across his teeth and knocked around his uvula before slipping back out and slobbering all over Zach's lips.

Zach had to do a double take to make sure Dylan hadn't turned into some overgrown dog trying to lick his face clean off. When Dylan looked back at him, his green eyes half shut in a dreamy passion that no longer coursed through Zach's body, he had to stifle a laugh.

Dylan actually thought this was hot. He made deep, guttural noises of pleasure as saliva continued to pour down their lips and chins. It was obvious from the passionate frenzy shining in Dylan's eyes that he wanted more.

All Zach wanted was a napkin.

When Dylan started to lick his way from Zach's mouth to his neck, he just had to stop him. Zach grabbed Dylan by the chin and held him fast, but Dylan's tongue darted wildly about, straining to continue on the path it had already begun.

"What's the matter?" Dylan asked as his tongue thankfully withdrew back into the hole that spawned it.

Could he be serious? Did Dylan not see the slobber dripping from his face? Evidently the answer was no. The only thing Dylan cared about was getting more of Zach. While his tongue might have been put away, he pawed at Zach's arms and chest, and his hips dry humped the air. It appeared to be some automatic response for him, like when someone holds a dog over the water and it starts paddling.

Except this wasn't cute.

This moment belonged on some bad reality show called *When Tricks Attack!*

"I want you real bad," Dylan told him. "I've wanted you since I saw you."

Dylan shook himself free from Zach's grip and pulled his white shirt over his head. He stood there, flexing in front of Zach, puffing out his chest and bulging out his lean biceps. Even though the younger man had a hot body, something looked weird. The angle of his chest looked off; he looked asymmetrical and that was when Zach realized why.

Dylan had three nipples.

He had two normal, healthy-looking nipples where one usually expected to find such body parts, but four inches below the left one sat a third nubbin that looked more like a dried-out, blanched raisin than anything else.

Zach fought the urge to flick it to see how it responded.

"You wanna touch me?" Dylan asked as he curled his bicep.

Could he really be that much of a prick and say no? Before he could respond, though, Dylan stepped out of his shoes, shucked off his shorts and underwear, and bent over the back of the couch. He'd entered waters from which there was no return. The only way to end this was to fuck him.

"Come on," Dylan complained as he handed Zach a condom. "Fuck me like the nasty bitch I am."

Zach almost lost it. With his spit-soaked muzzle and three titties, Dylan was already more like a female dog than anyone he knew.

"Do it," Dylan repeated as he wagged his tail.

"All right, already," Zach told him as he dropped his shorts and briefs. He left his shirt on, so he'd have less to put back on when this was over.

"I'm so hot for you, you fucking stud. I just love that you're acting all indifferent and shit. Making me feel like some worthless piece of trash."

Not worthless. This is priceless. This little clusterfuck would wind up in his next book.

Zach tried rolling the condom onto his cock, but it had lost all its hardness. Dylan immediately pounced on the situation. He slobbered up and down his dick, which refused to get hard. Zach closed his eyes, trying to recall how hot he thought Dylan was before he actually starting kissing him. All he could see now, though, was the third nipple and the lolling tongue.

Dylan jacked him furiously and started to get a little pissy and a bit too rough. "Come on, you fucker. You know you wanna shove it up my ass."

"Uh-huh," he told Dylan as he tried to will the blood in his body to his cock. It wasn't working. He was limper than a wet noodle.

Until Van sprung into his mind.

When he thought about the hot guy who helped him at the leather store, not the one who'd taken off with Mr. Perfect at tea, his cock started to slowly fill.

"That's what I'm talking about," Dylan mumbled.

"That's it," Zach told him. "Suck it."

When he looked down, he didn't see Dylan. Van knelt before him, taking his hard cock between his soft, pink lips. His steely-blue eyes looked up at him in desire, wanting, no, *needing* to be fucked by Zach's cock.

Zach stood him up and bent him over the couch.

"That's right. Ride my ass!"

After rolling the condom on his cock and using the spit that still coated his face as lube, Zach plunged inside. Dylan howled in a mixture of pain and pleasure.

"Yeah, Daddy!" Dylan screamed. "Make it hurt!"

Zach closed his eyes and worked his hips like a piston. He slid his cock in and out of Dylan's ass, but in his mind it was Van who he furiously skewered.

"Oh, God, yes!" Dylan moaned. He whimpered and screamed so much he actually started to sound like a dog.

Zach had to banish the image from his mind. If he lost his erection, he'd never finish, and right now, he wanted to see his fantasy fuck with Van through to the end.

So as Dylan howled and carried on like a suffering animal, Zach only heard the low grunts and whines he imagined Van would make as a cock slid up his ass. The warmth that clenched his erection belonged to the hottest man he'd ever seen. The butt cheeks he spread farther apart weren't pale or fair like Dylan's. They were tanned and firm, just how he pictured Van's ass would look.

Zach allowed his hands to roam over Van's body, delighting in the tense muscles of his back and the broad shoulders he used as handholds to shove himself inside faster and harder. He moved his left hand around to Van's chest before tweaking the left nipple and then the nipple just below it. This one was harder and smaller. When Zach realized he was rolling Dylan's angry third nipple between his fingers, his eyes fluttered wide open.

He wiped his hand on his shirt immediately. Zach wasn't sure why. Third nipples weren't contagious or anything, but he just couldn't help himself. It felt hard and crusty and almost made him lose his erection. Zach had to close his eyes quickly, and when he did, Van suddenly appeared in his mind, looking back at him, begging him to fuck him harder.

Zach did.

For a few more minutes, he continued his assault until the pressure within built up. His cock grew even harder, and Van clenched firmly upon his throbbing cock. He squeezed, obviously sensing the impending release and wanting to milk the cum out of Zach's dick.

"I'm getting close," he uttered.

The man who existed on the other end of Zach howled in satisfaction. "Me too," Dylan said as he furiously palmed his cock.

When Zach came, it was Van's ass that received his load, not Dylan who started screaming at the top of his lungs, "I'm gonna come now!" He then proceeded to shoot his spunk all over the back of the couch while howling like a wolf calling to its pack. After the call of the wild subsided, Zach withdrew from Dylan's ass and walked over to the trash can to throw away the spent rubber.

He'd done it. Now he could put an end to this debacle.

"That was awesome!" Dylan sighed from the living room.

"Yeah," Zach agreed when he crossed back into the room. He hoped he sounded more enthusiastic than he felt.

Dylan yawned and curled up on the couch. "Coming makes me sleepy."

Oh no! There was no way this three-nippled, howling motherfucker was spending the night. "Me too," he told Dylan. "And I really need to get some sleep. It's been a long day of traveling."

Dylan opened his arms. "Come lay down next to me."

Panic descended upon Zach. What else could he do besides grab Dylan by the nape of the neck and toss him out the door like an unwanted mongrel? Although that might be rude, it was Dylan who had crossed a line. Even Zach, who had rarely tricked, knew appropriate trick etiquette.

After you come, you go.

"I don't sleep on couches all that well," Zach finally said.

"It's okay," Dylan replied as he stood up. "We can go upstairs."

"I don't sleep well with strangers either."

Zach immediately regretted his words. Dylan's sleepy, come-happy face flashed in anger. "Oh, I get it!" he shouted as he picked up his shirt from the floor. "You're one of *those* guys."

Zach tried to explain, but Dylan wouldn't hear it. He pulled his shirt over his head and pulled up his shorts. "I thought you might be different," he told Zach. "You looked so innocent. Like Eliza fucking Doolittle being made over in the shop. But you're no different from all the other sluts in this place." After stepping into his shoes, Dylan bellowed, "God, I *fucking* hate P-town!"

He then turned on his heels and stormed out the front door.

He hadn't wanted to hurt Dylan at all. In fact, he usually went out of his way *not* to hurt people, but apparently in Provincetown, he was not only a slut but an ass too.

This trick was supposed to have helped him get past his inhibitions. Which he apparently had. Two fucks in less than a few hours was a new world record for Zach. Still, he hadn't planned on hurting anyone by it.

Apparently he still had a lot to learn about tricking.

Zach then closed the patio door that Dylan left wide open and locked it. It had been a long day, and he needed to rest.

Perhaps things would look better in the morning, but first, he needed to shower. He had to get all this fucking spit off his face. Zach turned off the downstairs lights and headed upstairs.

IT HAD been a long day. All Van wanted to do was sleep, but that seemed to be too much to ask. Nino was too busy fucking the shit out of some guy in the next room. Although he typically didn't get upset about Nino's tricking, which happened *at least* once a day, today he just couldn't handle it.

He had his fill of random sexual acts for one day.

Van pulled the pillow over his ears in a vain effort to drown out the grunts and whines from behind the much-too-thin walls. When that didn't work, he considered banging on the wall and telling them to shut the hell up.

How could he do that? It wasn't Nino's fault he was in a foul mood.

Van threw the pillow across the room as if that act of anger could somehow calm his temper. He only succeeded in knocking down a vase, which fell to the floor and shattered.

"Motherfucker!" he cursed. He jumped out of bed to clean up the mess and stubbed his toe against the bedside table. "Shit!"

Van hopped around on one foot, waiting for the pain to subside. As he waited, his anger only continued to grow. It needed to be released like the pressure inside of a boiling teakettle. If he didn't, he would likely rip his room to shreds, so Van opened his mouth and gave loose a cry of fury.

Afterward, his mind cleared. The red haze that dominated his vision slowly disappeared.

He sat at the edge of his bed in his yellow briefs and sighed. What the fuck was going on with him?

Suddenly, the door to his bedroom flew open, and Nino darted in naked. The condom he'd been using still clung tightly to his semi-hard cock. His best friend's gaze darted around the room, searching for an intruder. Finding none, Nino surveyed the broken vase shattered on the floor. "What the fuck, man?" he asked as he yanked off the condom and tossed it into Van's trash basket.

"Get back to your trick," Van told him with a grimace.

"I'd like to, but it's kinda hard to fuck when you're making such a ruckus."

"It's kinda hard to *sleep* when *you're* making such a ruckus."

Nino glared at him. He obviously sensed something was wrong. They had been friends long enough for Nino to be able to read him like a favorite childhood comic book. Without another word, Nino left his room and went back into his own.

Nino's muffled voice drifted through the wall. After that, someone screamed, "Fuck off!" before storming out of the place in a huff. A few minutes later, Nino, still naked, walked back into Van's room and sat next to him on his bed.

"You didn't have to do that."

"Do what?" Nino asked, feigning confusion. "That guy sucked in bed. He was one of those bottoms that just laid there like a frickin' corpse. For a man of my skills, I deserve much better."

Van didn't believe him, but he allowed his friend's sacrifice to go by without further comment. Nino hated for anyone, even Van, to know he had a kind and generous heart. Instead, Nino enjoyed everyone believing he was a heartless prick, so no one expected a damn thing from him.

Too many people placed too many expectations upon him already.

"Do you *have* to be naked on my bed?" Van asked, changing the subject. They both did better with humor than anything else. "I don't need your ass leaving skid marks on my Martha Stewart sheets."

Nino bore down and farted. "How's *that* for a skid mark?"

As always, Nino made Van laugh, even if he had to bury his face in the crook of his elbow to escape the eye-watering stench.

"You're so disgusting!" Van accused Nino as he chuckled. "That smells so bad I can actually taste shit!"

"I do my best," Nino replied, looking quite pleased.

After a few minutes, Van stood back up and tentatively sniffed, hoping enough time had passed for the fumes to dissipate. Thankfully, he was greeted with the lingering scent of vanilla from the candle he lit before bed instead of what had unfortunately escaped Nino's ass. "All right, let me clean up my mess," he stated as he motioned to his wastebasket, "while you take your nasty fuck rag outta my room."

Nino grabbed his wrist and yanked him back onto the bed. "Not before you tell me what's going on."

"Nothing," he told Nino, and though he didn't mean to lie, he *really* didn't know what the truth was. If he did, he'd likely not be pissy anymore.

"Most everyone else falls for your bullshit. Not me."

"What does *that* mean?"

Nino looked at Van as if he were stupid. "You keep everyone at arm's length. They ask how you're doing, and you lie to them. Tell them what you think they want to hear. I used to think that you did that for your benefit, so you didn't have to think about all you've been through, but that's not it. You do that so no one can get close enough to hurt you again."

"I do *not*!"

"Yeah, you do," Nino confirmed. "I'm not saying you're an asshole or anything. 'Cause you're not. You just usually act... you know... fake."

If he had the will, he'd have punched Nino right in his perfect, symmetrical nose.

Who the fuck was *he* calling fake? Nino was the fake one, working as a model and plastering on a phony smile to sell whatever stupidly overpriced outfits the designers wanted him to whore out in magazines.

Van wasn't fake. He stripped down to his flesh and bared all. He hid nothing from the camera. He exposed himself so people knew exactly what the fuck he was. He hid behind nothing. And no one. He didn't pretend to be something he wasn't like other people he knew or just met.

"Fuck you!" he shouted. He stood up and began picking up the glass shards on the wood floor. "I'm *not* fake."

"I didn't say you were," Nino replied. "I said you *act* fake. There *is* a difference."

"What the fuck does that even mean?"

Nino sighed. His scrunched-up face told Van he was thinking hard about his answer. He obviously knew that Van was on the edge of seriously losing his temper. "I'm not trying to make you upset," he finally said. "I'm just saying that I know you. Better than anyone else. And you can keep everyone else as far away as you want. But I won't let you do that to me." He stood next to Van and looked him square in the eyes. "I'm your best friend. I'm here for you. No matter what. I think I've already proven that to you."

Van couldn't deny that. Although his friends had rallied around him when he needed them the most, it was Nino who shouldered the majority of the burden. Nino had brought him back from the edge of despair, and when he told everyone he was getting into the porn business, Nino had championed Van's decision.

It was what Van needed at the time.

"I'm sorry," he said. "You're right. About everything."

Nino nodded. "Now tell me what's going on."

"Can you get dressed first?" Van asked. "It's weird having this conversation with you while you're butt-ass naked in my room."

"If you don't tell me, I'm gonna shove my balls in your face," he warned. "Now talk."

Nino was obviously serious, and he most definitely didn't want Nino's junk in his face. "I don't know," he begrudgingly admitted. "I'm just tired."

"Of?"

"Of people only seeing Hart Throb."

"I don't understand," Nino told him. "*You're* the one who wanted it that way."

"I know. I just don't know if I want that anymore." Van couldn't believe what he was saying. Just this morning, he'd been fine with his life. Getting fucked by Ram had been fun. He relished his notoriety and the nasty pig-sex he had onscreen. It made him feel powerful, but sometime after the shoot and coming home after tea, he longed for something far more dangerous.

Intimacy.

"Okay," Nino said with a nod. "Why now? What's changed?"

He couldn't tell Nino about Zach. Although Nino was a good sounding board, he sucked at relationship advice since he'd never been in one. Nino thought relationships were for people who lacked imagination, for those who needed labels established by society to define their lives for them.

Nino lived without such things and was quite happy doing so.

Besides, he couldn't exactly describe Zach as a relationship anyway. They'd just met, for Christ's sake! And he'd just seen Zach with his cock down some random guy's throat. Talk about jumping the motherfucking gun.

Still, meeting Zach breathed life into a part of Van he'd thought had died two years ago. The part that enjoyed taking risks with his heart.

That was what infuriated Van so much. He didn't even know this guy, except that he was crazy adorable and clumsier than the Three Stooges combined. And hadn't Zach just proven he was no different from all the other men who lived here?

This was Provincetown, after all.

The guys who came here usually wanted one thing—an ass for their cock or a cock for their ass. Love didn't live here; a never-ending hunger for hooking up did.

Still, there was something familiar within Zach's delicious brown eyes. It spoke to him as if it were his own voice coming out of someone else. Someone who knew nothing about Hart Throb. Someone who saw only Van Pierce.

It had been a long time since *any*one looked at him like that.

"You gonna answer my question?" Nino asked. "Or do you need my balls in your face?"

"I don't have an answer," Van replied quickly, and from the expression in Nino's eyes, he could tell his friend believed Van's words to be true. "I just know that right now I'm not happy."

"Fair enough," Nino told him. "Then, here's what we're going to do." Nino pulled back Van's covers and gestured for him to get in. "You're going to get a good night's sleep, and tomorrow, we're having a guy's day out. No work. No thinking. Just fun."

"I have a shoot tomorrow," he reminded Nino as he crawled into bed after having placed the broken pieces of the vase in the trash.

"You're canceling it," Nino said in a decidedly matter-of-fact tone. "You've done a lot for the studio. Giving you tomorrow off won't kill them, and if that troll of a director gives you trouble, just leave him to me."

"What are you gonna do?" Van asked excitedly as he pulled the sheets up to his chin. "Beat him up?"

"You never know," Nino replied. "You don't grow up in the barrio without having to bust someone's face in at least once in your life. But you don't worry about that. Leave Tripp to me. You rest and tomorrow, we'll have so much fun you'll piss yourself."

"It's a date," Van said.

Nino didn't reply. He nodded and left the room.

When Nino closed the door behind him, the gloom that had previously held him slowly released its grip. Maybe it was because he was giving Hart a break. Maybe it was because Van was going to take center stage, if only for a day.

But maybe—and this was a big maybe—maybe tomorrow he'd find what might actually make him happy.

Chapter Ten

"TIME to get up, bitch!" Nino hollered as he jumped up and down on Van's bed. "It's time for Nino and Van's day of fun!"

Van forced one eye open and cursed. "Fuck! Will you stop that?"

Nino responded by jumping faster. Apparently, the answer was no.

"I'm sleeping in," he told Nino as he dug himself deeper into his covers.

"On your day off?" Nino asked, still jumping and hollering like a fool. "Hell to the no! We're gonna go play!"

"No, I'm not," he pouted. He sounded like a child, but he didn't care. He was sluggish and in no mood for Nino's games. He'd hoped a good night's rest would cure what ailed him, but that had obviously been an epic fail. What happened to the harsh light of day making everything better?

"Oh, yes you are!" Nino hopped onto the floor and yanked the sheets off the bed. "I've already called Tripp and told him you were sick."

"You did what?"

Nino nodded as he pulled open Van's bedside drawer and pulled out a bathing suit. "You're suffering from explosive diarrhea, and since you're the big ole bottom, no one wants that shit on set." He threw the suit at Van. "Pun intended."

"Explosive diarrhea? Are you shitting me?" Before he had a chance to take the words back, Nino jumped all over them.

"No, but you are!" he added. "At least that's what Tripp thinks. Now get up and get showered. We're leaving for the P-town Inn in fifteen."

Van groaned. It wasn't that he didn't like the Provincetown Inn, it was that he *really* didn't want to go, but one flash of Nino's hallmark smile did Van in. There was no way he could disappoint *that* face. "Fine," he mumbled under his breath.

While Nino roared triumphantly, Van walked into the bathroom and shut the door behind him. He wanted to crawl back into bed, especially after looking at himself in the mirror. He looked like shit. No, worse than that. He looked like he *had* spent all night shitting out his guts.

Maybe Nino was right. Perhaps a day off would be best. The idea had appealed to him the night before, when he was in the middle of his emotional tantrum, but now all he wanted was to get back into his routine.

That might be the best thing for him. Apparently, Nino disagreed.

Van stepped into the warm spray, allowing the water to chase away the sadness that still clung tightly to him. He grabbed his bar of soap, worked up a rich lather, and then scrubbed his body vigorously. If the water wouldn't do the trick, then maybe a good exfoliation might slough away the gloom.

While he cleaned, Van allowed his mind to wander. Fixating on the problem didn't seem to help, especially since he had no fucking clue what it was, so he hoped just freeing his mind might release some of his tension.

That was when Zach popped into his head. He recalled him standing there in the leather shop, his white skin hidden underneath the baggy clothing. The way his lips parted in that big, goofy smile, and the gentle but firm hand that shook Van's in greeting.

As he remembered the sensation of Zach's warm flesh pressed against his, Van imagined what it might feel like coursing across his chest.

He closed his eyes, and suddenly Zach was there, standing before him naked and moving his hands over Van's body. Zach's strong fingers pinched at his nipples, handling them roughly, the way Van liked to be treated.

They turned rock-hard and burned from the pressure. Van had to bite his lower lip to stop himself from whining. When Zach released his nipples, he roamed down, surfing the water and arriving at the hard cock that bobbed before him. Zach took Van's hardness and jacked it slowly. He pulled the taut skin over the engorged head before slowly bringing it back and sliding his fingers around the base of Van's cock.

As he increased the tempo, Zach slid his fingers toward Van's balls and tugged on them, pulling them down so hard Van feared he might rip them off. He eased up a little but then went right back to torturing Van's balls, yanking the sac to the point of blinding pain before once again releasing the gathered skin.

Zach applied more soap to his cock, turning his prick into a white, foamy sword that he brandished expertly. He alternated between fast and furious strokes and a slow, steady hand job. Van enjoyed being kept on his toes, not knowing when he would be allowed to come, to be taken to the edge and then kept from falling over.

Zach played Van's body as if it were an instrument he'd been performing with his entire life. When he slid his thumb over Van's piss slit, teasing precum from the opening, Van's knees buckled. He'd never had anyone do that to him before. Then when Zach rubbed the head of his cock between his thumb and index finger, Van almost blew his load right there.

But Zach wasn't ready for Van to come yet.

He soaped up his other hand and then danced his fingers around Van's ass, teasing the opening. Zach tapped his fingers around his rim, causing his center to pucker in want. He'd never wanted to be filled by someone as badly as he wanted Zach to take him right there in the shower.

When Zach slid a finger inside, a desperate whine escaped from Van's throat. Zach worked his finger around in a circle, using the motion to open Van up, to prepare him for Zach's ultimate entrance, and Van gladly backed up into the exploring finger. He wanted, no, he needed Zach inside him, and the sooner he was ready, the faster Zach would make his way up Van's butt.

A second finger slipped past Van's ring, and Zach scissored them open and closed, using the motion to widen the passage. Van's legs trembled. He couldn't take much more. Although he had Zach's fingers wrapped around his cock and two of his fingers plugged in his ass, Van wanted the real thing, so he begged for it.

"Fuck me," he muttered. "Fuck me hard."

Zach needed no other invitation. He spun Van around in the shower and applied a generous amount of soap to his cock and Van's ass. Zach then shoved himself inside with one push.

Van had never been more filled, and he grunted in appreciation.

His insides expanded to take in all Zach had to offer. His cock felt at least a good eight inches and impressively thick. Van bucked backward, shoving Zach farther inside, and the spray from the shower drizzled off their bodies and out of the tub from the force of their moist collisions.

"Yeah," Van whined. "Just like that. Give it to me."

Harder, Zach pounded inside his guts, fucking him like a wild bull. His huge balls slapped against Van's ass, and while Zach pummeled him, Van stroked his own hardness as fast and furious as his wrist allowed.

Van was getting close to coming. Each time Zach slammed inside him, he massaged his button, which made him harder and pushed him closer to the edge he'd previously been hanging from.

He didn't want to go tumbling over. Van wanted Zach to stay plugged into him forever. It was *too* damn good to stop, but his body screamed for release. He had no choice but to shoot his load, so he yanked on himself harder, fanning the fire that burned in his balls.

With three final strokes, it was over. Van jettisoned ropes of white spunk out of his cock. As he watched it fall away into the tub and flow down the drain, Zach also disappeared from the shower, leaving Van once again alone under the spray.

Light-headed, he gasped for air as he slowly withdrew his fingers from up his ass and released his stranglehold on his drained cock.

He'd never come like that while jacking off before. If he wasn't already spent from a shoot, he typically sat in bed with his laptop and jerked off to clips on the Internet. He'd always preferred videos to photographs or fantasies. Rarely, if ever, did his imagination give him what he needed to get himself off.

Was he *that* hot for some guy he didn't even really know?

Judging from the sheer volume of cum he'd just set free, he was. He just didn't understand that. Especially after seeing Zach yesterday at tea. The reality didn't mesh with the fantasy. Besides, Van had a whole studio of good-looking, muscled men just waiting to fuck him. What was so special about Zach that it made his toes curl just imagining having sex with him?

Van had never needed fantasy before. His reality the past few years had been a walking wet dream. What did this mean? As he turned off the water and got out of the shower, he did know one thing.

He had no intention of finding out. He lived his life this way for a reason, and there was no way Van was changing that.

For anyone. Ever again.

ZACH couldn't believe that in the few hours he'd been awake, he had written four thousand words of a manuscript that hadn't existed a few hours before.

The idea just hit him while he was showering. One minute he was generously soaping himself up while fantasizing about Van, and the next moment, *bam*! His muse suddenly picked up a baseball bat and smacked him upside the head three times.

He quickly rinsed, threw on a new pair of shorts, opened up his laptop, and let his fingers fly. The story flowed quite easily. It was about a man who'd been dumped, flew halfway across the country, and while trying to figure out how his life got so fucked up had some pretty hot and not-so-hot experiences.

Where did *that* plotline come from? He couldn't help the smile that flashed across his face as he stared at the words on the screen.

Rereading what he had written made him feel better than he had in a long time. He didn't quite understand what had changed since yesterday. Ben had still dumped him, and his life still sucked worse than a bad *Twilight* parody.

That just didn't seem to matter right now. Sure, his life blew, and not in a good way, but he'd actually done things he'd never done before. He was no longer just watching his life go by while others did things he only dreamed about.

He got sucked off on a dance floor and fucked some random guy he met at a store. Sure, that last one had been a comedy of errors, but it had happened, and it had happened to him.

The man who dated men, not fucked them.

That was a far cry from the Zach Kelly he'd come to know and loathe.

Maybe that was the reason he'd been unable to write and why the few people who had actually read his books had hated what he had written. He'd been writing about things he'd never experienced. The scant reviews his books had received had bashed him for being over-the-top, for not being realistic. His characters had no heart or soul. That was painfully obvious to him now. They were basically stock characters no one gave a flying fuck about, and he couldn't blame them.

His stories and his characters *did* suck. He hadn't seen it before, but he now saw it as plainly as the third nipple that tarnished Dylan's perfect chest. He'd tried to write in a world he hadn't really lived in. Until now.

This story, the one where he poured out his frustration and fears, the one where he tore down the walls inside his soul to free all the crap he kept bottled in not only sounded believable, but it came from within, not from some random storyboard he tried desperately to fill.

This was him, raw and uncensored, and Zach liked it.

What he needed now were more experiences, more crazy adventures to fill his book. To live the way he always wanted to live.

He couldn't stop now that he had a taste of what life had to offer. The barn doors stood wide open, and Zach sat on his mount ready to break into a full gallop toward the world that waited outside.

Chapter Eleven

EVEN though Van had fought Nino tooth and nail about leaving their apartment, he was glad he did. The blazing summer sun not only warmed his skin, it also burned away his disappointment in himself for jerking off to Zach and in Zach for becoming another P-town slut.

Why did that change bother him so much? Van didn't go gaga for anyone anymore, and the fact that Zach somehow made him stupid redoubled Van's conviction to keep as far away from him as possible.

That started here. By the pool. Lying practically naked in the sun while surrounded by other barely dressed men. After all, what better way to not think about one guy than by diving headfirst into a sea of sweaty man flesh?

As Van surveyed the hard, oiled bodies packed into skimpy bathing suits around him, he realized this *had* been the right thing to do. It was what he needed. He just hated that Nino had been right to force him to do this.

As usual, Nino got what he wanted, and it made Van feel like one of Nino's tricks, who willingly offered up their asses in response to his seductive grin. One of these days, Van hoped Nino would meet his match and go up against someone immune to his disarming personality and Hollywood good looks.

"You're welcome," Nino announced from the pool chair next to him.

Van turned to Nino, who lay faceup to the sun. His curly locks fell across his forehead and off to the side as a sly grin spread across Nino's face.

"What am I supposed to be thanking you for?"

"For making you take a day off," Nino replied.

Nino's white Oakley sunglasses hid his eyes, but Van suspected Nino's usual shit-eating twinkle currently danced across them. That always happened whenever Nino felt vindicated.

"You just think you're so fucking special, don't you?"

"Think? I know."

Van rolled his eyes and then turned over on his stomach. He had no intention of stroking Nino's ego. His friend didn't need an even bigger head than he already had.

Now facing the pool, Van continued observing the other guests who had also decided to spend the morning relaxing poolside. The Provincetown Inn was very popular with the Townies and the straight families. Although some gay boys also sunned here regularly, most of them preferred the cruisier spots at the Boatslip or at Herring Cove, where guys typically sunbathed nude and cornholed each other in the dunes.

The Provincetown Inn proved tamer and not as crowded, but in recent years this once unknown destination had grown in popularity. Those who usually came here to get away from the hustle and bustle had to adjust to the increase in visitors, so they gathered in segregated pockets around the pool.

The families, both straight and gay, sat along the far right side of the pool with their troops of children. While their kids splashed around the pool, which was shaped like a pilgrim hat, the parents chatted each other up and shared stories. The childless gays who came to preen and find fuck buddies congregated around the front side of the pool or on the small beach just beyond the surrounding gate. There they could make dates and play kissy face without attracting too much attention.

Most of the Townies collected on the left side of the pool, which was closer to the bar. They could chat with friends or just lie on their pool chairs, nap, and drink the day away. Since most Townies worked two to three jobs during the summer, most wanted to simply be left alone on their days off.

That was why Nino brought him here. He wanted Van to be able to be himself in a place where Hart might not be as known, and where Van's Ray-Bans and Red Sox baseball cap might do a better job of disguising him than they did in the middle of Commercial Street.

He really did owe his best friend some gratitude, but there was no way he was traveling down *that* treacherous road.

"I'm going in," he told Nino. "Wanna come?"

"I always wanna come," Nino replied, his eyes still hidden behind his shades. "Just not with you."

"Whatever, Mary," Van replied as he rose from the deck chair. Nino retorted by flipping him off. "Yeah, I love you too."

"I know you do."

Without another word, Van took off his sunglasses and cap and then jumped into the pool. His flesh braced against the chilly water. The sun's warmth, which previously shielded him from his cold, prickly thoughts, faded away, leaving him completely defenseless and at the mercy of troubled ideas he'd managed to banish for a few short hours.

He still didn't understand what caused his sudden restlessness with the life he'd chosen. He'd been able to ignore it, to push it aside and let the warm sun liberate him from any reflection whatsoever, but those nagging doubts once again tugged away at him like a vulture trying to pick a carcass clean. What made things even worse was that as he swam underwater from one end of the pool to the next, he found himself once again thinking about Zach.

The sudden reintroduction of Zach into his thoughts caused him to break the surface in order to catch his breath. As he took in the heavy summer air, Van couldn't believe that the mere thought of that sexy, redheaded fucker had managed to take his breath away.

Again.

What was up with that?

Lately he'd only been attracted to the dangerous types. The guys who there were no futures with. The ones who fucked, came, and left. Just like his many costars.

His relationships had been reduced to casual dalliances of hot, sweaty sex, which were sometimes captured on video and sold all over America, and that had suited him just fine since.... Well, anyway.

Sex without intimacy had been what he preferred. No, what he sought. Yet one look at Zach yesterday had almost made him do something stupid like ask him out for coffee.

He didn't fucking do that. He wasn't some lame-ass, starry-eyed romantic. He had personal experience with love and its reality, and it sure as hell wasn't the crap Hollywood turned into movies.

Love was mean and spiteful, cruel and vindictive, and he had the scars to prove it.

That was why he loved the movies he made.

Porn told the truth. It reduced human relationships down to what they were really about—getting off.

People didn't want happily-ever-afters. They wanted a partner who could make their toes curl when they came. Once those toes uncurled or once someone else came along who could fuck an ass longer or swallow cock farther, it was time to exchange the old model for the new.

That was why Van didn't do dates and had sworn off them for over a year now.

It didn't matter that Zach had somehow spoken to a part of Van that he kept hidden. The part of him that longed for something more lasting than a come and go. He'd begun to hope that maybe one good guy existed in the world, but Zach had proven him wrong. Just like every other man in his life.

Time for a reality check.

Guys who pretended to be innocent destroyed him. The cocky motherfuckers never came close.

He needed to stick with the guys who treated him like a bitch. Lines couldn't be blurred there. Roles were clearly marked, and that kept him safe.

What more did he really need?

"SO, YOU'RE making progress?" Gary asked Zach as they sat on the deck in front of Gary and Quinn's condo, having a light brunch.

"I am," Zach responded. "I've written just over four thousand words this morning. That's unusual for me."

"How much is usual?" Quinn asked as he offered Zach more bacon, which Zach politely refused.

"Honestly, not much. I've published two books and they both took me about a year to write. I'd always thought I was just too busy with grading papers. Or committees. Or any of the other shit we have to do day-to-day. But I don't think that was it at all."

"What was it, then?"

"I think it was because I'd been living a pretty suck-ass life."

"Sucking ass can be a good thing," Quinn told him with a wink. "But I think I know what you mean. You just hadn't had the life experiences yet to be able to write?"

Zach agreed.

"Then I guess you have Dylan to thank for your sudden burst of writing," Quinn added with a smile. "We saw him leaving your condo last night."

"Not to mention your Tea Dance dalliance," Gary chimed in. "I haven't seen such a public display of depravity in weeks!"

A familiar blaze set a fiery path across his cheeks. Gary and Quinn silently chuckled.

"No need to be embarrassed," Quinn told him. "This is P-town. We don't judge. We save that for every *other* fucking town in America."

"I've never behaved like that before," Zach finally responded once the warmth on his cheeks cooled. "I pretty much save the sex for the bedroom and for my boyfriend. Hooking up just isn't me."

Gary peered at him dubiously. "I find that hard to believe. Besides the mountain of evidence that clearly shows that debauchery comes quite naturally to you, you are a man in your early thirties and in seemingly good health. Am I right?"

Zach nodded.

"Then how can someone as, oh, how can I put this respectfully?" Gary gazed into the sky as if the clouds held the response that escaped him. When he had obviously found the answer, his eyes widened in merriment and he continued, "How can someone as goddamn fuckable as you *not* have been hooking up constantly? I mean, look at you. You've got a gorgeous smile, an awesome personality, and a killer bod that I would happily let enter my honey pot for an hour or three."

"I thought you were shooting for respectful?" Quinn asked him with a frown.

Gary rolled his eyes at Quinn and snatched the last piece of bacon out of his hands. "That *was* being respectful. I didn't flash my ass at him like I *wanted* to!"

"Don't worry about it, Quinn," Zach announced with a laugh. "I take no offense."

"See," Gary pointed out as he proceeded to eat the stolen bacon with much relish.

"Truthfully, I don't see myself the way you do, Gary. I see the huge klutz who constantly falls down or knocks stuff over. That's been what everyone else has seen too. Including my dad. And Ben."

For a few moments, Zach quietly contemplated his relationship. Ben had slowly withdrawn over the years, as if there had been something about Zach he could no longer stomach. Maybe it was the clumsiness or his unwillingness to try new experiences. Perhaps the personality that had first attracted Ben to Zach had been the same one that ultimately pushed him away and into the arms of another man.

"After all this time I think I see that I've been my own worst enemy."

"That happens," Quinn announced as he stole some scrambled eggs from Gary's plate. "But the thing about that is it doesn't have to *keep* happening."

"That's right, Zachary. Besides, you're in P-town now. She's got a way of grabbing a hold of you and turning your life around. The impossible suddenly becomes possible."

Zach nodded because the words were true. In just one day, he'd changed profoundly. The man who was lost and miserable yesterday no longer took center stage. Although the breakup with Ben still hurt, it no longer crushed him. What other choice did he have but to move on?

It was easier said than done. Sure. But he had to let go of his grudge against Ben. What good did that do for him? He might not be ready to release the anger and the hurt entirely, but he was getting there.

The sex he'd been having had come a long way in helping with that. And why wouldn't it? It was hard to feel bad about life when coming inside some random hottie. That had a way of bringing his previously blurred world back into focus.

Did he still want to find true love? Eventually, yes. Right now, he simply craved no-holds-barred fun. With as many guys as possible.

Chapter Twelve

AFTER the Provincetown Inn, all Van wanted to do was go home and rest. Instead, Nino took him to lunch, then shopping, and finally back to the apartment to get dressed and ready for tea. He didn't want to go, but Nino had insisted. He couldn't back out of their day of fun, Nino told him, and as always, Van didn't have the heart to disappoint his best friend.

As it was, they barely spent time together these days between Van's porn shoots and Nino flying off to New York, Paris, or Milan for the designers who loved him almost as much as Van's rabid fans adored him.

Now, he was here. At tea. Just after four in the afternoon and the Boatslip was already packed, which was typical for a Saturday. That was why he didn't want to be here. There would be too many fans, too many people coming up to him and making goo-goo eyes at Hart Throb.

Why did that make him want to barf? He'd once again embraced the life that kept him safe just a few short hours ago. Why did being here somehow change that?

If he could just close his eyes, focus on the music DJ Mary Alice spun, and let the dance beat carry him to a place where Hart Throb didn't exist, he'd be fine. But as they wove through a crowd of men who looked at him as if he were a piece of meat thrown before starving lions, Van became resentful.

He'd never be anything more than Hart Throb to any of them. Could he really live with never being seen for who he was ever again?

"What the fuck's the matter with you?" Nino asked as he handed Van the rum and Coke he'd just purchased.

"I'm pissy," he told Nino after he downed half of the drink.

"No shit! This was supposed to be our day of fun, and you're acting like some prissy twink who can't find his next fix. What gives?"

Van didn't reply. Instead, he pierced the crowd that stood like a wall before him. Several guys said hello and tried to approach him, but Van brushed them off. He didn't have time to deal with their clumsy come-ons. He needed to get his shit together and pull on his big boy underwear. This was the life he willingly chose. He couldn't exactly freak out about that now.

After he finally broke through the horde of horndogs, he rested against one of the rails that looked out into the bay. With the tide out, hard-packed sand stretched before him, and the boats that typically bobbed on the surface rested on their hulls, which dug into the sand.

The boats looked the way he felt. Out of his element and incapable of finding the buoyancy that once kept him afloat. Could he be any more of a fucking mess?

"Jesus," Nino commented, once again at his side. "When did you turn into such a drama queen?"

"I'm not in the mood," he warned Nino. "Leave me be."

"That's exactly why I'm not gonna. There's obviously something chapping your ass, so you might as well just tell me."

"Not. Now."

Nino sighed heavily, and when he spoke next, his tone had changed. It no longer held exasperation, just concern. "Okay, you're not happy. I get it. Those guys back there saw Hart Throb instead of you, and it pissed you off. But why? What's going on? I really want to understand."

The sincerity in Nino's voice was unusual when compared to Nino's typically flippant personality. Van wanted to share what was going on with his friend, but he lacked the words to capture his feelings. How could he admit that the last person he wanted to be right now was the persona he'd grown used to hiding behind?

"Come on," Nino prodded. "It's me. We've been best friends for years. Don't shut me out now."

"I'm not trying to," Van responded, trying his best not to be heard by the group of men gathering behind him. "I don't know what's going on either."

"Okay. So when did it start?"

The day he met Zach, but he wasn't going to announce that. "Yesterday," was what he finally admitted.

"What happened yesterday? I was with you for most of the time. Except when I was fucking that college guy after your shoot."

"And that other guy later that evening."

A wistful expression fell across Nino's face. "Oh, yeah. Almost forgot about him. His ass was nice and tight too."

Van rolled his eyes. "That's part of what I'm talking about. I'm tired of the bedroom roulette. Getting fucked by one guy I don't know then having someone nail me at work because the studio's paying him to do it. It's one never-ending trick, and I'm getting bored."

"Are you serious?"

"As a venereal disease, which is what we'll get if we continue down this path." Van eyed the guys behind them. Why couldn't they just mind their own fucking business and leave him alone?

"I always use condoms, so no cock rot for me," Nino reminded him as he followed Van's stare to the congregating gaggle of gays. Nino blew kisses at the men, which embarrassed them enough to at least stop being so obvious and turn around. When they were no longer being so carefully observed, Nino continued, "And since I know you do too, that's just an excuse. What's the real reason?"

Van shrugged.

"Don't give me that 'I don't know' bullshit," Nino scolded. "*This* was the life you chose. You were done being used. And hurt. You were the one who said your heart got you into trouble that your cock never did. That's why when Tripp offered you the job, you took it. Now you're telling me that's somehow miraculously changed. *Some*thing had to cause it."

Van couldn't look at Nino for fear that he would spill everything, thanks to those damn eyes that made *everyone* do what Nino wanted. He was just too embarrassed to say that some guy he hadn't even fucked, much less known, had somehow managed to turn his world upside down. It wasn't even Zach's fault. Not really. There was just something he saw in Zach's eyes that restarted a flame that connected to his heart. Not just his prick.

How could he admit that what he really wanted was to get rid of Hart and maybe put his heart on the line one more time?

ZACH shoved his tongue down the throat of yet another guy who had started dancing with him at tea. How many guys did this make? He'd lost count somewhere around five, but he didn't give a flying fuck. He was having the time of his life.

This was what Provincetown was about, after all. Sampling the goods so generously offered, and the guy he was currently enjoying didn't seem to mind. In fact, the rock-hard boner that pressed against Zach's thigh told him the guy wanted more.

Zach wasn't quite ready to settle. Yet. He extracted his tongue from the guy's hungry mouth and boogied on over to where Gary, once again dressed as Penny Poison, shook her money-maker.

"Zachary!" Penny screeched as she hugged him tightly. "Are you done playing with your toys?"

"For now," he told her as he downed his second Planter's Punch. After the sting of the rum-heavy drink Tara so generously poured for him died down, a numbing cloud settled over him. Zach then positioned himself behind Penny and ground his pelvis against her leather miniskirt-covered behind.

"Such a nasty boy you've become," Penny squealed. "I love it!"

Zach loved it too. Finally, the rules he'd live by would be of his own making, not anyone else's, and that dawning realization caused him to spin around and gyrate on the floor while Carly Rae Jepsen told some guy to call her, maybe. The song reminded him of the guy he met after he had brunch with Quinn and Gary. He'd gone walking down Commercial Street and ran into some random shirtless hottie on the sidewalk. Zach started up a conversation, and fifteen minutes later, they were back in his trick's room, where Zach buried himself balls-deep up his ass. The guy, who Zach thought was named Chris, although he couldn't remember, asked Zach to call him sometime and maybe they could go out for drinks. He'd taken down Chris's information, knowing full well that he didn't intend to make that call. Not even maybe.

He wasn't here to date. Zach was here to fuck.

The admission jarred him. He sounded cold and callous. Not like himself at all.

Just what had Provincetown done to him?

"I'm ready for another drink," he told Penny as "Call Me Maybe" thankfully gave way to some song he couldn't identify. Perhaps a new song and another alcoholic beverage would chase away the unpleasant thoughts. "How about you?"

Penny held up her giant goblet, which was still half-full. "Not yet, dahling. But you go ahead. Just be careful. Planter's Punches can lead to Planter's Puking."

Zach nodded and cut a path through the sweat-drenched bodies that packed the dance floor and toward where Tara tended bar to the right of the stage. As she taught him, he went directly to the front of the line and winked at her as she slung drinks for the long line of people waiting for a moment with her.

"Hey, honey," she told him without missing a beat. She poured out three Planter's Punches and then filled four other cups with vodka and cranberry juice.

"Hey, good-looking. You look swamped."

She shrugged. "Not too bad. Yet." She told the customers at the bar what they owed her as she slid Zach's drink over to him. She took their money but refused to take anything from him.

"You're the best."

"I know," she told him with a wink. "We're still going to After Tea, right?"

Zach nodded. He'd never been to After Tea at Pied, but as Gary and Quinn told him at brunch, After Tea was a party not to be missed. "You betcha."

"You guys better wait for me."

"I'd never leave you behind," he said as he walked away. "Love you!"

"Love you too!" Tara yelled as more customers placed their orders.

Zach made his way back to the dance floor, which had grown even more packed than when he'd left. He'd planned on heading back over to Penny, but she was currently dirty dancing with some raven-haired twink. He walked outside instead.

The warm breeze swept over his sweaty body, causing his moistened shirt to cling to him. Without thinking, he pulled his blue muscle shirt over his head and tucked it into the pocket of his white shorts. Since when did he walk around half naked so easily?

Evidently starting right now. He didn't question it, though. He just went with it.

As he walked shirtless through the crowd on the tightly packed deck, Zach's thoughts turned to his actions over the last twenty-four hours.

He'd always been careful to think about other people's feelings. Too many people had hurt him for Zach to be acting the way he was. Sure, his relationship with Ben was over, and there was nothing wrong with some casual sex to get over being ruthlessly dumped. That didn't mean he had to turn into some uncaring manslut.

And that was what he had been doing.

Practically shoving Dylan out of his condo and then lying to Chris, or whatever his name was, this afternoon proved he was out of control.

He didn't have to stop having fun. Or hooking up. And he sure as hell wasn't looking for some relationship to replace the one he had with Ben.

Zach just needed to be smarter about his tricking. There was no reason he couldn't still be the nice guy he'd been before. He would simply be the nice guy who had lots of fun. And tons of sex with hot guys.

There wasn't anything wrong with that, right?

Now all he had to do was find the next guy who'd be the lucky recipient of a good-natured, no-strings-attached fuck session.

As Zach surveyed the crowd, he found plenty of candidates.

A blond-haired, Nordic-looking fucker, whose eyes also scanned the men around him. He was obviously on the hunt too, but he looked too desperate, as if he were on some timetable. Zach didn't want to have to rush.

Lingering close to the pool stood a couple, one Latino and one white. The taller white guy had a lithe body while his darker-skinned companion had a more solid, squat frame. He imagined heading over to them both and proposing a little three-way fun. Something far more intimate than his dance floor blowjob.

He just didn't know if they were the ones he wanted to break his orgy cherry.

As he made his way toward the railing that looked over onto the beach and ocean beyond, Zach caught a glimpse of familiar bronze skin. Was Van here again?

Zach fought his way through the mass of men, some of whom said hello and tried to strike up a conversation. Zach pushed past them.

He just had to know if it was Van, the perfectly tanned man.

When he finally broke through the last barrier of men, Zach found Van. He leaned against the railing, looking away from the crowd and toward the ocean beyond, which had retreated from the shore.

He couldn't believe his luck. Yesterday, he'd entertained the idea of taking Van in his arms, and he'd almost done it too. But that perfect-looking motherfucker had come along and swept Van away. He couldn't let that happen again. He'd never forgive himself for letting someone like Van slip through his fingers. He had to hope that maybe the guy wasn't Van's boyfriend and that maybe Van might be interested in him too.

That was a whole lot of fucking maybes, wasn't it? But what did he have to lose? Besides his self-respect. And his dignity. Did he ever really have those to begin with?

Zach crossed the distance between him and Van, and as he worked up the courage to tap him on the shoulder, he noticed that Van wasn't alone. Standing next to him was that same tall, Abercrombie-and-Fitch-looking motherfucker with flawless skin and boyishly charming brown curls.

He just hated that guy.

Still, Zach wasn't going to let Mr. Perfect stand between him and Van.

"Hey," Zach managed to say while lightly tapping Van's shoulder. When Van turned around, his gorgeous blue eyes widened in what looked like stunned horror. Zach immediately regretted his decision. Van's expression clearly told Zach he wasn't interested in him. At all. He needed to play this as cool as possible, if only to lessen the blow of rejection. "Long time no see."

If he could have, he would have slapped himself really hard. Long time no see? Really? How fucking lame was that?

Luckily, Van didn't comment on his weak greeting. He still looked to be schooling his face. "You look different. New clothes and product in your hair. I guess you've embraced P-town, huh?"

Zach nodded. "I suppose so. Some friends of mine convinced me I needed some sprucing up. I guess I looked pretty ridiculous back at the store."

Van laughed. It wasn't one of mocking, but of tentative agreement instead. In fact, the laughter seemed to ease whatever tension had previously gripped him. "I wouldn't say ridiculous. Your style was just different. Your own. Now you look like the rest of us."

He couldn't tell if that was a good thing or not. From the look on Van's face, neither could he.

"This is Nino," Van said, introducing his friend as if suddenly remembering he was there. "Nino, this is Zach."

"What's up?" Nino asked after shaking Zach's hand.

"Not much. Just enjoying tea."

Nino grinned. "I hear ya. There's lots of untapped potential here."

The way Nino leered at some of the guys as they walked by indicated that perhaps he and Van weren't a couple. Although in Provincetown, being coupled didn't necessarily mean monogamy.

Still, Zach secretly hoped Van was single. Where the hell did that come from?

"You here by yourself?" Van asked.

"Yes and no. I came to P-town by myself, but I'm actually here with G—" he stopped himself. "Penny Poison."

"Penny's here?" Nino asked, looking around. "I haven't seen that bitch in too long. Where is she?"

Zach shrugged. "I'm not keeping tabs on her, but I'm sure she'd be easy to spot."

"Damn straight!" Nino agreed as he continued to survey the crowd with renewed purpose. "There she is, macking on some twink. I'm gonna go give her hell."

Without another word, Nino took off, leaving Zach and Van by themselves. The last time that happened, he'd almost destroyed a store. He hoped something more embarrassing didn't happen this time.

"You okay?"

Zach swallowed hard. "That remains to be seen."

"What do you mean?"

"Well, the first time we met I wasn't exactly at my best. I'm just kinda hoping I don't knock into a load-bearing wall or something and bring this place down around your ears."

A smile stretched across Van's tanned face. His teeth were perfectly straight and white. The man really seemed to have no imperfections at all. "I've seen worse in my time. This *is* P-town," he told Zach.

"That seems to be the answer for a lot of things here."

Van nodded. "It is. This place isn't like anywhere else. It marches to the beat of its own drum." His blue eyes studied Zach. "That bothers you, doesn't it?"

Van's intuitive nature surprised him. Even though he'd embraced his recent lackadaisical approach to living, his recent actions *had* concerned him. The fact Van picked up on that intrigued him.

"Maybe," was all Zach admitted.

"Ah, you're one of those."

"One of those what?" he asked as he rested his back against the railing. Their conversation became easy. Whatever Van felt earlier had apparently disappeared on the ocean breeze.

"One of those guys who can't admit when someone else is right. Instead, you say 'maybe' as if that somehow allows you to save face or something."

Damn, he was good. He'd always hated acknowledging when someone might know him too well, especially someone Zach didn't know at all.

"Not gonna deny it?" Van asked.

Zach smiled. "Maybe. Maybe not."

Van laughed and shook his head. "Typical man. Can't admit when someone else is right."

"And what about you? Are you *not* a typical man?"

A naughty twinkle glinted in Van's silvery-blue eyes. "I'm *far* from typical," he admitted.

"How so?"

Van shook his head. "That's something you'll have to learn on your own."

"That sounds like a challenge."

"Maybe it is. You man enough for that?"

Zach liked the direction this was going. Not only was Van possibly the hottest man he'd ever seen, but his friendly, flirty, and confident behavior appealed to Zach. He'd never met someone attractive enough to be in movies who also didn't happen to be an unbearable prick.

Quite simply, Van appeared to be a wholesome, good-looking, down-to-earth guy, who Zach wanted to fuck *and* get to know better.

"Well?" Van asked.

"Challenge accepted," Zach answered with a nod.

"All right, then," Van said. "Let's get this party started."

Chapter Thirteen

WHAT the hell was he doing? Van had already decided not to pursue Zach. The man was just too damn cute for both their own goods. His goofy style combined with his endearing clumsiness had made Van want to rip the man's clothes off and ride him right there in the middle of the leather store. Now that Zach showed more skin in his shorts and muscle shirt, Van found it even harder to hold back as he and Nino followed Zach, Tara, and Penny Poison down Commercial Street to the After Tea party at the Pied Bar.

Could he just overlook what he saw at tea yesterday? As he ogled Zach's cute ass, the answer came back a resounding yes.

"I can't believe I let you talk me into this," Nino complained.

"Talk you into what?" Van asked, half paying attention to his friend. Zach's tight bubble-butt demanded his full concentration. He imagined how Zach's ass might clench as Zach pummeled his insides. Van's boner became even stiffer, and it made walking more than uncomfortable.

"Being your chaperone."

Nino's comment caught Van's attention, and he instantly shushed his friend. Though Zach, Tara, and Gary, dressed as Penny, walked ahead of them, he didn't want anyone to overhear that comment. He loved Gary and Tara to death, but if they even caught the slightest whiff of his attraction to Zach, the two of them would start playing matchmaker.

"You're not my fucking chaperone," Van replied through clenched teeth. He did his best to hide the fact that Nino was dead-on.

"Well good, then," Nino said, coming to a full stop. "Since our day of fun looks to be over now, I'll just go back to tea and see if I can find that hot piece of ass I'd almost scored with."

Van grabbed Nino's hand and jerked him forward again.

Nino smirked triumphantly. "So, you admit that I'm chaperoning this little shindig, then?"

"It's not a shindig. We're going to the Pied."

"Okay," Nino admitted. "Not a shindig, but most definitely a chaperone-type situation."

"Why are you being such an ass?"

"Am I now? Really? Does an ass go with his best friend on a date?"

Van stopped in his tracks. "What the fuck are you talking about? This isn't a date!"

Nino stared at him as if he were stupid. "Did you not ask the carrot top to go to After Tea? To, as you put it, get to know each other?"

"What's wrong with meeting someone new and getting to know him? And besides, I did not ask him on a date," he pointed out. "I invited Zach, which is his name by the way, *and* Tara *and* Penny to go to After Tea."

Nino wagged his finger at Van. "Not quite. You invited Zach. You knew Tara and Penny were going there anyway."

"Which meant that Zach was going with them, dumbass. I was just being polite."

Nino's face turned serious. Van rarely saw that expression darken his friend's party-boyish face. "You like him, don't you? I mean, you *really* like him?"

Van dragged Nino out of the street and into the parking lot of Bubela's, one of the more popular restaurants in town. "Will you stop that already? They might hear you. I don't want Zach to get the wrong idea here, and you know how Tara and Gary are."

"How did this happen?" Nino asked. "You don't even know this guy."

"Are you not paying attention to what I'm saying? I just said that I didn't like him."

"It makes sense, though. You've been a moody bitch all day, complaining about people only liking you for being Hart. How you're tired of all the fucking, when yesterday you'd been *all* about getting laid. Then when he comes up to us at tea, *bam*! Good-bye, moody bitch. Hello, happy Van. You practically pissed all over yourself you were so happy to see him. I wondered what the hell that was about, but I just figured you wanted him to nail you later. That this was just the standard booty call and you were trying to stake your claim before some other pushy bottom did. But it's not, is it?"

Van forced all the air from his body. "We're talking to each other but having two different conversations."

"Fuck! Did you meet him yesterday? Is that when all this *shit* started? What are you going to do?"

"Listen to me," Van said while placing his hands against Nino's caramel cheeks. He wanted to force his friend to read his lips if he wasn't going to pay attention to what he said. "I. Don't. Like. Him."

Nino placed his hands on Van's cheeks, mimicking Van's gesture. "Yes. You. Do."

Van released Nino and headed out of the parking lot and back toward Commercial Street. "I'm not having this conversation with you."

"I'm not teasing you, man," Nino called out to him. "I'm just worried."

Van stopped and turned around. He gazed into the troubled face of his best friend. Although he was still aggravated by Nino, he loved the man for being so concerned. "Don't be," he told him. "I got this covered."

"I hope so," Nino replied. "Your breakup with Jason almost killed you."

The mention of his ex-boyfriend's name cut through his heart like a rusty dagger.

"Zach's not Jason."

Nino nodded. "But the circumstances are awfully familiar."

Van turned around and rejoined the crowd of guys headed to the After Tea party.

It didn't matter if they were similar or not. He didn't do relationships anymore. Thanks to Jason. And even if he were attracted to Zach, it would just be for the fuck.

Not even if his heart told him he wanted more.

VAN walked into the Pied Bar pissed off. He hated that Nino had brought up Jason. They had a deal never to mention that asshat's name again. It was bad enough that he had to share this town with the heartless fuck; he wasn't going to talk about him too.

But what bothered him more than the mention of Jason's name was the fact that Nino guessed why Van had practically begged Nino to come with them to the Pied. After all, he never needed Nino to go anywhere with him.

The two usually came to tea together but left separately. Nino with his trick and Van with his.

Instead, he insisted that Nino abandon his conquest in order to come with him.

Could he have been more pathetic or transparent?

"Pierce!" A voice from within the bar yelled.

Van immediately bristled. He *so* didn't need this right now.

"You trying to ignore me, Pierce?"

He turned around and stared into the chubby face of his director. "If only I could, Tripp."

"Funny," the man replied, faking a laugh as two muscled studs appeared on either side of Tripp. Van pegged them as talent trying to break into the industry. The vacant expression in their eyes was a dead giveaway. He'd seen that look on many men before who'd realized if they wanted a part in one of Tripp's movies, they'd have to take a ride on Tripp's well-worn and crusty casting couch.

"I'm surprised to see you here at all," Tripp told him. "I thought you blew off work today because you had a bad case of the shits. You don't look like someone's who's spent all day on the can. You look like someone who's been laying poolside soaking up the sun. Isn't that right, boys?"

Cum Rag One and Cum Rag Two nodded obediently.

"That's funny. I felt fine before. I feel like throwing up now."

Tripp rankled at the insult, and Van regretted his words. The man might be the biggest ass he'd ever met, but he was still his boss. A boss he lied to in order to spend the day with Nino. He needed to be more careful, especially after already poking the bear yesterday.

"Sorry," he said. "It's been a rough day."

Tripp eyed him suspiciously. He knocked back the last of his beer before responding. "Tell me about it. Your dumbass friend cost us money yesterday, and your day off put us even further behind."

Van didn't want to argue. He had more important things to do, like head over to where Zach, Tara, and Penny stood on the outside deck. With exaggerated arm motions and her typically vampish manner, Penny busily introduced Zach to everyone she knew. Penny loved drawing a crowd because more than anything else Penny Poison enjoyed finding herself in the middle of a group of adoring men. With Zach at her side, she appeared to be attracting more than usual.

From the horny looks on most of the men's faces, Van could tell each one of them was trying to figure out how best to land Zach in their bed for the night.

That seriously pissed Van off.

Which pissed him off even more for being so pissed off.

He seriously needed to put some distance between him and Zach.

"What the fuck's gotten into you?" Tripp asked. He turned around to see who had captured his attention. "You found your toy for this evening?"

"Just looking for my friends."

"Is that what you're calling them now? Friends?"

"What does that mean?"

"You don't have friends," Tripp told him as he handed his beer to Cum Rag One, who dutifully took the empty bottle. "You have fuck buddies. Well, except for that hot fucker Nino. You really need to convince him to stop that print modeling shit and switch to film. He'd make tons." A slight smirk danced on his face. "Maybe even more than you."

"I have friends," he told Tripp. After the words came out of his mouth, he regretted how juvenile they made him sound. Van cleared his throat and continued. "Tara and Gary for instance. And Nino has no interest in doing porn. You know that already."

"You didn't want to do porn either, but you came around," Tripp reminded him. He looked over his shoulder again. "But I'm thinking the friend you're interested in has bright red hair and a pretty decent body. Maybe the two of you can do a scene for me?"

"Why do you have to be such an asshole?"

"You are what you eat," Tripp replied as he darted his tongue suggestively between his lips.

Could Tripp be more disgusting? Instead of replying, Van started to walk away.

"I'd be careful with that one," Tripp warned him. His usual caustic tone softened. He sounded as if he were sincere. Almost human. "I can tell from here he's not like you."

"What the hell does *that* mean?"

"I'm a director. I can tell right off the bat when someone's playing a part. Acting all cool and shit, but he's not. There's nothing but a wide-eyed innocent underneath. That's definitely *not* your type."

"You don't know what my type is," Van told Tripp.

"All the videos we've made together tell a different story. Why do you think I cast you with the rough fuckers who tear up your ass? Because that's what you like. That's what turns you on. You want the sons of bitches who don't give a rat's ass about you. Or anybody else." Tripp's typically confrontational gaze grew soft, as if he were suddenly experiencing human emotion. He then drew closer to Van and whispered, "If you're not careful, you're gonna get yourself hurt. Again."

Van wanted to tell Tripp he was wrong, but Tripp had never been more right about anything.

BY THE time Van finally parted the admirers grouped around Zach and Penny, he'd moved far beyond simply being pissed off. He was downright bitchy now.

He could handle Nino's concern easy enough, but there was no way he could stomach it from Tripp as well. It wasn't as though he didn't know he was headed in the wrong direction, but for both of *them* to see it told Van he was speeding the wrong way down that one-way road.

But instead of turning around, he swerved toward Zach and his ever-growing fans.

"Where'd you get off to?" Tara asked.

"Sorry. Got sidetracked on the street and then Tripp stopped me."

Tara wrinkled her nose in disgust. She hated Tripp. Van wasn't entirely sure why, but right now he was grateful for her protective nature. Tara might be small, but she had a fiery spirit few dared to cross. As long as he was with Tara, Tripp would steer clear. "Yeah, I saw that scumbag when we came in. Is he giving you a hard time again?"

"Nothing I can't handle," he replied before kissing her on her cheek.

"Well, you just let me know if that changes. Because I'll kick his fat ass all the way to Hyannis if he isn't careful."

Van gave her two more kisses for that.

"Well, there's our Van," Penny announced, waving around her empty, oversized goblet. She crossed over and practically poured herself all over him. Whenever Penny got drunk, she grew at least six other limbs that searched for a handhold on any man in her vicinity. "I'd begun to think you'd abandoned your dear sweet Penny."

"I was beginning to think the same thing," Zach said as he excused himself to the guys around him and came over to stand in front of Van. The innocence he'd seen before now had a hint of mischief. Van found that charming. "I thought we had a deal."

"Deal?" Penny asked. "What deal is this and why am I just finding out about this now?"

"Unbunch your panties, Penny," Van told him. "I just told Zach that I wasn't a typical man, and he wanted proof. I told him he'd have to find out on his own."

"First of all," Penny began, "I'm not wearing panties. My junk's too big. Second of all, unless my ears deceive me, that sounds like a date."

Van opened his mouth to tell everyone this wasn't a date, but no sound came out. He just stood there with his mouth opening and closing like a fish out of water.

"Does that sound like a date to you?" Penny asked Tara.

Tara snickered. She typically swooped in to save people in such obvious distress, but instead she just patted his back and continued to laugh. "It does to me too."

Van didn't like her anymore, and he told her as much when he gave her a raspberry.

"You know I love you," she told Van. "But a date's a date."

"Wait," Zach interjected. "Is it a date?"

Penny rolled her mascara-covered eyes. "What are we going to do with these boys?" she asked Tara. "I mean, they're obviously into each other, yet they pretend that they aren't."

"I think we should leave them alone to figure it out."

Penny nodded.

"Wait!" Van said as Tara and Penny prepared to leave.

They replied only with arched eyebrows that told him to shut up and have a good time.

As they departed, the pair laughed one final time and then walked out of the Pied. Van turned back to stare at Zach, who looked about as dumbstruck as Van. Was that a good or a bad thing?

Did Zach not want this to be a date? He sure as hell didn't, but now it seemed as if it was. What the hell was he going to do? He hadn't been on a date since he first met Jason at tea two years ago, and now here he was again, on a date with a man who made him stupid.

And what made it worse was that the effect Zach had on him after one meeting already surpassed the effect Jason had on him all those years ago.

Van was most definitely in a butt load of trouble.

Chapter Fourteen

VAN stood at the bar, waiting for the bartender named Doug to hand him the drinks he'd ordered—a water for Zach, who claimed he'd already had too much to drink, and a Heineken for himself, because he hadn't had enough.

He couldn't believe that after everything he'd said, he ended up being on a date with Zach after all. When he saw Gary and Tara tomorrow, he was likely going to kill them for doing this to him and then rip Nino a new asshole for not following him to the Pied.

They knew how hard he'd taken the breakup with Jason. They were there, helping him pick up the pieces, and though they hadn't supported his decision to do porn—well, except Nino who thought it would be wicked fun—Gary and Tara never judged him for ultimately deciding to do it.

Gary had said he understood it was something he had to do. Tara had told him that when his heart had repaired enough, he would stop.

Van didn't have the stomach to tell her that was bullshit.

"Here you go," Doug told him as he handed him the beer and the water. "That'll be fourteen dollars, sexy." The bartender batted his eyes uncontrollably. It was a nervous tic that people confused with awkward flirtation. He'd thought the same thing until Gary clued him in last season that the excessive blinking was a result of Doug's ADHD.

"Thanks," Van told him as he handed over the money and walked back to where Zach sat on a barstool overlooking the bay. Long shadows cast by the failing sunlight wrapped around him, which made Zach look sad and lost.

No, that was too kind a word.

He looked abandoned.

Van had never wanted to rescue someone more.

"Here you go," he said, offering Zach his water.

"Thanks." Zach took it and set it on the small shelf carved into the railing.

Unsure what to do or say next, he sat on the barstool to Zach's left. Was he intruding? Maybe Zach needed some personal space he wasn't getting. He had half a mind to just get up and walk out.

But that wouldn't be right. When he was at his lowest, his friends had rallied around him and refused to let the depression claim him. They made him go out, and they made him laugh. Although it didn't erase the pain Jason caused, it made him feel less alone. That seemed to be what Zach needed right now.

"Look," Zach said, turning his pensive, brown eyes to him. "I know you didn't want this to be a date. That's cool. Tara and Gary just kinda forced this on you, so it's okay to bail."

"Who said I wanted to bail?"

"You did. In not so many words. You looked like a cat about to be dumped in a tub full of water when they called this a date. And I'm okay with this not being a date. I'm also okay with being alone, which I can't believe just came out of my mouth. If you have somewhere else to be, I'll be fine." He paused and gazed back at the ocean. Zach peered far beyond the horizon, most likely to the home he'd left behind. "It'll give me time to think."

"What's there to think about? This is Provincetown."

Zach smirked. "You know, that phrase gets used an awful lot around here. It seems to be an excuse for everything. Bad behavior included."

Van nodded. "Won't argue with that."

For a few moments, they sat in silence, and Van joined Zach in looking out into the ocean. As the sun dipped below the water's edge, the sky burned a fiery red until moment by moment the sun sank beneath the waters, and darkness enveloped the world.

"So I take it you've been behaving badly?" Van already knew the answer. He'd seen it firsthand. It just seemed as if Zach might want to talk about it. How the hell did he know that?

Zach didn't answer. He simply continued to stare into the dark surf that rolled under the deck on which they sat. Van was about to repeat his question when Zach finally spoke.

"Maybe."

Van laughed, and Zach grinned. They both knew that was Zach's way of saying yes.

"Tell me."

"I don't think I can talk about it, especially on a date."

Van nodded. "Okay, so let's not call this a date, then. Let's call this two guys getting to know each other better."

"Sounds like a date to me."

Van frowned. "Why is everyone saying that?"

Zach's brow furrowed. "Who *else* is saying that?" He looked around. "Is there someone else speaking besides me?"

"Forget it," Van said. He certainly didn't want Zach to know that Nino thought this was a date too. "What's important is that this doesn't have to be a date."

"Especially since you didn't want it to be," Zach reminded him.

Van sighed. "Okay, I was sorta transparent about that. I confess. It took me a little bit by surprise."

"A little bit?"

"Fine. A lot," he admitted. "I just haven't gone out on a date in quite some time."

This got Zach's attention. He shifted his gaze from the ocean to Van, and he was once again able to stare into Zach's sandy-brown eyes. "And why's that?"

"Not uh," Van answered, waving his finger at Zach. "You're not talking. Why should I?"

"Fair enough," Zach told him. "Silence it is." He then turned back to stare at the ocean.

Van grew frustrated. Zach was proving almost as stubborn as he was, and it was a trait he wasn't particularly fond of at that moment. If they were going to get to know each other, they were *both* going to have to give an inch or two.

"How about this?" Van asked after he took a sip of his beer. "You answer my question. I'll answer yours."

Zach nodded. "Tit for tat? That seems fair."

"Since I'm the one who came up with the idea *and* asked the first question, that means you have to answer my question first."

"I don't recall agreeing to that rule."

"Oh my God, this is the worst date ever!"

Zach smirked. "I thought this wasn't a date."

Van lightly banged his head against the shelf where Zach's water bottle rested. "I'm not very good at this sort of thing. You're gonna have to help me out here. What should I be saying?"

Zach patted him on the shoulder. The warmth of his touch was even better than the first time they'd shaken hands at the leather store. The heat and weight of Zach's hand almost turned Van to jelly. Why did he suddenly feel like a lovesick schoolgirl? He didn't like that. At all.

"If I were any good at this," Zach told him, "I wouldn't be here alone."

Van lifted his head from the shelf and frowned. "Gee, thanks."

"You know what I mean."

He did, so Van nodded. "What now?"

"First, we have to clear up whether this is a date or not," Zach told him. "I think it's important for both of us to know the type of social situation we're in."

"I like that." Van stared at Zach, who gazed back at him. Apparently, they were both waiting for an answer neither of them was willing to give. "Let's try this. On the count of three, we both answer whether or not this is a date. How's that?"

"I can live with that, but what happens if one says yes and the other says no?"

Good question. That sort of wrong answer would likely bring the whole evening to a grinding halt. And if it did, well, then maybe it needed to be stopped. After all, Van couldn't believe he was still here to begin with. "I think that's a risk we're both going to have to take. If we have different answers, then we get up and part ways. No hard feelings. If we have the same answer, then we stay and talk. No matter what that answer is."

Zach seemed impressed with Van's logic. "Sound reasoning. Besides, this is Provincetown, right? If something is meant to happen, it will."

"Exactly." He moved on the barstool so his body pointed directly at Zach, who did the same. As they stared deeply into each other's eyes, Van said, "Now, on the count of three, we answer this question: is this a date or not?" He held up his hand, prepared to begin the countdown. "You ready?"

Zach nodded.

He held up one finger, then two, and when the third finger was revealed, they answered in unison.

"No."

IT WASN'T a date after all. Thank God. That released some of Van's anxiety. If they were just two buds drinking beer and shooting the shit, he could handle that, and if they happened to have sex at the end of the night, well, he could fucking handle that too.

Not being on a date meant he wasn't returning to the person he used to be, the one Jason had destroyed and cast aside. He was still safe and protected.

"Now that that's settled, it's question and answer time," he told Zach. "You start."

"Why me?"

"Because I said."

Zach glared at him. He clearly wasn't going to accept that answer.

"Okay, then if you don't like that response, how about because I just answered a question from you?"

"What question have you answered?" Zach asked. The arch to his red eyebrows expressed his confusion.

"Your 'why me?' question. This makes two questions of yours I've answered to your none." He flashed his trademark grin at Zach, who clearly wasn't buying it. "Hey, you agreed to the rules. Tit for tat, as you said. We each answer a question, and I've answered two of yours. Now, you have to answer mine."

Zach frowned. "Fine. Ask away."

"You hinted that you've behaved badly. What have you done?" Van leaned closer to Zach. Even though he already knew some of the details, he suspected there was more he didn't know. Why he wanted a blow-by-blow account was beyond him.

After letting out a long exhalation, Zach replied, "It's embarrassing, and just so you know, I don't usually open up to people like this. I'm pretty shy and reserved. The thought of spilling my guts to someone I don't even know goes against everything I believe."

Shy and reserved? That certainly wasn't the guy he saw getting sucked off on the dance floor. Maybe Zach preferred spilling his seed in public instead of his guts. Still, he went along with Zach's self-appraisal. "So noted," Van replied after taking a long sip on his beer. "Now spill. And just so you know, I don't judge." That wasn't entirely true, since he had been silently condemning Zach's actions since yesterday, but Zach didn't need to know that.

Zach nodded and reluctantly told Van about tea yesterday, Dylan from Bravo, and the guy from this afternoon.

Could he have been any more wrong about Zach? He had suspected there was more than just the dance floor blowjob, but he hadn't expected all this. Zach apparently was a bigger slut than he realized.

The man he met at FK Leather, the one who was awkward, unsure, and dressed in the most god-awful clothing imaginable had struck a chord within Van. Zach had been so different from everyone else that he'd been intrigued and wanted to know more. After all, Zach still didn't even know he did porn for fuck's sake! How much of an innocent was that? Or at least that's what he'd thought. Especially since pretty much everyone Van ran into in this town had seen him take at least two cocks up his ass.

But now Zach wore the standard P-town uniform of tight clothing and had confessed to numerous sexual encounters in just over twenty-four hours. Did the man he helped clean up after at FK ever really exist?

Had he misjudged someone again? That certainly seemed to be how Van did things.

"You can say something now," Zach told him. "Staring at me in silence doesn't exactly make me feel like I'm not being judged."

"Sorry," Van told him. "I'm just surprised."

"Why's that?"

"You just don't strike me as *that* type."

Zach chuckled. "I'm not."

"Then why do it?"

"It's P-town, right?"

Van didn't like the answer because it told him that the man he thought he'd met had been a fake. That disappointed him.

"Your turn," Zach told him. "Why haven't you been on a date in so long? Is there something that horribly wrong with you?"

Van looked away. Although it had been a good-natured tease, the phrasing of the question hit him hard. Was there something wrong with *him*?

"Jeez, man. I'm sorry," Zach said. Suddenly, Zach reassuringly rubbed up and down Van's exposed thigh. He halfway hoped Zach would proceed farther up. God, he was just as much of a slut as Zach apparently was. "I was just kidding. I didn't mean to be an ass."

"I know," Van replied, trying to ignore the warm flesh that pressed against his own. Instead, he focused on how easily Zach had read his emotions. He really hated that. There was no point in denying Zach did, though. Even though that was what he typically did. Why did he not want to cover up his true feelings around Zach? He still questioned the innocence he sensed before Zach's sexual tell-all. He'd be a fool not to. But why did he feel like he could tell Zach anything?

The only other person he'd ever felt that way about was Nino.

"No worries," Van finally told him. "It's nothing I hadn't thought about myself."

This time, Zach placed his hand on Van's shoulder and massaged it. Zach's touch made his body burn, and if he didn't stop, Zach might just find himself being sucked off at After Tea too. Yup. Definitely *more* of a slut than Zach. "It's cool," he said. Van let out a deep breath when Zach pulled his hand free. "It's just a sore subject. One that I don't really talk about."

"You don't have to if you don't want to. I can ask something else."

Van shook his head. "A deal's a deal." He stared off into the darkness since there was no way he could look at Zach and tell his story. This way, he wouldn't have to school his face, and he could just be honest. It was something he hadn't done in longer than he could remember. "I haven't had the best of luck with relationships. No, that's not right. I suck at them. I really don't know what it is, but being with me seems to turn men into assholes. Maybe it's because I give of myself so completely or something. I don't really know.

"Anyway, I've had three pretty serious relationships. I mean, these were guys I loved with everything I had, and who I thought loved me back, but it never turned out that way. It started in high school. Timothy was his name. Damn, he was fine. Baseball jock. Strong, lean body. The boy really knew how to fuck. He even challenged the school when they threatened to cancel the prom rather than allow us to go as a couple. But after only a few weeks, he wanted more."

Van stopped. He found it hard to continue, and he even toyed with the idea of just walking the fuck out of there. Zach brought his barstool closer and took Van's hand in his. He appreciated the gesture.

"What did he want more of? A commitment?" Zach asked.

Van laughed. "Ha! I wish." He shook his head and continued. "He wanted more ass to fuck. He said he was young and that we were getting too serious. We needed to slow things down. Take a break." Tears formed in the corners of his eyes, and he forced them back. "I didn't understand why. I loved him, and I thought he loved me. I even imagined us moving in together after graduation, but I just wasn't enough. He broke up with me. After he left for college, I never saw him again."

"That's not your fault," Zach said. "You did nothing wrong."

"Wait," he told Zach. "It gets better. After Timothy, I met Scott. I wasn't in school or anything, so I took lots of odd jobs to make money. I'd been working the grounds of Boston College, and Scott was going to school there. That's where we met. After dating a year, I asked Scott to move in with me. And you know what he told me?"

Zach shook his head as he gripped Van's hand even tighter. "He said he had no idea we were that serious. He thought we were just having fun. We'd spent almost every weekend in bed together, and he thought we weren't serious? Hell, we even drove to New York City one weekend and had the time of our lives, but he just saw me as a regular fuck buddy. Nothing more."

Van slowly withdrew his hand from Zach's touch. For this last part, he needed no support. It was where the real pain lived, and to overcome it, he needed to be in complete control and on his own. "I moved to Provincetown shortly after that. After about a month here, I met Jason. He'd just moved to P-town. When I saw him at tea, I couldn't believe how beautiful he was, and he even came up to me and asked me for my phone number. I thought, wow! Someone is chasing me for once. We went out on a few dates, but this time I was careful. I didn't let him in too quickly, and Jason liked that. He pursued me, like the way men used to woo women. He was *that* romantic, flowers, candy, mixed tapes. I was like, is this guy for real? Eventually I gave in and gladly gave him my heart. We moved in together, and that's when things changed.

"He started coming home late. Going out with his friends. He'd flirt with people we'd meet on the street, and I thought, I'm going to lose him if I don't do something. So I thought, why not give him what he obviously wanted? The same thing that Timothy and Scott wanted that I couldn't give to them. If I did, then maybe he might stay."

"What was that?" Zach asked. "What did you give him?"

"I told him it was okay for him to fuck others if that's what he wanted. I didn't care who he shared his body with as long as I had his heart."

"I take it that didn't work out so well?"

"For Jason it did," Van replied. "He fucked around at least two or three times a week, but he always came home to me. Surprisingly, I was okay with it because it only mattered to me that I still had Jason, had managed to keep him with me. But one night, he brought a friend home. A friend he had promised to let fuck me."

"Are you serious?"

Van nodded. "And I went along with it, even though I didn't really want to. I figured if he was doing it, then why not get in on it too? But then he'd bring home more and more friends. One night, six guys I didn't even know fucked me, and not one of them was Jason. After that, he started to take me to private parties where other guys got to fuck me too. It made me feel worthless and completely degraded. But I did it for Jason. Because I loved him."

Zach shook his head. "That sounds awful."

Van huffed. "You'd think so, right? But that doesn't even come close to what finally clued me in to the fact that he didn't love me. You see, I'd text him or call him throughout the day. He rarely answered, claiming to be busy or something. One day, I wanted to surprise him. I don't know, take him to lunch or something. So I went to his office. He's a dentist, by the way. That alone should have told me what a sadist he was. Anyway, he wasn't there. In fact, no one knew where he was. I called his phone, and this awful noise came out of the desk in his office. I remember thinking, can that be his phone? I opened the drawer, and it was. He'd left it behind. I stared at the phone as it rang and rang. Not because of the fact that he'd left it but because of the ringtone. Jason had picked a tone for me that sounded like a nuclear meltdown, like some hazardous event that you try to avoid at all cost, and all I could think about was that I'd let him fuck all these guys and even allowed all those guys he brought home to fuck me. Just to prove that I loved him. And he had assigned me such an awful ringtone. One that showed me how little he actually thought of me. I knew then that he didn't love me or value me. I was just a toy he'd grown tired of playing with. I went home, packed up my stuff, and moved out. He never called me to ask why. He never tried to get me back. In fact, a few days later, some other guy moved in."

Van blew out a quick breath and turned back around to face Zach. "And that's why I don't date. I have no desire to feel that way ever again."

Zach looked stunned, as if he'd just been punched twice in the face. Van wanted to laugh, but telling his story drained him. All he really wanted now was to crawl into bed and forget.

"I can certainly understand why," Zach said at last. "And I have to apologize for giving you a hard time about not wanting this to be a date. After what you've just told me, I think you handled yourself better than I could have under similar circumstances."

Van nodded in reply. What more could he say? He'd just unloaded his entire pathetic life story on a virtual stranger. Frankly, he was surprised Zach was still there.

Suddenly, Zach stood up and grabbed his hand. "Let's go," he said as he pulled Van off the barstool.

"Where we going?"

"I don't know about you," Zach told him, "but after all that, I could use a treat. How about some ice cream?"

Van loved ice cream. He loved it more than sex. Well, it was a close second. "Double mint-chocolate chip?"

"Is there any other kind?"

"Not in my book," Van replied as Zach held on to his hand and led him out of the Pied.

Chapter
Fifteen

AS THEY strolled down Commercial Street eating their double mint-chocolate chip ice cream cones, Zach realized neither of them had spoken since placing their orders. What was that about? They had shared some rather personal stories. Well, Van's had been extremely private. His bout of public indecency and descent into whoredom in no way compared to what Van had been through.

Had they shared too much? Were things now going to be uncomfortable because of it?

He hoped not. The quiet didn't appear to be a bad omen for some weird reason. It seemed they were both at peace, as if they'd somehow settled into a miraculously comfortable relationship.

When he had approached Van at tea, he'd been angling to score some action with a hot guy. Secretly, he still hoped that might happen, but he found it odd that he'd been thrown completely off the hunt that had enraptured him since his first tea.

What they now shared seemed even better than chasing ass.

How could he have forgotten how much he truly enjoyed connecting with another person? It had been too long since that had happened to him. He and Ben had a connection, but it always seemed forced. Whatever was going on between him and Van wasn't forced. It made things a little frightening.

He'd never met a man who opened himself up so freely. Although he could tell the story had been difficult for Van to recount, it hadn't stopped him from doing so.

A sense of security he'd never experienced around anyone else wrapped its arms around him. Like a big, unseen hug.

Van had nothing to hide, which was a rare commodity in Zach's world. His life had been rife with secrets, from the ones that destroyed his family to the one that ultimately ended his time with Ben.

If he wanted to know something about Van, all he had to do was ask.

"We've been quiet for a while," Van said as they approached a building called the Crown & Anchor. "Anything on your mind?"

"It's silly."

"Well, I have to know now," Van said as he playfully nudged his shoulder into Zach. The sudden move almost made Zach drop his ice cream, but he managed to save it. His surprisingly adept speed astonished him. He rarely recovered from such bungles.

"Look at you," Van pointed out. "You didn't make a mess like you did yesterday."

"I must be getting graceful in my old age."

"Either that or you *really* love ice cream."

Zach thought about it. "It must be the ice cream."

"That's what I thought," Van chimed in.

"Smartass."

Van chuckled. "You have *no* idea."

As they walked in front of the Crown & Anchor, a bevy of activity buzzed around the building. People packed the courtyard to the right. Most waited to be seated at the hotel's eatery, the Central House restaurant, which comprised the patio and main floor of the hotel. The structure itself was remarkable. Painted yellow and white, the building extended to three stories, with balconies at each level of the façade.

Those not in line at the restaurant were either purchasing tickets to one of the shows currently housed at the hotel or bypassing dinner and entertainment for cocktails at one of the three bars—the Vault, the Wave Bar, or the Paramount—that made up the far back wall of the hotel.

In front of the courtyard, entertainers hawked their shows, passing out flyers while trying to entice passersby into coming in to see their performance. One drag queen, who looked like a bastardization of Liza Minnelli and Michael Jackson, pranced around in a skintight blue unitard. She sported the worst case of camel toe Zach had ever seen. Which was truly unfortunate for anyone with eyes.

"She's a mess," Zach whispered to Van.

Van turned to where Zach nodded and laughed. "You mean Suzy Wroughtinkrotch? She's great!"

"Oh my God! Is that a friend of yours?" Zach asked, completely mortified that he had insulted someone Van knew.

"She sure is. Great gal. Even better performer."

"I'm sorry."

"For what?" Van asked.

"For saying she's a mess."

A huge smile spread across Van's face, once again revealing his perfect set of teeth. "Are you kidding me? She is a mess." He pointed at Suzy, whose hairy back lay exposed, a result of a huge tear in her outfit. "That's how she markets herself. She's definitely not your typically glammed-up drag queen."

"That's no lie," Zach added.

Van grabbed his hand and pulled him across the street. "Come on, I'll introduce you."

"That's really not necessary," Zach told him, but Van didn't listen. In no time at all, he was standing in front of Suzy Wroughtinkrotch. Her Liza Minnelli wig sat askew on her head, and the white makeup she had painted on made her look as though she just stuck her face in a bowl full of chalk. To make matters even worse, her thick lips were coated with bright-red lipstick that also ran across her teeth.

The girl looked seriously fucked up.

"*Van!*" she screamed at the top of her lungs, making her sound like a very butch Marilyn Monroe. When she pulled Van into a hug, her sweat-soaked pits became visible to the world. Did she smell as funky as she looked?

"How are you, Suzy?"

"Oh, you know," she replied, now quite demurely. Apparently, she fluctuated her voice between a screaming bull-dyke banshee to a coquettish teenage girl. "I'm just here prostituting myself like always."

"Business good?"

"Not bad, not bad," she answered while eying Zach instead of Van. "But I see you've brought me some fresh ginger. It's always been one of my favorite spices. I try to add it to my diet as much as possible."

Zach laughed uncomfortably as Suzy undressed him with her eyes.

"Suzy, this is Zach."

"Just Zach?" she asked. "Is that like just Cher?"

Van grinned. "Maybe. We haven't exchanged last names yet."

"I'm not surprised," she said with a nod. "It's P-town, after all. The most you've probably been able to exchange is body fluids. And really? What else matters?"

"No body fluids have been exchanged," Zach told her. "And my last name is Kelly."

"Well, if the two of you haven't played poke the butt yet, that must mean this is quite serious. Only tricks and benefriends jump straight into bed."

"Suzy!" Van warned.

"Oh, hush, Van. Let's do this right. Zach Kelly, let me introduce you to my friend Van Pierce. Van, this is Zach Kelly."

She arranged the two of them so they stared into each other's eyes. Zach stood there, embarrassed yet entranced by Van's gorgeous features. He imagined licking his way down Van's brown beard and toward his perfect lips.

"Well, say hello or something," she commanded. "Jeez!"

"Hi," Van said with a slight blush to his tanned cheeks.

He'd never seen humiliation look quite so sexy. "Hi," he responded to Van.

"There. That wasn't so bad now, was it?" Suzy asked.

"No," Van answered. "Just completely degrading."

Suzy cackled. "If you want degrading, come see my show."

She put her arms around their shoulders and pulled them close. Zach definitely caught a strong whiff of sweaty armpit. The musky smell of man typically turned him on, but coming from Suzy and her rotten crotch, his balls crawled up inside his body instead.

"What do you say?" Van asked. "Want to go?"

"Why not?" Zach answered. "I'm up for some depravity. Are you?"

Van laughed. "The fact that you can ask me that proves there's a lot more you still need to learn about me."

"Another challenge?"

"Yup," Van happily replied.

"Challenge accepted."

"All right, break it up," Suzy told them. "Before I turn the hose on the both of you. Now go buy the tickets, and I'll see you inside."

Zach and Van nodded as they made their way past Suzy, who returned to hawking her show. As they walked over to purchase the tickets at the ticket counter, Zach couldn't help but wonder what Van meant.

What type of naughtiness did Van usually enjoy?

Zach didn't care. He just wanted to find out.

ZACH and Van sat together on the first row of the small theater where Suzy Wroughtinkrotch's show was slated to begin. He hated being so close to the stage, especially during a drag show. The performers typically picked on those closest to them, and he disliked being put on the spot. But when Van led him to where they now sat, he found himself incapable of telling him no. He simply looked too excited, and Zach didn't want to burst that bubble.

"You're gonna love this," Van whispered in his ear. His hot breath rushed against the sensitive skin between Zach's ear and neck, causing him to shiver. "You cold?"

Cold? He'd never been so hot for anyone in his life. Instead of admitting his cock was rock hard, he lied, "A little."

"Well, buck up," Van told him. "I don't have a jacket to loan you and even if I did, this isn't a date so—" Instead of finishing his sentence, he stuck out his tongue.

Zach laughed. Could Van be more adorable? The laughter spread from Zach's face to his entire body. The silliness they shared validated his previous assumption. An unexpected ease did exist between them.

Had their shared stories done that? Or was it perhaps something else?

"It's nice to know I'm with such a gentleman," Zach finally said, pretending to be offended.

"Yeah, well you're not, so get over it!" Van bared his perfect teeth to punctuate his response.

Before he could stop himself, Zach asked, "Do you even know how cute you are?"

Van's cheesy grin slowly withdrew across his face as his cheeks burned a bright red. What the hell did he say that for? If he had a hammer, he'd thump himself over the head with it for potentially ruining such a fun evening. Why did he have to say exactly what he was thinking? He'd never done that before. His responses were typically well thought out. He'd rarely, if ever, made such conversational blunders. Sure, he fell down and broke things. All the time. But his words had never failed him before.

As Van fumbled with a reply and squirmed in his seat, Zach had to say something to bring back the ease they'd previously enjoyed. At least until he stuck not just his foot but his whole fucking leg into his mouth.

But every time he opened his mouth to say something, no words formed.

Then Suzy Wroughtinkrotch saved him when she came onto the stage amid much applause and musical fanfare. Her blaring entrance as she took the microphone and thanked the crowd for coming forced the both of them to put the uncomfortable awkwardness on pause.

Zach had never been a fan of drag shows before. They typically either did bad lip-sync renditions of popular songs or screeched so much through perfectly good lyrics that his ears bled.

That hadn't been the case with Suzy Wroughtinkrotch.

Her show was predominantly stand-up with occasional breakout numbers that punctuated the jokes she told. Since it was Twink Week in town, she ripped into the bad behavior of the younger set of gay men, calling them cheap, anorexic divas. She then broke into a parody of "No Scrubs," which was made famous by an all-girl R&B group called TLC in the 90s. Suzy's version, though, was called "No Twinks."

The crowd, who were mostly the gay men she was making fun of, ate it up. Apparently, being insulted onstage was a good thing. Throughout the song, Suzy wove through the audience, pushing the young men away every time she said "no twink," which elicited howls and whistles from the audience.

By the time the song was over, the crowd was on its feet, and Suzy was coated in so much sweat that her white make up bled onto her blue unitard.

The rest of her show followed the same format until the last fifteen minutes, which she dubbed audience interaction time. Zach sunk into his chair. He had no interest in being asked questions or being brought up onstage. The thought of standing up there in front of everyone made him want to bolt.

Van must have sensed his apprehension because he patted Zach's hand and smiled. Then, instead of removing his hand, he simply left it resting atop Zach's. He made no effort to lift it. As if them holding hands was no big deal. As if it was something they'd been doing for years.

What did that mean?

Zach could now only focus on the weight of Van's touch. It draped perfectly over his hand, and the warmth of Van's skin pressed against his gave him a raging boner. It made his already tight shorts even tighter and more uncomfortable.

"For those of you who've never seen my show before," Suzy said from the stage, "this is where I choose one lucky audience member to come onstage with me. Naturally, whoever I choose must obey my every command, and I'm a pretty demanding bitch." The audience laughed as she smiled broadly. "Now, normally, I just ask Rey, who runs the lights for me, to randomly shine the spotlight on one audience member. But not tonight."

The audience oohed around them, but Zach was only half paying attention. He'd been transfixed by how Van's tanned skin looked so natural next to his pale, white flesh. Like a work of art that demanded a photograph to capture the moment.

"Tonight, I'm going to choose my victim—I mean, my volunteer."

Suzy giggled while the audience laughed.

"You see, right before the show, I ran into a good friend of mine. A man who I love so much. Because he's given *so* much of himself to all of us."

Van's hand tensed. What caused that? When he gazed over at Van, a small bead of sweat broke from his temple and slid down his cheek until it became lost in the tangle of brown facial hair. Van definitely looked distressed. In fact, instead of holding Zach's hand, he now squeezed it.

"Some of you don't know who I'm talking about because, well, maybe you haven't seen him yet in the room with us. Or maybe because he's wearing far more clothes right now than we're used to seeing him in. But he's quite a celebrity around town."

Zach turned around, trying to see who Suzy was referring to. He expected to find someone like John Waters or Lance Bass in the crowd, but all he could see were ordinary guys just like him and Van.

"And for those of you who know who I'm talking about, your eyes have no doubt been glued to him for much of the evening. I mean, why not? He's fucking hot. Much hotter than my hairy, fat ass, that's for sure."

The crowd erupted into laughter as Zach continued to scan the people in the small theater. Most everyone else was looking forward, toward him and Van and the stage. Just who was Suzy talking about?

"Zach," Van whispered. "I need to tell you something."

He turned around. Van's blue eyes appeared twice their normal size. "What's wrong?" he asked. "And who is Suzy talking about?"

Just as Van was about to answer, Suzy interrupted them by announcing, "Of course, the man I'm talking about is P-town's own Hart Throb!"

Suddenly, the theater's spotlight shone on him and Van. Why was the fucking light on them, and why the hell was Van P-town's heartthrob?

"Come up on stage with me, Hart," Suzy instructed as she held out her hand to Van.

Van flashed him a smile filled with regret as he released Zach's hand and took Suzy's before ascending to the stage. As soon as he was up there, the crowd went wild. Guys started whistling and barking. Some even asked if he'd get naked.

What the hell was going on here?

"So, Hart, are you enjoying the show?"

"Of course, I am, Suzy," Van responded. He looked nervous and unsure.

"I hope you don't mind that I'm picking on you today, but I just couldn't help myself. It's not often that you're out and about. For someone who apparently enjoys the limelight, I rarely see you at any of the shows."

"I'm just too busy, I guess."

"*Very* busy, I'm sure," Suzy told Van with a wink to the crowd, who erupted into raucous laughter. "That's why I just had to pull you onstage. I mean, besides the fact that I could just eat you with a spoon, I just had to acknowledge the fact that you decided to grace *my* show with your fabulous presence."

"Thanks, Suzy. I just love your show. You know that."

She pretended to be flattered by hiding her face behind her gloved hand. "You know flattery will get you anywhere," she told Van while presenting her ass. "And I do mean *any*where." She gawked at the crowd with her eyes wide and mouth agape. It was evidently her way of admitting her naughty behavior. "But who am I kidding?" she told Van as she once again faced him. "We all know you're a big bottom."

This admission was met by applause.

How the hell did everyone here know that? He thought Van was a top.

She then ducked behind Van and dry humped him, much to the crowd's enjoyment. "Have you ever been fucked by a drag queen before?" Suzy asked, this time in a booming male voice instead of her quiet, demure tone.

The theater exploded with amusement.

"No," Van told her. "That would be new. Even to me."

From up on the stage Van stared down at him with wide, apologetic eyes. What was Van sorry for? And why did he look as if being up there was killing him?

"Take off your shirt," some guy in the back screamed.

"Fuck the shirt," another man argued. "Lose the pants."

The catcalls were treated to a resounding applause. If he could, he'd walk around the room and tape all of their mouths shut.

"Now, now," Suzy scolded the crowd. "This is a family show. Besides," she said, looking down at Zach, "Hart has brought a date to my show. That wouldn't be appropriate, now would it?"

Suddenly, the spotlight shone on Zach, and the crowd teasingly booed him.

"This goes against what I typically do, but why the hell not?" Suzy asked. "Come on up here, Zach." She held out her hand to him. Zach's body immediately petrified. Since he had no clue what the hell was going on, he had no desire to get up onstage and add humiliation to his already crushing confusion.

"Ooh, he's shy," she cooed as she looked back at Van. "Not like you at all."

Suzy walked down the stairs from the stage and grabbed Zach's hand. She then gently, but also with more strength than Zach believed her to possess, pulled him onto the stage and stood him next to Van.

"My, my," she told everyone in the theater. "Don't they make a good-looking couple?"

The audience replied with applause.

"If Hart could shit kids out of his ass, the two of you would make beautiful babies."

Laughter once again filled the theater.

"So how did you two meet?" she asked Zach.

"At FK," Zach responded quickly into the microphone, which screeched in response.

Once the feedback surge subsided, Suzy took her fingers out of her ears and responded, "How sweet! Leather stores are like Hallmark cards for gays. When you care enough to send the very best, you dress it up in leather and assless chaps and then whip the shit out of it."

Once again, everyone laughed.

"Do you have a favorite Hart Throb video?"

Okay, so he was an actor. That cleared up some of his confusion, but since he'd never seen one of Van's movies, he had no clue how to answer.

"All of them," he replied as more of a question than a statement.

"Good answer," she told him. "Especially if you want the date to end well."

"This isn't a date," Zach told her.

"It's not?" she asked, looking at Van for clarification. When Van nodded in agreement, Suzy snickered. "Then, this changes everything!"

"How so?" Van asked, looking even more nervous now.

Suzy moved Zach to the side of the stage. "Well, if this was a date, I wouldn't dare do what I'm about to do." She gave a sly wink to the crowd. "But since it's not, I just gotta."

"Suzy!" Van warned as she placed her microphone in the stand and then yanked Van's shirt from his chest. The audience thundered with appreciation.

Suzy rubbed her gloved hands up and down Van's tense, bare torso. This was the first time Zach had seen Van shirtless, and it was an amazing sight to behold. His pecs were perfectly chiseled, and Suzy teased the dark-brown nipples with her gloved hand. The audience howled even louder as she progressed farther down his flat, hairless stomach and halted just inches above his waistband.

Even though he *really* wanted to see Van naked, this wasn't right. He didn't appreciate Van being treated like some mindless piece of meat who was there for everyone else's pleasure. It reminded Zach of the story Van had just told him about his ass of an ex-boyfriend. The pained expression in Van's eyes as he stood there looking at Zach instead of the crowd spurred him into action.

He walked over to Suzy and took her traveling hand off Van's body. The crowd expressed its displeasure by booing him rather loudly.

"Not liking the show?" she asked Zach.

"I was," he told her. "But it just went a bit too far."

"Too far?" she asked him and the crowd. "We were just getting to the good stuff!"

Zach didn't respond. He grabbed Van by his hand and led him off the stage and out of the theater as the men's boos echoed around them.

Chapter Sixteen

ZACH led Van all the way to the Provincetown Town Hall before he stopped. The stunning building, painted a light blue with white trim, had been recently refurbished according to a sign in front, and hosted a mass of people. They sat on its perfectly manicured grounds or on the many park benches that lined its perimeter.

Had this been a date, this would have been a romantic spot to sit under the stars and lounge in each other's arms. But this wasn't a date. Both he and Van already agreed on that. Still, he'd managed to make an ass out of himself by dragging Van offstage in what could only be described as a fit of jealousy and then marching him through town like some naughty child in need of a time-out.

He had to say something, to salvage this evening and repair what damage he may have done. Instead, he plopped himself down on one of the park benches facing Ryder Street, one of Commercial Street's less populated offshoots.

Van quietly took the seat next to him. His heavy sigh told Zach how upset he obviously was.

"I'm sorry," Zach told Van. "I shouldn't have done that. I don't know *why* I did that. I had no right."

Van stared at him, apparently dumbfounded. "Are you serious right now?"

Zach nodded. "Look, I know you have every right to be upset. I wouldn't blame you if you were furious with me. After all, this isn't even a date, and I act all stupidly jealous and possessive." He smacked his forehead with his palm. "I mean, what the fuck is *that* all about?"

"Jealous and possessive? *That's* why you did it?" Van asked. He looked as though he couldn't believe his ears.

Zach bit his tongue. Once again, he had spoken without thinking. He hadn't meant to admit what he was feeling. He simply wanted to apologize. Now, he'd more than likely screwed this up even worse. He entertained the idea of biting clear through his tongue. Then maybe he could shut himself up.

"Can you just accept my apology and leave it at that?" he finally asked Van.

"No, I can't," Van answered as he scooted closer to Zach on the bench. He took Zach's hands in his. "I'm the one who should be apologizing to you."

"What in the world do you have to apologize for?"

"For not telling you that I'm Hart Throb."

Zach shrugged. "So, you're an actor? That's no biggie. It's not like I've told you I teach college English or that I'm an author. Well, I'm not a good author, apparently, but it's what I do. We *did* just meet, so it's not like we know everything about each other or anything."

Van smiled. His perfect teeth shone like stars in the moonlight. "True," he admitted. "But I should have told you about Hart sooner than this. It's not like something I can hide. Or even something that I want to. I'm not ashamed about what I do."

"Why would you hide being an actor?" Zach asked. "I think that's pretty cool. I'm not one who watches a lot of movies or anything, so I hope you'll forgive me for not having seen any of your films."

Van's smile practically took over his face. "You keep apologizing when you shouldn't be."

"I'm sorry," Zach replied. When he realized he'd just apologized again, he flashed Van an impish grin. "I can't seem to stop."

"No, you can't," he said. "But that's okay."

"So, what's it like being a big movie star?" Zach asked.

Van averted his eyes and blushed. "I'm not a big movie star."

"Yeah, right. The way those guys were fawning all over you. They wanted you to take your clothes off!"

Van swallowed, hard. "That's because that's what I do."

"Oooh, so you do nude scenes, huh?"

Van turned back to him. His eyes were serious. "The movies are one big nude scene. With plot and occasional clothes sprinkled in between."

Zach was just about to ask what that meant, when he realized the answer. Hart Throb wasn't Van's stage name; it was his porn name. How stupid could he be? That's why Suzy and the audience knew Van was a bottom. And why they treated him like a sexual object. Because he basically was.

He sat back against the park bench. At least he no longer needed to chew off his tongue. Van's revelation made him quite speechless.

"I don't know how to take your silence," Van told him.

He didn't know either. He'd never met a porn star before. Hell, he didn't even watch porn. Sure, he sometimes beat off to X-rated clips on Dude Tube, but those instances were few and far between. He preferred to use his imagination. It just made jerking off better. For him at least.

But here he was sitting next to someone who was not only a porn star, but who apparently was pretty popular. He'd always thought porn stars were disgusting, lecherous men incapable of keeping their pants zipped up, much like the way he'd been acting lately. But he'd become loosey-goosey enough to finally toss some fun into his rather mundane life. He figured porn stars were different. They fucked on screen because they either suffered from sexual addiction or self-esteem issues. As he stared into Van's blue eyes, he saw neither sexual deviancy nor low self-esteem.

Sitting next to him was a confident man, who looked just like everyone else.

That meant one of two things for Zach.

He either had judged porn stars unfairly or Van wasn't the man he thought he was.

"Will you say *some*thing?" Van asked.

Zach wanted to, but he hadn't processed what he'd learned yet. That meant he couldn't say *any*thing until he did. He needed to think this through before he responded and said something they both may regret.

Could he have judged Van incorrectly? He knew nothing about him, after all, except what he'd seen at the leather shop. The man he met there looked like the next-door neighbor, all-American boy. He'd been so captivated by his looks that Zach had tried to not be his usual clumsy self, even though he created a disaster anyway. When he did, Van had helped him clean up.

Van didn't poke fun at him. He even tried to defuse the situation with Andrew, the store employee. He'd been a good guy then and all throughout their evening together. Somewhere along the way, they'd even become quite comfortable with each other.

Until now.

"Okay," Van said as he stood. "I get the message."

What message? Had he spoken without realizing it? "What do you mean?" he finally asked.

"Don't worry about it," Van told him. "I've run into people who can't get past what I do. I hold no grudge." Van extended his hand out to Zach. "It was nice to have met you."

Zach took Van's hand and held it. With Van's warm flesh in his grasp, he had no intention of letting this man get away. Sure, they had only shared a few hours together, but in that short time, he'd managed to forget the fact that life had recently crapped all over him.

He stood up and stared into Van's liquid blue eyes. They gazed back at him, confusion clearly reflected within. It appeared as if Van didn't know whether to yank his hand free from Zach's grip or decrease the distance that separated their bodies by taking two short steps forward.

To make his intentions clear, Zach stroked Van's face with the tips of his fingers. They danced around his tanned flesh, scratching through the toffee-colored beard before arriving at the cute dimple at the cleft of Van's chin. Zach pressed into the crevice with his thumb at the same time he turned Van's face slightly to the left.

Zach then slowly closed the space between them, taking a step toward Van and wrapping his left arm around Van's waist to bring Van's body even closer. At the same moment their bodies pressed against each other, he pressed his lips against Van's.

Since Van seemed such a tough man, he hadn't been prepared for how soft and dainty Van's lips felt against his. They reminded him of rose petals, and they tasted sweet like nectar. He lighted upon the fragile lips carefully, delivering long, leisurely kisses to velvety flesh that eagerly brushed back against his own.

But his dainty flower quickly grew thorns. Van caught Zach's lower lip between his teeth and bit down, not enough to draw blood but enough to add a bit of zest that communicated to Zach that his flower was definitely not easily broken.

It fact, his flower liked it a bit rough.

Zach brought his right hand up to Van's throat and held him tightly. His grip was just enough to inform Van who was in charge without seriously constricting his airways. The devilish twinkle in Van's eyes told Zach that Van liked it.

When Van pushed himself further against Zach's body, Zach darted his tongue inside the open folds of Van's mouth. Their tongues tussled, slipping and sliding past each another while trying to grasp and pull the other farther within. While their tongues dueled, their hands went just as wild.

Van's strong hands massaged his shoulders, back, and ass. They wove through Zach's hair before Van scratched a path down Zach's cheek and throat. In response, Zach held Van tighter against him, forcing his straining erection against the hardness within Van's shorts before resting his left hand on the gentle slope of Van's firm ass.

As their kisses grew deeper, they each inhaled the other's breath, taking the air in by the lungful as if they were suddenly inhaling the first scent of spring. Their bodies responded in kind. An awakening stirred deep within Zach's soul, far deeper than the lustful desires that raged through his groin, and the same emotion that permeated through him radiated from Van as well.

Their kiss triggered some long-forgotten wellspring that filled them to capacity. Before he lost control right there in front of everyone, he tentatively pulled away and rested his forehead against Van's.

"You kiss good."

Van smiled. Zach wanted to lick each polished pearl individually.

"Not as good as you," Van replied.

For a few moments, they said nothing else. They stared into each other's eyes, their arms wrapped around each other's waists, as people continued to parade up and down Commercial Street, searching for something Zach had just inexplicably found.

ZACH held Van's hand as they walked back down Commercial Street. Where they were going wasn't important. All that seemed to matter rested within the hand that held firmly on to him.

They had both been silent since their kiss because words seemed incapable of communicating what had occurred.

A comfortable silence floated between them. Was that good or bad?

That got him thinking, though. Had his relationship with Ben *really* been as important as he thought it was? Or was there something wrong with *him*?

Was he capable of sustaining a long-term relationship? He had no role models to follow. His parents had hated each other for as long as he could remember, and when his father was shoved out of the closet, which destroyed any semblance of family he had, Zach had come to realize that relationships weren't anything like they were supposed to be.

They contained deceit and betrayal. Happily-ever-afters seemed impossible, relegated only to the fiction he loved to read but couldn't write.

Was that why he sucked at relationships? Because good relationships were only found in fiction?

And what exactly did he feel for Van? It certainly was too soon to call it love, but it was obviously a very serious case of *like*. He'd never been so protective of someone before as when he thought Suzy Wroughtinkrotch was unfairly taking advantage of Van.

Plus, Van got him rock-hard. Guys had turned him on before, but he'd never wanted to devour someone whole as he did with Van.

And then to find out he was a porn actor. Well, that just threw him for a loop.

How could he feel this way, whatever *this* was, for someone who sold his body?

"You look a thousand miles away," Van commented as they strolled past a seedy-looking hotel called Crew's Quarters. It looked run-down, which was unusual for most of the Provincetown establishments he'd come across. The men who smoked by the front door did nothing to improve the sleaze factor. They looked to be tweaking out.

"I guess I am," Zach finally replied.

"Care to share?"

Zach had no intention of admitting his reservations about Van's chosen profession. After all, he barely knew Van, even if he felt a strong bond forming between them. It was much too soon for *that* discussion. "I was just thinking about home," he answered. Since it was only a partial lie, the justification made Zach feel less guilty.

"I see," Van said. "And I take it there's someone special waiting at home?"

Zach sensed disappointment in Van's response, and it intrigued him. It meant that whatever Zach was feeling, Van might somehow feel something quite similar. "Would it bother you if I said yes?"

"Not at all," Van replied, but he could tell from the faraway look in Van's eyes that he was lying. "It happens a lot here. Guys come for a vacation, and whether they have open relationships or not, they dip their wicks in as many willing holes as humanly possible."

Zach laughed, and Van stared at him crossways.

"Did I say something funny?" Van asked.

"Yes, you did 'cause that's *so* not me. I've never cheated on anyone in my life. But most everyone in my life has cheated on me."

"Does that include your boyfriend back home?"

"Ex-boyfriend," he clarified. "He dumped me, and although he didn't say it, I think there might have been someone else."

"Ouch," Van replied while gritting his teeth. "That's tough."

"It was, but not so much anymore."

"Why's that?" Van asked. A hopeful sparkle twinkled in his eyes.

"Honestly?"

"I always expect honesty," Van told him. "It's how I live my life."

"It's this place," Zach told him as he waved his arm around Commercial Street, where people still zigzagged back and forth. The setting of the sun did nothing to abate the frenetic energy Zach witnessed this afternoon. In fact, the rising moon seemed only to amplify it. "You can't really be sad here. There's just too much happiness, and the people here, well, they've been great."

"I know what you mean," Van replied. "Gary and Tara are awesome. They're some of my best friends here."

"Yes, they are awesome," he admitted. He then squeezed Van's hand even tighter. "But you've been pretty awesome too."

"That goes without saying," Van teased as he increased his grip on Zach's hand. "I'm a pretty remarkable person."

Zach rolled his eyes while Van bared his full set of teeth. "Who would have thought that you and I would be walking down Commercial Street holding hands after the way we first met?"

"Stranger things have happened here," Van told him. "It's P-town."

"It certainly does cast its spell, doesn't it?"

"You have no idea."

Zach stopped in the middle of the street, forcing the people behind them to walk around. He pulled Van closer until their noses touched. "That sounds like another challenge."

"I don't know," Van told him. "You've already accepted two."

"And I've met them."

"Have you now?"

Zach nodded. "I know how very far from typical you really are *and* I've got a pretty good idea how wicked you can be."

A smile parted Van's lips, which Zach once again craved to kiss. "You've only seen the tips of both of those icebergs. I don't think you're ready for much more."

"Try me," Zach dared. "I never take on more than I can handle."

Van arched his eyebrows at the suggestiveness of his comment. "Oh, really?"

"Really."

"Now *that* sounds like a challenge," Van said.

"Maybe it is."

"Well, then. Challenge accepted."

Zach then brushed his lips tenderly against Van's. The sweetness of his lips combined with the scratchiness of his facial hair made Zach want to gobble him up. When he kissed his way to Van's tanned neck and inhaled the muskiness of the day lingering in Van's pits, Zach almost passed out.

The man's sweat smelled heavenly. While he found most people's body odors disgusting, Van's stink attracted him even more. He wasn't sure if it was the pheromones Van gave off or what, but he wanted to bottle up Van's fragrance and sell it. It turned him on so badly he had to fight his desire to lift up Van's arm and shove his face into his underarm to not only get more of the scent inside his lungs but to spread Van's smell all over his face.

When did he turn into an animal in rut?

"God, you smell good," he told Van.

Van inhaled deeply at Zach's neck. "I was just thinking the same thing about you. No trace of deodorant whatsoever."

Zach pulled back and smiled. "You like that?"

"I do."

"The tips of those icebergs get bigger and bigger by the moment."

Van grinned. "Well, then, maybe it's time we both dove deeper. Get to the bottom of the challenges we've accepted."

Zach liked where this was heading, and so did his cock. It was at full mast. "What do you have in mind?"

"Underwear shopping," Van announced as he tugged Zach forward down the street.

Zach and his erection became confused. "I'm sorry. What now?"

Van snickered. "We're going underwear shopping."

"That's *so* not what I thought you were going to say," Zach admitted.

"I know." Van beamed. "I'm full of surprises."

"And *why* are we going underwear shopping?"

"For the underwear party," Van told him in mock exasperation.

"Naturally," Zach replied, pretending to be annoyed. "Why else would *anyone* go shopping for underwear?"

"Exactly," Van agreed. "You need underwear for the underwear party."

"I've got underwear."

"Who says I'm talking about you, silly?"

Zach's eyes immediately scanned downward to Van's shorts. He squinted, trying his best to see the outline of Van's shaft. Even the swell of his balls would be enough, but the ambient light proved too dim. Right now, he hated himself for being a gentleman and not trying to grab Van's cock earlier while they kissed. If he had and with no briefs constraining Van's treasure, Zach would have definitely gotten a good handful.

"It's not polite to stare," Van scolded as he lifted Zach's chin up. "My eyes are right here."

"I know where your eyes are," Zach told him as he strained against Van's hand to once again be able to gawk at Van's basket. "That's not what I was looking at."

"Let's go," Van ordered as he pulled Zach forward again. "After we buy some new undies we can grab a quick bite to eat before the party."

Although Zach pouted, he allowed Van to lead him forward. "I've never been to an underwear party before."

"You'll *love* it," Van announced. "It's the best party of the week."

Zach seriously doubted that, considering the party currently under way in his shorts, but he was willing to give it the old college try, something he'd never have done before Provincetown.

Or Van.

Chapter Seventeen

VAN had refused to let Zach see the underwear he'd purchased for the party, no matter how many times Zach practically begged at the store or during dinner at Jimmy's Hideaway. Luckily, they had a quiet booth in the corner, so no one else was subjected to Zach's never-ending pleas, which he found pretty damn cute.

Even when Zach made his brown eyes get all big and sad like Puss in Boots did in *Shrek*, he managed to stay strong. When Zach jutted out his lower lip like a pouty child while doing his Puss in Boots imitation, Van had almost given in entirely.

He'd been reaching for his bag to pull out his skimpy skivvies when they were interrupted by a couple who wanted to take a picture with Hart Throb and get his autograph.

After that, Zach let the matter of the underwear drop.

The change worried him. Zach hadn't gotten all cold and distant, which Van appreciated. He hated to be frozen out by anyone. But the ease they'd enjoyed for most of the evening seemed less uncomplicated.

For a few moments, some unseen phantom drifted up between them.

It didn't last long. Before either of them knew it, they recovered and went back to more casual conversation.

Did Zach have a problem with his job after all? He didn't dare ask. It was certainly much too soon to talk about it, and even if Zach did, what could he do?

Sure, Zach was adorable, and he hoped that later tonight, they might see each other in less than just underwear. But if Zach had a beef with what he did for a living, it wouldn't change anything.

Not only was Van's profession his choice, but Zach didn't live in P-town. By next weekend, Zach would return to his life back home, and their time together would be nothing but a memory or perhaps a stray comment on each other's Facebook pages.

"I'm getting nervous," Zach told him as they lined up to get into Club Purgatory, where the weekly underwear party was held. "I'm not used to walking around in my briefs."

The slight panic he saw darkening Zach's brown eyes made him want to cradle the big redheaded baby in his arms. "Pretend you're in your swimsuit at the beach and you'll be fine."

"Yeah, great," Zach replied. "I'm uncomfortable at the beach too."

Van rolled his eyes. "Stop whining, ya big baby."

Zach pouted. "I'm not whining. I'm informing you of my general state of distress."

"Also known as whining," Van told him.

"Is not." Zach stuck out his tongue in reply.

"Real mature."

Zach answered with a raspberry.

Van couldn't help but laugh. He'd never met someone so insecure and confident at the same time. While Zach saw himself as a complete screw-up, something he had mentioned at dinner, Van saw someone else entirely.

Sure, Zach was a klutz. He dropped his fork at the restaurant twice and knocked over the small table vase once. Even though no object lay in their path as they walked down Carver Street to get to the club, Zach managed to trip. He claimed it was some pesky flea after Van managed to stop him from flying face-first into the pavement.

Despite Zach's occasional blunders, he had enough self-assurance to not only challenge an audience full of Van's admirers and pull him from the stage, but to also act like a fool in front of a line of hot guys.

Zach had more balls than he gave himself credit for.

"Van!"

When he looked toward the front of the line, Van saw Sean Monroe, one of the co-owners of the club and also a dear friend, smoking his Virginia Slims to the left of the front door.

"Hey, Sean!"

Sean waved Van toward the front of the line, so he grabbed Zach's hand and led him over to where Sean stood underneath his private white cloud.

"How are you?" Van asked as he hugged Sean and kissed him on his cheek.

"Better now that you're here," Sean replied in his usual throaty voice. "You'll be good for business. What fag doesn't love dancing mostly naked next to a porn god?"

"I guess I'm one of those fags, then," Zach announced as he introduced himself to Sean.

"You don't do porn, do you?" Sean asked Zach. When Zach shook his head, Sean added, "Too bad. You should."

"Is Ken tending bar?" Van asked, attempting to move the conversation away from porn. He didn't want that unseen phantom from dinner to follow them to the club.

Sean nodded as he took a deep drag on his thin cigarette. "Where else would that bastard be?" Even though Sean talked badly about his partner of twenty years, Van, and pretty much everyone else, knew it was all a charade. Sean just hated being nice to anyone. "You know Ken. If there's a chance he'll see some cock, he'll be around." He blew out another plume of smoke and then waved Van and Zach toward the door. "You boys go on in. I'll see you inside."

"We haven't paid cover yet."

"Oh, please," Sean told Van. "I plan on using your name to drag the horny fuckers in here, so it all comes out in the wash. Now, get in there!"

Van smiled as he and Zach headed through the front door and into the already packed club. The roar of the men crammed inside the basement bar almost overpowered the rhythmic beat of the music blasting from the speakers. Men paraded about in their underwear everywhere. Some hot. Some not so much. But all of them looked to be having a good time as they wandered about holding drinks or each other.

"Do we just strip here or what?" Zach asked as he nervously surveyed his surroundings.

"No," he responded while nodding to the far right corner. "They have a clothes check. You put your clothes in a bag, and you get a paper bracelet with your bag number on it. After that, you walk around, dance, drink, or whatever floats your boat."

Zach nodded in reply and followed Van over to the small area where guys were hurriedly shedding their clothes. When he got their bag, he escorted Zach over to a small leather chair where they could disrobe and where Van could get his first look at Zach's body.

He was more excited than a kid on Christmas morning, waiting to unwrap his present. Except in this instance, the gift would be unwrapping itself. Van didn't care. He just wanted to see the bounty.

"So what now?"

Van chuckled and pulled his T-shirt off and then undid the button of his shorts.

"Oh," Zach replied. "I guess we just do it, huh?"

Van nodded as he pulled down his shorts and started to fold his clothes. While he placed them in the bag, Zach just stood there ogling him. He obviously liked the low-rise blue briefs. When Van tried them on at the store, he fell in love with the fact that they looked like denim and that they proudly displayed his package and the ass he enjoyed showing off. He'd been told his butt was his best feature, so he wanted to highlight it for Zach.

He'd been nervous that Zach wouldn't like the underwear, but by the drool collecting on Zach's chin, it seemed he didn't have to worry about that after all.

All Van had to do now was get Zach out of *his* clothes. "Come on, you big baby. I don't even know why you're so nervous. From what I can see, you've got nothing to be embarrassed about."

"I'm *so* white." Zach frowned. "People make fun of me for it."

The miserable look on Zach's face told him how much Zach hated not being covered up. Van guessed he must have been teased relentlessly about his fair skin, but Van enjoyed the creaminess of his flesh. It looked soft and gentle just like his eyes, but the ruggedness of his facial hair told him Zach also had the edge Van craved in his men.

"No one's going to make fun of you," he assured Zach. "Look around. There are guys with beer bellies walking around in jockstraps and thongs. Their asses have more cottage cheese than a Weight Watchers meal. Do *they* look worried?"

As Zach looked around him, Van could tell he felt a little better but not much.

"How about this?" Van asked as he closed the distance between him and Zach. "How about I undress you?"

Zach whipped his head back to look at him. "Are you serious?" he asked with a wicked glimmer in his eyes. "That might make me…," he stammered, unable to finish his sentence.

"What? Hard?"

"Well, yeah." He nodded. "I don't exactly want to walk around with a boner."

Van laughed. "I doubt yours will be the first hard-on these queens have laid eyes on. Besides, you didn't have a problem getting sucked off at tea. I bet your boner was plenty on display then."

Zach glared at him in mock anger. "Hey! You're not supposed to use that against me!"

"Says who?" Van asked as he placed his hands on Zach's waist and leisurely lifted the shirt free from his body. For the third time in just over twenty-four hours, Van couldn't breathe. The coppery fur that fanned from Zach's washboard stomach and firm chest glistened next to his white skin. It resembled spun gold more than body hair.

Van couldn't help but run his fingers through it.

"You like?" Zach asked, his voice a deep whisper.

He nodded, since speech seemed impossible.

"Well then, I guess you better finish what you started."

Van nodded again as he fumbled to open Zach's shorts and let them fall to the ground. Zach now stood in front of him in a pair of red briefs that tented outward from the erection that strained to get free. Van wanted to set it loose and work what looked to be a big, fat fuck-stick inside his ass, but he couldn't move. All he could do was stare, not just at the amazingly attractive man before him, but also at the clever design of the briefs. As part of the pattern, a pair of yellow fireballs shot across the front.

"Hope you like my fire crotch."

"I do," Van responded in a breathy voice.

Zach turned around to show him his ass. Across his perky, round cheeks were stamped the words FIRE RESCUE.

"I bought these yesterday," he told Zach as he spun back around, apparently no longer worried about his appearance.

"Great purchase."

"I'm glad you think so," Zach said as he took Van into his arms.

As they stood there, bare chest to bare chest, Van completely forgot about where he was. The randy men milling about and the music blaring from the dance floor disappeared. Right now, his whole world existed within Zach's arms.

Not only did Van like the way it felt, it also scared the shit out of him.

SWEAT dripped down Van's body as he and Zach danced amid the swirling sea of men packed onto the dance floor with them. Although they'd been dancing since they got there and undressed, Van didn't want to stop. Yes, his feet hurt, and his body craved liquid refreshment, but he couldn't pull himself away from Zach.

He couldn't get enough of Zach's wet, hairy body sliding against his skin. It made him happy and hard, and apparently Zach felt the same way. Their erections either dueled against each other as they danced and gyrated their pelvises together, or they were rubbed up and down the other's crack.

What Van found fascinating was that they hadn't grabbed hold of each other's cocks or slid their hands underneath the waistbands of each other's briefs. They surfed and slid their hands across chests and stomachs and over arms and backs. They'd even cradled each other's asses, but they steered clear of the throbbing dicks between them and the bare flesh hidden from view.

It wasn't that Van didn't want to touch Zach. Hell, he wanted to suck Zach's cock down his throat and then shove it up his ass, but he didn't want the first time he touched Zach in so intimate a place to be shared in such a public setting.

That confused the crap out of him.

Van enjoyed getting his freak on in public, and obviously Zach did too. Why didn't he just shove his hand underneath the fabric and grab a hold of what he most wanted?

As he contemplated doing just that, Zach licked a trail from Van's ear to his neck. "Your sweat tastes good." He then lifted Van's right arm and shoved his face inside his hairy pit, which hadn't been touched by deodorant that day. Zach lapped up the collected beads of sweat before he rubbed his cheeks and face against the damp underarm.

Van had to fight back the rising cry of pleasure that wanted to escape his throat.

When Zach pulled himself out of Van's pit, he had a crazed look on his face. "You smelled so fucking good. I just had to get it all over me."

How fucking hot was that? He wanted to yank down Zach's undies and fuck himself silly right there on the dance floor.

"You're driving me crazy," he told Zach.

Zach smirked. "You are too. I *so* want to grab your cock, but I've never wanted someone so badly. I kinda want the feeling to last."

Van couldn't help the smile that drew itself across his face. He thought for certain he looked like an idiot, but he didn't care. Zach had managed to express what Van had yet to understand.

He'd never been this attracted or this in sync with someone before.

"There you are, you fucking crazy bitch."

Van didn't have to turn around to know who was now standing behind him. No one but his best friend ever greeted him with such endearing terms.

"Hey, Nino," Van said as he turned around in Zach's arms. Zach held him close, pressing his chest against Van's back and grinding his hardness against Van's ass. He enjoyed the fact that Zach appeared to not want to let him go.

"Where've you been?"

"Where've *I* been?" Nino asked as he stood there in his black bikini briefs and his hands on his hips. "Where've *you* been?" He eyed Zach, and then arched his eyebrows at Van.

"We've been to a show and dinner," he told Nino. "Now we're here."

"That's a long-ass date."

"It's not a date," both he and Zach replied in unison.

"Are you boys *still* on your date?" a voice next to them suddenly asked.

When Van turned to his left, Gary and Quinn were beside them. Gary, who currently had both his legs wrapped around Quinn's midsection, wore blue boxer briefs while Quinn had on a white jockstrap.

"We're *not* on a date," Van repeated while Zach nodded in agreement.

"How's the date going?" Quinn asked.

Van glanced over his shoulder to look at Zach. "Am I speaking English? Because no one seems to be understanding me."

"Oh, we hear what you're saying," Gary chimed in. "We're just not buying your bullshit."

Van growled in frustration while Zach kissed the back of his neck. It was such a tender and loving gesture that it did what Zach evidently intended it to do. Van's annoyance all but disappeared.

"Call it whatever you want," Quinn told them. "We're just happy to see you both, well, happy."

Gary winked. It was his way of agreeing with Quinn. Nino simply shrugged.

"I don't really care," Nino announced, once again pretending he didn't have a soul. "Just as long as the Debbie Downer from this morning doesn't return, I'll be happy."

"I love you too," Van told Nino.

"I know you do," Nino replied with his trademark grin. "Now, if you'll excuse me, not only am I bored by this conversation, but I've got to find me a nice tight hole for the evening."

Without another word, Nino turned around and disappeared into the crowd.

"We'll let you get back to your... evening," Gary said as he motioned for Quinn to carry him away. Quinn waved good-bye as they walked three more steps to the right and were swallowed up by the dance crowd.

"Those guys are incorrigible," Zach said as Van turned around in his embrace to once again dance face-to-face with him.

"I know. I'll have to kick the shit out of them later."

"So why have you been Debbie Downer?" Zach asked as they returned to dancing, their bodies once again matching not only the beat of the music but each other's rhythm.

Van didn't want to talk about his recent problems with his porn gig, especially not while at the underwear party or with Zach. "Not now," he said. "Maybe later."

Zach nodded as he slid himself up and down Van's slick torso. Van loved the way Zach danced, pressing the entirety of his body against Van. The sweat that poured off their bodies was shared between them.

It was as if they were dogs marking each other, and the animalistic quality appealed to Van's primal, sexual nature. It made him want Zach even more than he already did.

"Are you ready to get out of here?" Van asked.

"Are you not having a good time?"

"Of course I am, silly. I just thought we'd have more fun somewhere less crowded."

Zach smirked. "What*ever* do you mean?"

Van wrapped his arms around Zach's neck and gave him a long, deep kiss. "Does that clear things up for you?"

Nodding, Zach grabbed Van's hand and led him off the dance floor, but before they cleared the area, a group of young guys blocked their path.

"Fuck me!" one of the guys said. He wore a blue wrestling singlet. "It's Hart Throb!"

"Oh my God," another one squealed. "You're like my fucking favorite porn star."

Van eyed Zach, whose blank expression he couldn't read. "Thanks, guys," he told them. "But we were just on our way out."

"Can we get a picture?" a third guy asked. He was taller and more muscular than his twink friends. Most definitely one of the newer breed of gym twinks, who rebelled against the typical waifish younger man look by packing on muscle mass. Still, even though he was twice his friends' size, he looked the most childish of them all, almost begging Van for a picture.

"I really can't."

"Oh come on!" they whined in unison.

Zach leaned over to Van and whispered in his ear. "Go ahead. You don't want to upset your fans, do you?"

Did he hear Zach right? He looked into Zach's smiling brown eyes. "Are you serious?"

Zach nodded. "You're just a fantasy for them," he told Van. "I get the real deal. After all, you're coming home with me."

"You're right," he replied. "I am."

When he told his fans he had time for one picture, they cheered, and while they set up the shot the way they wanted, he never once looked at the camera, not even when it finally flashed. He could only focus on Zach, who stood off to the side in his hot red underwear, watching him with a huge smile stretched across his face.

The fear that had gripped Van earlier disappeared completely.

Chapter Eighteen

WHEN Zach closed the door and turned around to see Van standing in his condo, he suddenly found himself very nervous. He still wanted to ravage Van. He'd never wanted to be with a man more than he did with Van, but Van was a fucking porn star who'd done scenes with probably more attractive and virile men than he.

How could he compete with that?

"What's wrong?" Van asked. He too looked anxious, as if he didn't know whether he should sit, stand, or run. Van's unease made him feel a little better.

"I don't want to say," he told Van. "It'll make me look stupid and insecure."

Van laughed. "I could use that. I'm feeling a little stupid and insecure right now too. Maybe we can help each other out."

Zach crossed over to Van and took his bronze hand in his. "It's just that, well, sex is what you do for a living, so I'm gonna assume you have a lot of it."

"This from the man who's had four tricks in the last twenty-four hours."

"I have not had four!" Zach protested.

"Oh, yes you have. The guy whose name you can't remember from earlier today. The three-nippled Dylan, and the two guys on the dance floor at tea. That's four."

"The couple counts as one."

"Were they conjoined twins?"

"What?" Zach asked. "Of course not!"

"Then that's two separate people. Which makes four."

Zach rolled his eyes at Van.

"Hey, don't get hateful because you can't count," Van announced with a grin. "Now, what were you going to say about me and all the sex *I've* had?"

Zach pulled Van into his arms and ran his fingers through his short-cropped hair. "I guess I'm just worried that compared to your costars, well, I won't be very good for you."

Van nodded. "You're right. You won't be good." He rested himself against Zach's body, chest to chest and groin to groin. "You're going to be great. I know it."

He stared into Van's eyes, and Zach's anxiety fell away under his steel-blue gaze. He no longer worried about Van's past or his profession. All he cared about was right now. This moment in time that had brought the two of them together.

Everything else drifted away as he lowered his lips onto Van's, and the building storm of their passion from the evening together swept through their bodies, thundering in their chests and in their shorts.

Zach feverishly drank in Van's abundant kisses, and they sparked within him a passion so rich it was like being kissed for the first time. Upon Van's lips rested some miraculous wellspring he'd never before known and which he'd never again live without.

As his tongue shot into Van's open mouth like lightning, a rumble of desire resonated deep within Van's throat. Van lifted Zach's shirt, and his fingers danced like raindrops across Zach's chest, lighting on his stomach, flickering through his chest hair, and eventually descending upon his nipples, which he rubbed and rolled beneath his fingers.

Zach followed the trail of muscle and sinew from the expanse of Van's back down the curve of his spine until Zach rested them at the dip of his lower back, just above the swell of his round ass.

He used his hands to bring Van's body closer against him, to force the rigid erections they hadn't yet touched against each other's bodies. Van's hot, hard cock throbbed against his own, a storm of a different kind obviously churning inside his balls.

"I want you so bad," he told Van as he yanked Van's shirt free from his body. He gazed down at the tanned, broad chest, and Zach reached out to tease the brown nipples to attention. He then kissed his way from Van's lips down his neck until he took the left nipple inside his mouth. He flicked his tongue over the area, teasing it with moist flutters that caused the sensitive skin to harden.

"Me too," Van said, his voice breathy and deep. "Since the moment I saw you."

Van then ripped Zach's shirt from his body and pushed him against the living room wall. He raised Zach's hands over his head and then dove into his pits the way Zach had done to Van on the dance floor at Club Purgatory. He licked frenzied circles through the matted hair. He then gnawed at the sensitive flesh of each underarm before rubbing his cheeks and chin through his stink.

"Now I smell like you too," Van announced with a grin before pressing his lips back on Zach's.

As they kissed, Zach could scent his own smell lingering in the air between them. He had difficulty discerning where Van's natural odor stopped and his began. It made him want to howl, thinking they had marked each other like animals, and it reignited within him a fire that had always burned far too bright and far too hot.

His sexual urges had frightened him before. He had run from them because he was taught to be afraid and embarrassed of what he couldn't control.

That fear no longer existed. The embarrassment vanished.

In Provincetown, he'd found the courage to push the boundaries that constrained him, but in Van's arms he found what existed on the other side—a never-ending frontier, where everything suddenly seemed possible and within Zach's reach.

And this time, nothing was going to get in Zach's way. Not even his own blundering self. He reached out to grab Van by the neck with loving forcefulness and then used the leverage to pin him against the adjacent wall. As he held Van secure, Van's eyes flashed with wild abandon. He obviously loved being dominated, and now that he had marked himself with Zach's musk, Zach planned on showing Van just how much he owned him.

"Take off those shorts!" he commanded Van after he bit down on the nipple he'd already roughly tweaked.

"Yes, sir," Van meekly replied as he hurriedly fumbled the buttons open and let his shorts fall to the ground.

Van's body trembled before him and his cock strained against his blue, skimpy briefs. The whole time at the underwear party Zach had wanted to tear them from his body, but now that it was time, he hesitated.

He didn't want the moment to end. He wanted to savor the sight of Van pressed against the wall and obeying his every command. For many painful minutes, he studied Van, committing every curve of muscle, every bead of sweat that snaked down his torso to memory.

"What do you want me to do now?" Van asked. His voice was low and subservient.

"Lose the underwear," he ordered. "But do it slowly."

Van nodded in understanding as he swallowed hard. The muscles in Van's throat shuddered as Van hooked the waistband of the briefs and began their leisurely descent.

The small brown treasure trail that extended down from Van's belly button to his crotch spread into a manicured patch of pubic hair. The light dusting of fur fanned out from just over the bulging crotch, still covered by fabric, and toward the sensitive flesh where the exposed, muscular upper thighs joined the pubic area.

As Van lowered his briefs to midthigh, the root of Van's cock came into view. Its thick base, nestled amid his hair, made Zach want to bury his nose in the thatch and inhale the intoxicating aroma.

Finally, after agonizing moments, he shoved Van's briefs off his thighs. As they fluttered to the floor, out sprung the most beautiful cock Zach had ever seen in his thirty-plus years. It stood out about seven inches with a bright-pink mushroom head. The shaft bobbed up and down as Van's still-shuddering body forced more and more blood into the already engorged dick. His smooth balls, gathered up between his legs, looked filled beyond capacity and ready to bring forth their sweet milk.

"You're beautiful," he told Van. He then returned his lips to Van's while reaching out to take Van's hardness in his palm. Upon contact with Van's cock, Van moaned while pumping his hips into Zach's firm grip.

"I'm glad I please you," Van uttered before wrapping his arms around Zach's neck and forcing their bodies closer. Unbridled lust coursed through Van's flushed skin.

Van evidently wanted to be wanted, which explained why Van did porn. After everything he'd been through in his past relationships, Van turned to the sex industry to fulfill what the men in his life had been unable to offer.

For as much as Van had just given him, he wanted to return the favor and give to Van what Van had been searching for as well.

"You do please me," Zach said in between their passionate kisses. "Very much."

Van practically whimpered in response.

"In fact, I'm gonna show you," Zach announced as he led Van toward the stairs to their left. He motioned Van to stand on the third step before Zach sank to his knees. "I'm gonna worship you with the devotion you deserve."

He grabbed onto the base of Van's cock and flicked his tongue across the weeping slit. He slurped the honeyed juices before licking along the top of the shaft and up to the base of the throbbing dick. Once there, he thrust his nose into the root, nuzzling as far into Van's pubes as he could manage and inhaling deeply. A heady mixture of musk and sweat filled his body and threatened to drive him crazy.

Zach reached down to grab his own cock, still confined between the fabric of his underwear and his body. He longed to pull the material from himself, but right now it wasn't about him. This moment belonged to Van.

From the base of the cock, Zach rained kisses upon Van's crotch, nibbling at his groin and gnawing his way down the curve of his leg until arriving at Van's balls. He jacked Van's meat as he popped Van's cum-heavy sac into his mouth. He rolled the jewels around inside, using his tongue to massage the taut flesh. In response, Van yelped, and his thighs trembled incessantly.

"That feels so good," Van panted.

Zach allowed Van's balls to slip from his mouth. "Just wait."

He then stuck the head of Van's cock in his mouth and sucked hard, using the suction to milk more precum from the throbbing prick. Van shuddered in delight and threw back his head as Zach slid more and more of the shaft down his throat until the full extent of Van's cock lodged down his gullet.

With his nostrils once again shoved against Van's sweaty crotch, he inhaled sharply as his throat massaged Van's hardness. He pulled off the cock and then rested the head on his tongue before he slid all the way down the hard dick again. He worked Van's prick until his spit slid off Van's meat and down Zach's hands.

When he noticed Van's breath quicken, he abruptly stopped. He didn't want Van to come. At least not yet.

He released Van's cock and then resumed kissing Van's crotch before snaking a trail with his tongue up to Van's belly button, around both nipples, and back up to his sexy mouth filled with his perfect, white teeth.

"You almost made me come," Van muttered as he greedily descended upon Zach's lips.

"I know. That's why I stopped."

Van grinned. "I like that. A lot."

"Good."

"But you know what I'd love even more?"

"Tell me."

Van slid his hands under the waistband of Zach's briefs and grabbed his ass. "For these to come off."

"Is that an order?" Zach asked. He made sure his voice sounded stern and authoritative.

"A request," Van answered before tenderly kissing Zach's lips.

"Good boy," he said. "Request granted."

A boyishly innocent smile danced across Van's face as he pulled Zach's underwear down and off his body. He then hopped onto the floor in front of the first stair and dropped to his knees. He gazed in admiration at Zach's thick nine inches. "Oh my God!" Van exclaimed. "It's big, and it's beautiful."

"And it's all for you," he told Van as he ran his fingers through his hair.

Van looked up appreciatively before he swallowed Zach's dick whole.

"Fuck!" Zach hollered as Van expertly worked his hard cock. His tongue swirled around the head while his hands gripped the shaft, jacking it in time to the measured beats of the lovemaking Van's mouth provided his dick.

While he slid back and forth on Zach's cock, Van locked eyes with Zach. He never broke contact, obviously wanting to make certain that what he was doing was giving Zach the pleasure Van intended.

Zach caressed Van's cheeks, lovingly reassuring him of a job well done. His eyes twinkled in satisfaction, and Van's suction increased exponentially.

With his heart thundering in his ears and his toes about to curl, Zach tried to force Van off him. His mouth had brought Zach too close to the edge, and if Van didn't stop now, there'd be no turning back.

"I'm too close," Zach warned.

Van came off his cock long enough to say three words. "Just do it."

"No," Zach complained as his hips instinctively thrust forward. He was supposed to be the one in control, not Van, but by the way Van continued to stare at him, his eyes reflecting a hungry need for seed, he realized this was part of being the submissive.

Van saw himself as the vessel through which Zach pleased himself, and Van wouldn't stop servicing him until he was spent and dry.

"Fine," Zach told him. He grasped Van's shoulders and force-fed him his cock. His hips rocked back and forth, his dick sliding between Van's soft lips. He pushed himself down Van's throat until his body tensed and his lungs burned from the exertion. "You want it?"

Van nodded, his eyes begging Zach to come.

"Here it comes!" Zach bellowed as his cock spasmed inside Van's greedy mouth. His lips wrapped entirely around the base, as he guzzled down the thick, creamy load Zach jettisoned from his body until after five heavy spasms, Zach had nothing left.

Van finally released Zach's softening cock from his moist grasp. "That was good," he said as he rose within the stairwell, wiping the spittle from his chin.

"Good?" Zach asked. "That was fucking great!"

"I'm glad you think so."

Zach nodded, completely out of breath. When the air returned to his lungs, he said, "But you disobeyed me, and you must now be punished."

Van chewed on his lower lip. "I like the sound of that."

He turned Van around and forced him onto all fours on the small landing of the stairs, a few steps up from the lower level. "Present yourself," he commanded, and Van arched his back and lifted up his ass to Zach.

"Now *that's* a good boy," he said as he dove between Van's ass cheeks and ate out his center. Van groaned as Zach worked his tongue in and out of Van's sweat-moistened ass before Zach alternated between nibbling on the rim and sliding his tongue up and down Van's crack.

The musky taste of Van's butt quickly got Zach hard again. He hadn't been able to come twice in a row since his early twenties. Right now his cock was so hard, he was more than capable of blowing another load. Perhaps even another two.

"Yes," Van mewled. "Eat my ass. Oh, God, please keep going!"

Zach immediately stopped. "No more eating ass."

"What?" Van asked. "Why?"

Zach didn't respond. Instead, he inserted a finger and wiggled it around. Van moaned in response. His arched back and quivering ass told Zach that he understood it was time to prepare him for Zach.

With his index finger inserted to the third knuckle, he twirled large circles inside Van's butt. Each rotation created a bigger arc as Van's puckered flesh relaxed. When Zach inserted two fingers and began working them together inside Van, Van called out his appreciation.

When Zach was satisfied that he could take him with ease, he rose onto his knees and slapped his hardness against Van's pulsating center.

"It's time to fuck."

"That's right," Van told him as Zach retrieved the condom from his own shorts. "Fuck my ass hard. Fuck it 'til you fill me up."

"I will," Zach announced as he rolled the condom on and positioned himself behind where Van's ass wagged in anticipation before him. "I'm gonna fuck you stupid."

Van's low moan told him how much he was looking forward to that. When Zach slowly pushed his way past Van's tight ring until he was buried all the way inside, Van's moans turned into cries of ecstasy.

"Oh fuck, yeah!" Van groaned. "You feel great inside me."

Zach couldn't respond as he worked his cock furiously in and out of Van's tight ass. Van bore down on him with each thrust, using his muscles to increase the friction.

Beads of sweat sprung out across Van's skin before sliding down and collecting at the small of his back. Zach slid his hands up from his grasp on Van's ass and skimmed across the surface of Van's slick flesh. He fluttered his fingers across the contracting muscles, massaging Van's exterior as Van's interior massaged Zach's cock.

When he surfed his hands to Van's shoulders, he gripped them firmly and used them as leverage to slam himself harder and faster inside Van's clenching ass.

Their grunts and groans filled the staircase, making it sound as if a dozen people were fucking in the condo instead of just the two of them.

This made Zach even hornier. He increased his rhythm, slamming into Van with even more power, and Van matched his beat by ramming his ass backward with equal if not more ardent force.

Their bodies, now drenched in sweat, made wet, sloppy noises, a symphony to their lovemaking.

"You're gonna fuck the cum right out of me," Van moaned as he furiously beat his meat. "I don't think I can hold back any longer."

"Me either," Zach grunted. "I'm about to come again. Up your ass."

"Yes," Van pleaded. "Do it! Fill me up."

Once again, Zach's body grew tense as he prepared to shoot for the second time in less than twenty minutes. "Take it all!" Zach shouted as he hovered over Van's body, shoving his cock deep inside while he emptied his nuts within the condom.

Van howled as he no doubt felt the violent force of Zach's dick spasming inside him. His convulsions brought Van over the edge as he pumped himself to creamy release.

After they caught their breaths, Zach hesitantly extracted himself from Van, who turned over and curled up on the small, carpeted stairwell landing.

"That was an amazing fuck," Van told him as he smeared his cum across his chest.

Zach tossed the condom into the kitchen wastebasket and then joined Van on the landing. He ran his fingers through Van's cummy mess and then licked them clean. "Tastes like candy," he announced. "And I like candy."

Van laughed. "You're nasty. I like that."

"Good," Zach said. "I like that too. I never thought I could do that before."

"Do what? Fuck?" Van asked, eying him as if Zach were crazy.

"No," he told Van. "I can fuck, but I've never…. Well, I've never fucked like *that* before."

"Are you kidding me?"

Zach shook his head.

"Wow," was all Van responded with.

"Kinda makes me want to do it again."

Van drew closer and kissed his lips. "Really?"

Zach nodded.

"I'm fine with that. Let's just try somewhere other than the stairs this time. I'm not a big fan of carpet burn."

"I don't know," Zach said. "You might make it as far as the top of the stairs before I have to crawl back inside you."

"That sounds like a challenge." Van smirked.

He chuckled. "Maybe it is."

"Challenge accepted," Van replied and then got up and bounded up the stairs.

Zach immediately chased after him, and when he caught up to Van at the top, he took Van again one more time. Afterward, they finally collapsed in bed, where they drifted off to sleep in each other's arms.

Chapter Nineteen

THE bright morning sun streaming between the slats on the window blinds woke Van. He didn't want to get out of bed. His insides were too warm and fuzzy, and that had nothing to do with his aching muscles or sore ass. Well, that wasn't *entirely* true. His happily numb butt was part of the reason. Just not the *only* reason.

He'd had a great time with Zach the night before. The sex had been fucking incredible. He couldn't remember the last time he'd gotten nailed four times in a row. He hadn't even managed that onscreen yet.

But he was more than just sexually satisfied. The cloud that had hung over him the past twenty-four hours had moved on. He'd been so depressed that people only saw Hart Throb when they looked at him. He worried that perhaps his alter ego had replaced him in the world, making Van somehow obsolete.

Zach reminded him that wasn't the case. He only saw Van, not Hart. Zach really didn't even know who Hart was.

But as he glanced over at Zach, who lay on his side facing away from him, Van had to face the cold, hard reality of the new day. Whether he wanted to or not, it was time.

The morning after spending the night with someone, something he hadn't done since Jason, proved difficult sometimes. With the passion fulfilled and the cum dry, one of the two who were so into each other the night before always looked for the easiest and tidiest excuse that provided the quickest exit. At least that had been his experience.

Although he longed to stay in bed and snuggle into the warmth that radiated from Zach's side of the bed, he couldn't bring himself to scoot over the few inches.

What if Zach complained and swatted him away? What if he woke up and looked surprised to see Van still here?

He couldn't take that kind of disappointment.

It was better if he simply got up and slunk away. He pulled the covers slowly aside, but before he had a chance to get out of bed, Zach turned over to face him and wrapped his arm around Van, drawing him close.

"Good morning," Zach said with his eyes still closed. "Were you planning on leaving without saying good-bye?"

"Not at all," he fibbed. He settled next to Zach, wrapping his left leg over Zach's waist and resting his head on the same pillow as Zach. His warm morning breath washed over Van's face. Why in the world did inhaling Zach's morning breath comfort him? Was it because that was how a couple who'd been together for years woke up every morning? If that was the case, it made them more than just relative strangers who met a few hours ago.

Was he really ready to travel down that road again?

"You're such a bad liar." Zach's accusation brought him out of his thoughts. His beautiful brown eyes fluttered open, and the edges of Zach's mouth hooked into a sly grin. "You were about to make the great escape. Admit it."

Van laughed. "Maybe."

"As I thought," Zach said before grabbing him and pulling him on top of his naked body. Zach's morning wood pressed against his stomach. He liked that even after a night of wild sex, Zach still appeared ready for another go-around.

"I understand leaving first thing is proper etiquette," Zach told him. "But I'm okay with you hanging out for a little longer."

Staring down into Zach's eyes, he noted that Zach looked just as surprised to have said those words as Van was to hear them. He did want to stay and was actually quite relieved that Zach didn't want to immediately boot him out of bed. What did all this mean, though?

It was entirely unprecedented for him.

On the rare occasions when he stayed over at a trick's house or let a trick sleep in his bed, he'd been more than happy when the fucker put his dick back in his pants and they went their separate ways.

But this didn't feel like a usual tricking. What made it different?

It wasn't as though there was a future in this. He lived here, and Zach lived, well, wherever Zach lived. They had yet to discuss where Zach called home. If he didn't even know where Zach lived, how could he be deluding himself that this *wasn't* a trick?

But as Zach ran his fingers through his hair with one hand while the other played with Van's still-lubed butt, Van realized it wasn't just him. Zach was doing this too. Whatever the hell it was.

If Zach was willing to go with the flow, why shouldn't he?

"No pressure," Zach said after a few moments of silence. "I completely understand if you've got things to do." He broke eye contact, obviously embarrassed that Van had yet to respond to the invitation.

"I'd love to," Van said.

"You sure? You were quiet for a long time. I didn't know how to take that."

He traced the outline of Zach's delicious lips with his fingers. He hoped his touch would deliver the reassurance he meant it to bring. "I was just running through my schedule for the day. There's nothing so pressing that I can't put it off for a few hours."

When Zach smiled, he couldn't help but return it with one of his own.

"I am confused, though."

"About?" Zach asked.

"What are we going to do with ourselves?"

A salacious grin crept across Zach's face. "I can think of a few things."

Zach then craned his neck upward, and he found Van's lips once again. Like last night when they kissed outside the town hall and then again later downstairs, Zach's kiss made his body tingle. As if he'd been plugged into a power source and thousands of volts of electricity now coursed through him.

He just had to go in deeper, so he forced his tongue farther into Zach's mouth, drinking in the sweetness he remembered from the night before. Except this time, the taste was even more pleasant than before. Some secret ingredient had been added that made Zach even more delicious.

In fact, Van craved more.

He moved from Zach's face to his neck, biting on the smooth, creamy skin hard enough to leave a trail of red marks as he chewed a path to Zach's pits.

"Fuck, yeah," Zach told him with a sharp intake of breath. "Make it hurt good."

By the way Zach furiously ground his hard cock up against Van's own painful erection, he could tell he was driving Zach as crazy as Zach was driving him. He squirmed and moaned underneath Van, and when Van arrived at his pits, he gasped as Van kissed and licked his way through the coppery hair that smelled ripe with musk collected from dancing and fucking all night long.

Zach smelled the way he liked his men to smell. Like a man.

Before departing Zach's pits, he rubbed his cheeks and chin within them. He wanted to get a good stink on himself before moving on. It got him hot thinking that he'd go about his day later smelling like Zach, feeling as if he'd been marked as someone else's property.

Even though Zach might not be with him later, his smell would linger on Van's beard.

The idea made Van even hornier than he already was, so he slid down Zach's body to his gorgeous cock. He took the pink dick in his hands. Its warm weight felt good in his grasp. It throbbed and pulsed, leaking a steady rivulet of clear liquid from the tip.

Van immediately lapped it up, and Zach practically came off the bed as a result.

"Damn!" Zach said. "Your tongue's like magic."

He shook his head. "It's your cock, not me. I could play with this all day and all night."

"I'd be okay with that," Zach responded.

"I bet you would," he told Zach, and then he placed the head of Zach's dick in his mouth and started to suckle. The move elicited incomprehensible groans of pleasure from Zach, so he shoved Zach's entire hardness down his throat. As he massaged Zach's cock with his mouth, he tasted a steady stream of Zach's juice on his tongue. It made him want to get Zach off right then and there, but that wasn't how he wanted Zach to come.

He wanted Zach to shoot up his ass.

He took Zach out of his mouth and then rubbed his face in Zach's crotch. He needed more of Zach's odor. When he smelled enough like Zach to satisfy him, he reached for the box of condoms on the bedside table.

"It's time for you to fuck me again," he told Zach after rolling the rubber on Zach's prick and lubing his ass and Zach's sheathed cock.

"About time," Zach told him between breaths. "I was trying my best to hold out."

He squatted over Zach's hardness and slowly lowered himself onto Zach. His sore ass protested further invasion, but Van exhaled through the discomfort. Once Zach was again firmly within him, the pain ebbed away slowly as pleasure rolled throughout Van's body.

"You feel so good inside me."

"You feel so good inside."

He rode Zach's cock like a cowboy trying to keep from being thrown off a bucking bull. He slid his hands up and down Zach's heaving chest, feeling every tense muscle. A thin sheen of sweat covered Zach's body, matting his fiery hair to his chest and stomach. He bent forward, taking care to make sure Zach stayed where he placed him, and lapped up the sweat that coated Zach's body.

Zach's left hand rested on his hip, keeping the loud collisions of their bodies timed to their frenzied beat while his right hand held Van's head to his chest. The gesture made Van feel cradled and protected but dirty and used at the same time.

The combination caused him to leak a small pool onto Zach's furry belly.

While Zach continued to pummel him and hold him close, he bit down on Zach's left nipple. He scraped the sensitive skin with his teeth, causing Zach to growl. "God, I love when you do that."

In response, he increased the pressure, gnawing so hard that Zach's left nubbin turned as red as the hair spread across his creamy flesh.

"Oh, God," Zach moaned. "I'm getting so close."

He sat upright on his haunches so Zach could thrust upward as hard as he needed to bring him over the edge. "Do it," he told Zach. "Give it to me!"

Zach needed no further instruction. He slammed upward inside his body as Van bounced up and down on Zach. The whole time Zach nailed him, Van palmed his cock and stroked it furiously.

"I love coming like this," he told Zach. "Shooting my load while my ass gets pummeled."

"You like that?" Zach asked. He gritted his teeth as he continued his upward assault inside Van's guts. "You like having your hole used?"

"Yes," Van pleaded. Having someone take complete control had been what Van used to enjoy, but it was something he rarely allowed to happen as Hart. On film, he was the bossy bottom who told the top what to do and how to do it. It was what made him famous and the studio rich.

But what he enjoyed was different from Hart. He preferred for the men in his bed to use him and to own him. It had been too long since he had allowed another man to do that. For some reason, he was safe with Zach. Zach wouldn't misuse the power he willingly relinquished.

Instead, it would be shared.

"Fuck!" Zach screamed. "I'm coming!"

Zach thrust upward, and Zach's cock pulsed wildly inside him, filling the condom with his reward. The vibrations created by Zach's orgasm stimulated him. He furiously jacked his dick until he exploded. Jets of white-hot sperm splattered across Zach's fair skin, caking the hair on Zach's body with Van's spunk.

When their bodies had stopped convulsing, Zach brought him down to rest on his chest. Their sweat and cum cemented their bodies together.

He'd never been so wonderfully full in his life, and that wasn't just from Zach's cock still lodged up his butt. It came from something that started in his heart and spread like the sun's rays throughout his body.

"I don't know about you," Zach said after a few moments. "But I'm famished. After all this fucking, I could eat a horse or two."

Although he hadn't been hungry before, the mere mention of food made his stomach grumble. "I could go for some food."

"The bad part of that, though, is we'd have to actually leave the bed."

He giggled. Did that just come from him? He hadn't giggled in years. "Well, we haven't done it in the kitchen yet."

"Good idea," Zach said before kissing the top of his head. "Then let's go see what we can cook up downstairs."

He smiled as he slid off Zach's chest and cock. "Should we shower first?"

"Nah," Zach said as he got off the bed. "We're only gonna get all sweaty and cummy again anyway. Besides," he began as he sniffed his pits. "I'm starting to smell like you, and you smell fucking great. Why wash that off?"

When he took a deep whiff of himself, he scented more of Zach's odor than his own. "I couldn't agree with you more," he answered and followed Zach out of the bedroom and down the stairs to the kitchen.

Chapter Twenty

ZACH couldn't help but watch as Van stood naked in the kitchen, drying the dishes Zach had used to serve their ham-and-cheese omelets. Even Van doing such a mundane task turned him on. The way his muscles flexed as he moved or how his tanned body absorbed the morning sun cascading from the front window and reflected it outward like an angelic aura. Even his slightly tousled brown hair looked golden, making Van resemble a Grecian god bathing in the daylight.

Could Van be any more stunning?

As he reached down to stroke his hardening cock, he realized for the first time how raw and sore his dick was. They'd been fucking like animals in heat, and though he wanted to continue the marathon fuck fest, they might need to give it a break.

For an hour or two.

Van turned to him and eyed his boner with a seductive arch to his brow. "What do you want to do now?" he playfully asked.

He crossed over to Van and took him in his arms, delivering a soft peck on his neck and then on his lips while grinding his boner into Van's stomach. "I know what I want to do, but my cock's a little sore. Would you mind if we took a small break?"

"Mind?" Van asked incredulously. "How do you think my ass feels? I'm the one that gets that fat monster shoved inside me!" He pulled lightly on Zach's cock to punctuate his point.

"Are you complaining?" Zach asked as he pretended to pout.

Van answered with another tug on Zach's tender dick. "Never!"

"Good."

"So what do you want to do, then?" Van asked as he released his hold on Zach's cock and tossed the damp towel on the counter.

He had no clue. He didn't want to venture down Commercial Street, that was for sure. Although he now enjoyed the chaos of the main thoroughfare, he had no desire to trek through it, especially not when he had such an attractive man in his condo.

He wanted Van to himself for the day.

"Or if you'd like me to leave so you can get some rest, I'd completely understand."

"No," Zach answered quickly. When he realized how distressed he sounded at the mere thought of Van leaving, he cleared his throat and tried to be more casual. "Unless you want to go."

From the grin that slid across Van's face, he understood that he hadn't been successful at sounding offhand. "Okay, then, how about we snuggle on the couch and watch some TV?"

"I could stand to veg," he admitted with a nod. "Can we stay naked? Just in case, you know, inspiration strikes?"

"Of course. It's my one requirement."

"I like that being naked is a requirement."

"Why wouldn't it be?" Van asked as he grabbed his hand and led him into the living room.

He fell back onto the sofa and opened his arms for Van to lie in them. "Well, my ex preferred to have on clothes. Unless we were doing it, obviously. Then, I'd just wear my shirt."

Van settled in his arms with a sigh of contentment. After getting comfortable, he asked, "You wore a shirt while you fucked? Why?"

"My white skin bothered him, apparently. Plus, he wasn't a fan of the body hair. I was like a shedding dog it seemed."

"He sounds like a jerk," Van told him as he handed over the remote. What was he supposed to do with the remote control? With Ben, he rarely had charge of what they watched.

"I'm starting to see that quite clearly. He wasn't always that way, though. At the beginning of our relationship, he was a pretty good guy. Kinda sweet actually. Then, somewhere along the way, he changed."

"Why do you think that was?"

He shrugged. Why did people expect him to know the answer to that question? He didn't live inside Ben's head. Thank God. All he did know was that the man he'd been living with hadn't been the man he first fell in love with. Something had happened to Ben that changed him and his perspective on life. He grew dark and controlling, and Zach had done nothing about it. He just went along with the new persona, not questioning it or trying to find the reason. He simply accepted it and altered himself for the relationship.

It was just something he had been taught to do.

"You have to have *some* idea," Van insisted.

"I wish I did," he replied. "Maybe he got tired of me and didn't know how to tell me."

"Well, some guys aren't good at discussing their emotions. You're kinda like that. You tend to hold your emotions close to the vest. Like you're playing poker or something. I've always done the opposite. I tend to wear my heart on my sleeve. I envy your ability to keep a part of yourself back from everyone else. It must keep you safe."

"It does, but it's also a little lonely," he admitted. "And I find it amusing that you envy me when I wish I could be more like you."

"What? Fabulously handsome and equally humble?"

Zach rolled his eyes as Van bared his teeth in that beautiful shit-eating grin Zach had come to cherish. "That too," he replied before he kissed the top of Van's head and ran his hand down Van's smooth stomach. "But what I was going to say was that I wish I could care less what other people think of me. Just do what I want to do. Be who I want to be. Feel what I want to feel."

"I don't think you're giving yourself enough credit. From what I've seen, you seem to be trucking along just fine doing what you want to do. You've had some tricks, none as great as me, of course—"

"Of course. There's that humility you mentioned."

"I know, right?" Van asked with another grin. "But as I was saying, I've seen no real trace of the man you told me about at dinner last night. The big, clumsy buffoon who doesn't know his asshole from his elbow. Sure, you're not the most graceful man I've ever met, but so what? We all have our shortcomings."

"Except you," he pointed out with a grin.

"Well, duh," Van added with pretend annoyance. "That goes without saying. But for those who aren't like me, perfection isn't possible. So if people can't be perfect, it just makes sense to be, do, and feel what makes us happy. At least that's the way I've tried to live."

Even though the advice sounded simple, he took it to heart because Van was right. He *had* been living for himself the past few days, and it had been wonderful.

In fact, he didn't want it to end.

"So, what are we gonna watch?" Van asked as he turned toward the television and pressed his naked back against Zach's bare chest.

He sniffed at the back of Van's neck, taking in his intoxicating scent as Van wiggled his uncovered butt against his ever-hardening cock. "If you keep that up, I'll fuck you again. Right here. Right now."

"What about your sore cock?" Van asked as he reached around and massaged Zach's ass.

"I'd risk it," he responded as he turned Van's head to the left and kissed his soft, tender lips. "But I don't want to hurt you," he admitted when their lips finally parted. "I know you're sore."

"I'm a big boy." Van grinned. "I can take whatever you dish out."

"That sounds like a challenge."

"Maybe it is."

He turned Van over onto his back and rested between his open legs. "Challenge accepted."

"COME on me!" Van told Zach as Van furiously jerked himself. "I want you to shoot your load all over my chest."

Zach ripped the condom off his cock and tossed it over his shoulder. He didn't care that his sore cock protested its constant mistreatment. It hadn't been abused this much since he was a teenager, and his tender cockhead and shaft burned a bright red from more than just the impending orgasm that churned in his balls.

His body screamed for a respite, but it wasn't going to happen. At least not until he granted Van's request.

He pumped himself furiously, bringing himself ever closer to the edge, and he could tell from Van's heaving chest and the dreamy look in his eyes, that Van was about to blow too. "Come with me," Zach told him. "Both of us. At the same time."

Van nodded, and they both timed their strokes, pumping their shafts and tugging on their milk-rich balls. Doing whatever was necessary to get them both flying over the cliff together.

"I'm coming!" Van grunted as his body grew stiff beneath Zach.

"Me too!" he replied as he sat on his haunches and delivered the final stroke that took him where he needed to go.

They both shot simultaneously. Dual eruptions of spunk streamed through the air. Van's spray flew across his sculpted abs all the way up to his chest while Zach's splashed across Van's balls and trimmed pubic hair.

Van looked like a cummy but yummy mess.

"You look delicious all covered in spunk," he told Van.

"You're just saying that 'cause it's true," he answered and held his arms open for Zach.

With a pretend look of exasperation at Van's comment, Zach fell into Van's embrace. Zach rubbed his body up and down their sticky goodness to make sure it covered as much of their flesh as possible. He'd never before craved the feel of someone's cum against his skin, but with Van, it was quickly turning into an obsession.

He just had to taste, smell, or feel the cream that came from Van's body.

In fact, he'd be happy to have Van's sperm wherever Van wanted to put it.

"That was good," Van said, his voice dreamy.

"Even though your ass is sore?"

"Are you kidding? That made it even better. It brought the sex to a brand new level of intensity."

He had to agree. Despite his sore dick, the pleasure mixed with the pain made the release that much sweeter. Now, though, exhaustion took hold. He doubted he'd be able to move for quite some time. "I don't think I'm getting up from this couch for a while."

"That's fine by me and my numb asshole," Van admitted. "How about we watch some TV like we were originally planning to do?"

He nodded and slowly slid off Van, who moved over to lie on his side. Their cum still clung to their bodies. When Van pressed his back against Zach's naked flesh, the seal that formed earlier once again bound them together.

Van found the remote on the floor where it fell during their lovemaking and handed it to Zach, who clicked the television on. As he flipped through the channels in search of something to relax to, he found a station advertising a musical marathon set to begin in a few minutes.

He loved musicals, and when he saw that *Chicago* was first up to bat, he tried to rein in his excitement. At least until Van asked if they could watch it.

"Really?" he asked.

"Yes, really," Van told him. "I love *Chicago*. Well, I love musicals in general, but *Chicago* is one of my favorites."

He tried to contain his joy. He'd gotten so used to Ben's hatred of the genre that he almost clicked past the channel when he saw the station's announced programming.

"Why? Do you not like musicals?"

"I love them!"

"What's not to love?"

"To me, nothing. But to Ben, well, he hated them. He preferred action and adventure to most everything else. He claimed to never understand my fascination with musicals. He didn't think people dancing or singing their way through life was realistic."

"And surviving multiple car crashes or explosions without a scratch is *so* much more believable?"

He laughed. "That's what I used to tell him. At the beginning of our relationship, he tried to sit through them, but after a few months, he gave up. Whenever one came on that I wanted to watch, he either left the room or the apartment."

Van turned to stare at Zach over his left shoulder. "And you were with this guy for three years?"

"Yup."

"Why did you put yourselves through that?" Van asked. "You two had nothing in common. At least nothing that you've told me about. It sounds like a waste of three years of your lives."

He couldn't disagree with that logic. He and Ben were polar opposites, and though they had tried to make things work, they should have cut their losses and gone their separate ways a long time ago.

Although he didn't feel bad about his breakup with Ben, he'd still held on to some minor regret before Van's comment. Now, he realized that being dumped by Ben had been the best thing for them both.

"You're wise beyond your years," he whispered after he kissed Van's cheek.

"Tell me something I don't know," Van responded. "Now be quiet. It's about to start."

Without another word, Zach pressed his lips into the back of Van's neck and settled in behind him to watch the show. He found, however, that all he could watch was Van, who tittered with glee as Catherine Zeta-Jones strutted her stuff as the vaudevillian murderer Velma Kelly during her "All That Jazz" number.

Sharing this guilty pleasure with someone who also enjoyed musicals warmed him from the inside out. More than that, though, being with Van made him truly happy. Inexplicably, he had found himself by finding Van.

But what would that mean in a few days when he had to leave Provincetown and head home?

WHEN *Chicago* ended, Zach and Van cheered as Velma Kelly and Roxie Hart brought down the house with their "Nowadays" number. They had just enough time to pee and grab some snacks before the next musical, *Dreamgirls*, began.

They munched on chips and dip as Jennifer Hudson and Beyoncé duked it out for the role of lead singer for their all-girl 1950s group, but when Jennifer Hudson began belting out "And I Am Telling You I'm Not Going," they sat in silence as Hudson's character Effie White had a breakdown on the television before them.

When *Dreamgirls* ended, they curled up on the couch to watch *Moulin Rouge!*, where Nicole Kidman and Ewan McGregor fall in love in 1899 Paris. But as the movie went on, Zach became troubled.

The plot, a struggling writer falling in love with a beautiful courtesan, seemed far too familiar. He couldn't help but draw parallels between him and Van. Technically, Van wasn't a prostitute, but as a porn actor, he did come close. Christian grew insanely jealous over Satine's profession. Even though he promised her he wouldn't. Would he be any different? Could he accept that Van was also Hart Throb? In theory he had. But when put into practice, he doubted he could be that strong.

Christian and Satine had attempted to overcome it regardless of Christian's objection, but they didn't get a happily-ever-after. What did the tragic ending for the romantic leads mean for him and Van?

After all, no matter how much Christian and Satine loved each other, their love wasn't destined to last. Fate, in the cruel way it does, brought them together only to tear them apart.

While the plot made excellent cinematic material, in terms of real life, it blew chunks, and it got Zach thinking.

What was he doing with Van? Where was this *really* going to go?

In a few days, he'd have to head home to Texas to pick up the pieces of his life that he'd left behind. His time in Provincetown was almost over, and the reminder splashed across his face like a bucket of cold water. He'd actually started to think this was his reality and Texas had been nothing but a bad dream.

Baz Luhrmann's musical brought him back from fantasyland.

Churning waters of regret pooled around Zach as the swirling current attempted to carry him away. He needed something to anchor him before he was dragged underneath by the weight of his melancholy.

As if he sensed something wrong, Van turned around in his arms to look at him. "You okay?"

"Yeah." Zach nodded. Although he didn't want to lie, he couldn't discuss what he felt right now. It was too real, too raw. "The movie just always gets to me."

"I know what you mean," Van said. His lips then pressed against Zach's. "You know she's going to die, but you can't help wanting to see them fall in love. And hope that by some chance she beats the tuberculosis."

"But she's not going to beat it," he told Van. "Why do we keep hoping that she will? Why do we keep wishing for a different ending every time we watch this?"

"Because we want the love to last."

That was childish. They had to be more mature than that. They had to see that they couldn't have a future. How could they when as soon as he left P-town, Van would shed his clothes and ride another cock for the camera? "Even though we know it won't?"

Van nodded. "Even though."

"That's pretty dumb of us, huh?" Although he now referred to him and Van, Van was oblivious to the reference.

"Not really," Van answered after a few seconds of thought. "They're in love, and even though we know it's going to end tragically, the pain seems worth it."

"Is it?" He didn't think so. He came to Provincetown to escape pain, not find a hurt more gut wrenching than the one he left behind.

"I think so," Van answered with complete certainty before turning his attention back to the characters, who now sang "Come What May." It was the song Christian and Satine used to tell each other that no matter what happened, their love would overcome it.

As Zach listened to the words, he tried to find the faith Van blindly clung to. Every other time he'd watched this show before today, he had nurtured the rising swell of love and hope that the characters' voices breathed into the lyrics. It was what made the musical so powerful for him.

Now, he heard only the promise of the pain to come.

No matter how perfect this might feel with Van, it couldn't last. Just like Christian and Satine. He didn't want to think about their end. He wanted to banish the thought from his mind, but he realized he had no choice but to think about his future.

His feelings and their reality had to be put into perspective. For himself and Van.

Just as he was about to open his mouth to tell Van they had to talk, Van brought his arm around his body and rested it on his chest. Van held his hand and sighed in happiness.

It wasn't the time. One more day together couldn't hurt, but tomorrow, well, tomorrow, he would have to do what needed to be done.

Chapter Twenty-One

VAN had never before spent a whole day naked in another man's arms. It had made him feel special in a way no one had ever done for him before. When he and Zach went to bed after *Moulin Rouge!*, he couldn't have been happier. He would've been content simply going to sleep, but Zach was a man on a mission.

Zach was bound and determined to have sex one final time before bed, and Van couldn't deny him. They fucked with even more intensity than they had previously. Where Zach found the energy and the stamina was a mystery, but he applauded his sex drive. Then, in the morning, they did it again.

The enthusiasm from last night had carried over to this morning in a big way. Zach had almost drilled him into the next condo. It had reminded him of getting fucked by Ram the other day at the shoot, as if Zach was pummeling him to prove some point.

What could that be?

Unlike Ram, Zach had no technicians or director watching. No one to prove anything to. It was just the two of them, so even though it confused him, he let it go, especially when Zach announced they were having breakfast outside on the patio.

After all the sex they'd been having, he definitely needed to refuel.

So after making a small feast of eggs, bacon, bagels with cream cheese, and orange juice, they spread the fruits of their labor across the table on the patio deck. Even though it meant having to put on clothes, they both decided eating outside on such a beautiful day was worth the annoyance of slipping shorts over their ripe, unshowered, cum-drenched bodies.

Zach did request that they remain shirtless, so they could ogle each other. The suggestion was sweet and pretty fucking hot. It was also quite the departure for Zach, who previously preferred to remain covered. If his stomach hadn't grumbled loudly at that moment, he would have made Zach do him right there.

"Well, look what we have here," Gary said as he sauntered down the walkway connecting their two condos. "It appears to be a veritable smorgasbord."

"Hey, Gary," Zach said before he took a bite of his bagel.

Van noticed the slight blush that spread across Zach's cheeks. His innocent reaction to their pretty obvious night of fucking turned him on. Was there anything Zach could do that wouldn't give him a painful erection?

"Pull up a seat and join us."

"Don't mind if I do," Gary said. He took the seat next to Zach and across from Van. He looked back and forth between them, and a devilish twinkle flashed across his eyes as he held his nose to the air. "The two of you reek of sex and man stank. I guess this means the date went well."

"It wasn't a date," Zach reminded Gary while pointing a piece of bacon at him.

"Now, now, Zachary. Don't go pointing your meat at me unless you intend to let me eat it."

Zach rolled his eyes and deposited the bacon inside Gary's wide-open mouth. Gary moaned in pleasure, which sounded to Van more like a good orgasm than anything else, as he crunched. "I so love it when hot men force-feed me their meat."

"You and me both," he chimed in.

"I swear I always walk up at the wrong times," Quinn announced as he joined them on the patio. "Now who's been feeding my man his meat?"

Without missing a beat, both he and Gary pointed at Zach.

"Traitors," Zach told them after he stuck out his tongue.

"It's okay, Zach. Next time, though, I get to watch. I'm quite the voyeur."

"And an even bigger exhibitionist," Gary added.

"What's *that* supposed to mean?" Quinn asked, pretending to look deeply hurt.

"Oh, Bobby Quinn," Gary said as he snatched another piece of bacon off Zach's plate. "How many hookup apps do you have on your phone? I know you've got Cyber on it for sure, and I bet there's more naked pictures of you floating around on Cyber than there probably are of Van on the Internet."

Quinn cleared his throat and glared at Gary, whose shocked expression clearly communicated that he understood what he'd done. He had unintentionally let Van's career out of the bag.

"Don't worry about it," Van told them as he glanced over at Zach. Although he didn't look upset, Zach didn't return anyone's eye contact. "Zach knows all about Hart Throb. I was outed the other night. By Suzy Wroughtinkrotch."

"That spiteful little bitch!"

"It wasn't like that, Gary. She was just doing her show, and she brought me up on stage. It was an innocent mistake."

"Innocent my ass," Gary fumed.

Gary's history with Suzy Wroughtinkrotch, also known as Jeffrey Moore when she wasn't in drag, wasn't pretty. When he looked over at Zach, who appeared clueless, he made a mental note to fill Zach in on the whole sordid affair.

"Forget about Suzy," Quinn told Gary. "What have I told you about speaking before thinking?"

Gary glared at Quinn before he turned back to Zach and Van. By the time he looked at them, his eyes had softened. "I'm really sorry about what I said"—this time only staring at Zach. "I hope you're not upset."

When Zach looked up, Van could tell that Zach had schooled his face. He wasn't angry, but Van saw an emotion he couldn't recognize. "Not at all," he finally told Gary. "It's all good."

"Great!" Quinn exclaimed before he changed the subject. "What are you boys going to do today?"

"Don't know," Zach admitted. "We don't have much of an agenda."

"You should go to the beach," Gary advised. "It's such a good day for it."

Van nodded as he stared out into the cloudless sky. "That might be fun."

"I'm up for it if you are," Zach responded after he finished eating. "I've heard that Herring Cove is beautiful."

"Forget beautiful," Gary told him. "It's spectacular. Plus, there's tons of hot men sunbathing nude. It's a visual banquet of assorted meats of all colors and sizes."

"And endless porking in the dunes," Quinn added.

"That's my Bobby Quinn," Gary sighed. "The exhibitionist."

"I take it you two have played hide the salami on the beach a time or two?" Van asked.

"You know it," Quinn replied with a wink to Van.

"So we going?" he asked Zach before he placed a fork full of eggs in his mouth.

"How could I pass up the opportunity for a beautiful beach packed full of assorted meats of all colors and sizes?" Zach asked in response.

"Don't forget the porking," Quinn reminded him.

"I haven't. That's what sold me on going," Zach announced as he winked at Van.

Gary and Quinn chuckled while a large smile stretched itself across Van's face. It embarrassed him that the idea of having sex with Zach again made him so obviously happy, but what made him even more uncomfortable was that Gary and Quinn both noticed. They looked at each other knowingly, communicating silently the way couples in long-term relationships typically did.

Before he had a chance to respond, his cell phone in the pocket of his shorts started buzzing. He took it out and noticed he had five missed phone calls and eight text messages—all from Nino and Tripp.

Fuck! He was supposed to be on set an hour ago, and now Tripp was calling him, most likely to chew him a new asshole. Van excused himself and answered the phone as he walked into the condo.

"Hello."

"Where the fuck are you?" Tripp screamed. "You're fucking late! I've got the fluffer here keeping Ram hard, but without the bottom for this scene, all Ram's gonna end up doing is blowing his load down this kid's throat."

"I'm not feeling good," he told Tripp and feigned a moan of pain. "Must've been something I ate."

"Don't bullshit me, Pierce. I saw you at the Pied. Remember? You looked fine, especially when I caught you eyeballing that redhead." Tripp laughed. "Unless that's what you ate that made you sick."

"Not even close," he replied, which was most certainly the truth. Zach's meat was tasty, and he wanted Zach back in his mouth or up in his ass for as long as Zach wanted to slip it inside. In order to accomplish that for today, though, he needed to find a way to get out of work. "I went home right after I saw you. Started feeling queasy. Been sick since, and I haven't slept well. I'm gonna have to take another day or two off."

"Do you think I'm fucking stupid?" Tripp asked. "You're blowing the shoot off because you want to keep blowing that redhead."

He hated that Tripp had grown so intuitive all of a sudden. Usually, the man couldn't spot his asshole if he were bent over looking at it in the mirror. "I'm sick," he repeated. "I can't come in. Besides, I thought Brick Hard was flying in today anyway. Shoot his scenes until I feel better."

"Are you telling me my job, Pierce? 'Cause I don't remember you being made director of this fucking film."

Van took a deep breath. Arguing with Tripp would get him nowhere except fired. No matter how popular he might be with the fans, Nasty Boy Studios was a business and two reshoots wouldn't endear him to anyone. He just needed a day, maybe two, before he went back to Hart's world.

"Please, Tripp," he pleaded, hating the fact that by doing so Tripp was getting the upper hand. "I *really* don't feel good. Give me one more day. Two at the most."

Tripp exhaled loudly on the other end. "Fine. If *you're* begging *me*, you must be feeling like crap. I'll give you two days," he told Van. "That'll give me enough time to shoot with Brick, but if you're not here by ten in the morning the day after tomorrow, we're done. Do you understand?"

"I do," Van said. "Thanks, Tripp."

"I hope the redhead's worth it," Tripp told him. His voice sounded unusually kind and warm, as if he somehow sensed how Van felt about Zach. Could Tripp be somehow growing a heart?

"Thanks" was all he could manage in his astonishment before Tripp hung up.

Van put his phone back in his pocket and gazed out the patio door at Zach, who was laughing with Gary and Quinn. As he watched Zach, Van couldn't help but think about Tripp's words.

Zach *was* worth it.

And perhaps so much more.

Chapter Twenty-Two

VAN couldn't remember the last time he made the twenty-minute trek to Herring Cove Beach. During his first summer in Provincetown, he and Jason made a weekly pilgrimage from the bike rack on Route 6 and through the rolling dunes until they found the perfect spot on the beach, where they could spy on the cute boys as well as gaze out into the cobalt sea.

After their relationship disintegrated, he'd only been back a couple of times, and each visit had been difficult. It reminded Van of the pain and humiliation he suffered from a man who was supposed to love him.

But today, as Zach spread out the huge beach blanket he had found at the condo, none of those old feelings resurfaced. Although he'd always remember the times he and Jason shared out here, neither the pain nor the love associated with this place seemed vivid. Instead, they existed as faint echoes.

That made him extremely happy. He'd finally moved on, and perhaps Zach had a little something to do with that.

But how was that possible? He stretched out on the blanket while Zach opened up his backpack to retrieve the sunscreen. They'd only spent a couple of days together. Sure, they had been filled with hot sex and good times, the musical marathon taking the cake on that one, but how could such a short amount of time with Zach so quickly erase the pain he'd carried with him? Maybe it was because he had trudged around with it for far longer than he should have.

"Okay, blanket hog," Zach complained loudly. "Scoot over."

He moved, and Zach plopped next to him. A smile dangled from the corners of his mouth as he waved the bottle of Banana Boat in front of him. "Who goes first?"

"I'd say you," he replied as he scanned Zach's white skin. Although Zach had just taken his shirt off a few moments before, tiny scorch marks spread across Zach's shoulders. "In a few minutes you'll look like a lobster."

Zach grumbled as he lay down on his stomach. "I know. I hate being so fair."

"I kinda like it," he told Zach as he took the sunscreen bottle from Zach's outstretched hand. He straddled Zach's butt and thrust his hips forward as if he were trying to hump Zach on the beach. His gesture elicited a growl of appreciation from Zach and the applause of some of the men sunning around them. Zach chuckled, obviously embarrassed. Not fazed by the attention, he simply squirted some of the contents of the bottle into his palm and massaged the lotion onto Zach's freckled back.

"You really like my almost albino skin color?"

He couldn't believe the surprise in Zach's voice. Apparently, he still had lingering self-image issues. "Would you stop that already?" he asked Zach as he worked more of the sunscreen across Zach's shoulder caps and down his biceps. "You really need to stop doubting the way you look or how you act. It shouldn't matter what anyone else sees or thinks. Your opinion should be the only one that matters."

"I know. That's what people have told me for years. Including Ben."

"Then why haven't you changed your perspective yet? I mean, if the man you've spent the last three years of your life with has told you the same thing others have been telling you for years, why keep hating on yourself?"

"Learned behavior, I guess."

"You've mentioned that before. From who? Your parents?"

"My father, actually," Zach sighed. "I never quite lived up to his standards. As a doctor, he prided himself on being perfect, and he wanted me and my sister Sami to be perfect children for the perfect doctor who were all part of a perfect family."

Van chuffed. He had some experience with that too. "Perfection's overrated. I've already told you that," he reminded Zach.

"I know. Apparently, it was for my dad too," Zach said with a grimace.

"What do you mean?"

"Turns out my perfect father wasn't so perfect after all. It was all a sham, as my mother discovered when she came home early one morning to find my dad getting sucked off by the gardener, the *male* gardener." Zach glanced over his shoulder at Van, and even though he was admitting a very painful story about his family, a mischievous twinkle glinted in his eyes. "And to top it off, the guy was fucking hot. I would've let him blow me too."

"I bet you would've," he told Zach before leaning over Zach and looking into his eyes. Was Zach pulling his leg? "Are you kidding me with this shit?"

Zach shook his head. "It's true," he replied, holding out his fingers in the Boy Scout salute. "That was one smoking-hot gardener."

"Not that, you ass," he chided as he playfully smacked Zach on his head. "What you said about your father? It really happened? He's really gay?"

"Very gay, apparently," Zach retorted with a sigh. "After he was literally caught with his pants down, all of my father's past indiscretions came out. My parents divorced and have been bitter enemies ever since. My sister Sami gets stuck in the middle, but I've distanced myself from the whole crap storm." Zach's annoyed tone turned wistful. "I haven't seen my parents in years."

"That's unbelievable," he said after a few moments of silence.

"Yeah," Zach agreed. "That's what happens when you try to be perfect."

"I gave up trying to be perfect, or anything my parents wanted me to be, a long time ago," he admitted. "The only person I can be is me, and at the end of the day, it's my face staring back at me in the bathroom mirror. Not theirs."

"Yeah, I guess I'm just not as smart as you," Zach mused, his voice low and dejected. "I tried to be perfect for my dad back when I thought he was some ideal to be modeled. I came up with a plan to show him that I could make something of my life, but it didn't quite work out the way I imagined. When he was revealed to be as defective as he'd made me feel since childhood, I felt even more like a failure."

"Why are parents so good at making their kids feel that way?" he asked as he proceeded to coat Zach's legs and feet with the lotion. "My father was an officer in the navy. Made it all the way up to captain. He commanded his own vessel, and he damn well tried to call the shots as if I were one of his crewmen. My mother wasn't much better. She's a shrink, and she imagined me going to college, becoming some kind of egghead, while my dad expected me to go to Annapolis. Boy, were they both pissed when I didn't even go to college, much less enlist. They were disappointed in me, made me feel as if I was some worthless piece of shit they found on the side of the road. They cut me off financially as some kind of punishment. I told them I didn't need their fucking money, and that they couldn't bribe me to do what they wanted. It was my life, so I left."

"Are you happy with the way your life turned out?"

Good question. He wasn't the happiest he could be. At least not yet. But he was a lot closer today than he was yesterday and certainly closer than last year. He might have bounced from job to job and from man to man after he left home, but his life was his own. He had no regrets, and if given the choice, he'd do it all over again. "I'm content with my choices so far," he finally replied. "They haven't always worked out for the best, but they've been my decisions. *That* makes me happy."

He sat next to Zach and watched him stare off into the dunes. His usually happy brown eyes looked dark and contemplative, as if he were peeling the layers of his life apart and inspecting each section. "What about you?" he asked.

Zach snorted. "Not even a little bit. I used to be a completely different person when I was younger. I tried to live life my way, and I remember being that little shit who challenged everything. God, my father hated that. And when I think about how far I've fallen from that person I used to be, it makes me sad."

Having finished thoroughly coating Zach's back, Van slapped his shoulder. Zach immediately turned over. He interpreted exactly what Van wanted him to do. Van liked that, but not as much as he enjoyed now squatting on Zach's crotch. The pressure of his bulge against Van's ass made Van instantly hard.

"You can be that person again," he told Zach as he squirmed on Zach's cock, which hardened underneath him. "You can be whoever you want."

"I'm beginning to realize that," Zach replied. "Being here in P-town. The people I've met. They've opened my eyes to a lot of things. To possibilities I thought had long since passed me by."

While the meaning of Zach's words was a mystery to Van, the spirit they expressed made him smile. "Like what?" he asked as he finished rubbing the sunscreen all over Zach's chest and stomach. He teasingly allowed his fingers to slip beneath the waistband of Zach's trunks and stimulate the head of Zach's cock.

Zach grabbed him by the shoulders and in one quick motion had Van pinned underneath his body. He then forced his hardness against the firmness growing in Van's suit. "Like maybe heading into the dunes with the hottest man on this planet and using the Banana Boat to help put my banana in his boat."

Van giggled. Even though he couldn't believe he was laughing like a kid again, he didn't stop. He embraced the joy Zach brought to his life. It was better than clinging to the sorrow of the past year.

"What do you say?" Zach asked as he reached between their bodies and squeezed Van's stiff prick. "You up for it?"

"That sounds like a challenge."

"You bet your sweet ass it is."

He rolled over on his side, causing Zach to slip off him. He then sprung to his feet and ran for the dunes. "Challenge accepted," he yelled back over his shoulder as Zach chased after him.

AMONG the tall reeds of one of the most secluded dunes they could find, Van did a quick scout for park rangers on dune buggies and then shucked his suit. He bent over to touch his toes, exposing his bare ass for Zach. "Give it to me good," he announced. "But just keep an eye out for the party poopers."

On their search for the perfect spot, he filled Zach in on how the park rangers sometimes snuck up on the dunes to catch people either sunbathing nude or fucking the snot out of each other and issuing steep fines.

Apparently, Zach loved the added hint of danger, because his cock about popped out of his skimpy swimwear in response.

But now after rolling on the condom he brought with him and squirting a generous amount of sunscreen on his throbbing cock and on Van's crack, Zach's only response was to shove the full length of his hardness deep within his ass in one quick motion.

He yelped in both pleasure and pain as Zach burrowed inside him. His ass, already more than sore from being fucked five ways from Sunday for the past two days, screamed for mercy. Still, he wasn't going to let the discomfort ruin his fun. He breathed deeply, and after a few mind-over-matter moments, the pain disappeared completely.

When his ass opened up to once again take Zach all the way to the root, he came to life in a way he'd never before experienced. Not only did he have a hot man plugged into him—again—but it was a man he could trust, based on what they'd shared since their first heart-to-heart at the Pied.

He hadn't connected with someone like that in quite some time, and the realization made this joining in the dunes, with the wind whipping around their primal act, seem as natural as the sun shining down on them from above.

"I can't get enough of you," Zach grunted as he drove his hips harder into Van.

"You can have as much as you want." He reared back on Zach's cock, forcing his big head passed the second ring of muscles. When he popped even farther inside, he cried out once again.

"You like that, don't you? You like being fucked where people might see?"

"Yes," he panted as he lifted his head to take a look around. There was no *might* about it. Their fucking had drawn a couple of onlookers, who stood a few feet away down the path. They stroked themselves through their suits as their lustful eyes cheered them on.

Van shoved himself backward on Zach's cock while Zach just stood there, making Van fuck himself. "Use me in front of these boys," he begged. "Make them see how I have to work for your cock."

When he realized they had spectators, Zach stopped, his cock still hard and deep inside Van, but when Zach noticed the couple on the path and the three newcomers watching on the opposite side of the dunes, Zach's previous unsure nature appeared to return.

He apparently couldn't decide whether he should stop or continue.

"Fuck me," he told Zach, wiggling his ass up and down Zach's dick. "Show them how a man fucks another man."

Zach switched his gaze from the voyeurs around them and back onto him. When their gazes locked, the previous apprehension faded away. Zach evidently let go of the man he'd been turned into and once again embraced who he used to be as a boy, someone who lived without fear of consequence.

With a loud growl, which he expected was more for those around them than for him, Zach picked up his pace once again. Zach slammed into him with such intensity that his teeth rattled together. He had to brace his hands in the hot sand to prevent being fucked right over.

As Zach continued his assault on his butt, Van completely surrendered to the moment. Zach's faraway, dreamy stare told him Zach had done the same. Hesitation and fear no longer lived in their bodies. Just as he'd finally opened himself up to the potential Zach brought to his life, Zach had cast aside all the obstacles that stood between what Zach wanted and who he thought he should be.

"This is fucking great!" Zach said. "My cock is so hard knowing all these people want you, but that it's me that's buried inside your ass."

He peered over his shoulder, locking eyes with Zach as he rammed into him even harder and faster. "That's right," he responded in between deep breaths. "It's you inside me. No one else."

Those words caused Zach to grow even harder inside him, which meant Zach was on the verge of blowing his load. "Fuck yeah, baby," he told Zach as he jacked himself to the beat of Zach's thrusts. "Come on me. Come on my ass."

"Oh fuck," Zach bellowed as he yanked his cock out of Van's butt and ripped the condom free. After a few tugs, hot blasts of Zach's seed splattered all over his lower back and butt. The wet warmth carried him over the edge as he sprayed his own sperm all over the sand around them.

He stood up. Zach wrapped his arms around him, pulling his back against Zach's chest while turning Van's head to the right. Zach's lips found his, and in the kiss and the strong hands that held him close, an overwhelming sense of security took root in Van's heart.

It banished all the other times he'd been used and mistreated by the men he'd once believed he loved. He'd been nailed for public consumption before. Hell, he'd been so good at it that he turned it into a career, but with all those men and in the numerous sexual encounters he had experienced, he'd never had sex with anyone like Zach.

He had never met someone who not only unleashed the horny bastard inside him but who also cradled him as tenderly as Zach now did. Men like Jason and Scott and Timothy had always been as rough with his heart as they were with his body.

Zach apparently knew the difference, and Van's heart, which had stopped beating for another man since Jason, throbbed to life.

VAN lay his head in Zach's lap, watching the sun set on the ocean. For the past few hours, they'd shared more stories about their pasts and what they wanted for their futures.

He learned Zach lived in Houston, Texas, which came as a surprise since Zach didn't have a Southern drawl. Zach claimed that his father made sure that the South Texas twang never took hold in his children's speech. He wanted them to sound intelligent, not like hicks.

Zach also wanted out of teaching and to become a full-time author. Apparently, there was a manuscript he'd recently started about his life, and it appeared to be going well.

When it was his turn to share, he told Zach stories about his adventures rock climbing in California, scuba diving in Hawaii, and skydiving in New Zealand. Zach grimaced during each story, telling Van he was crazy. Zach preferred having his feet firmly planted on the ground. So when he told Zach how his parachute didn't open properly on his third jump in New Zealand and that he broke his leg upon landing, Zach about had a fit.

When Zach asked him about what he wanted for his future, Van suspected Zach's real question. He wanted to know how long Van planned on doing porn. What was he supposed to say? As far as he was concerned, porn was his future, despite the misgivings he had earlier. He didn't think that was the reply Zach was looking for. He had also intuited that part of the reason behind Zach's question stemmed from his curiosity on how safe Van was while working. He reassured him that he always played safe. As for his future, well, he gave a vague response about going wherever life took him.

His answer hadn't been a lie. That was the way he approached life, coasting along until something new presented itself.

After their discussion, a silence settled over them, and as he looked around, Van realized they'd been pretty much left alone on the beach. A few couples spotted the area on their blankets, and every now and then a head or two could be seen poking up from the dunes as other horny guys got their freak on.

For the most part, though, he and Zach were alone. Like castaways on a deserted island with only their bodies to offer for shelter and sustenance.

How hot was that? He could see them foraging for food and building a shelter. Only the two of them, naked on the beach and fucking for hours. When he turned his head to get Zach's take on his little fantasy, the words died on his lips. Zach gazed upward at the darkening sky, and his white skin and red hair set against the dusk above took his breath away.

Zach looked down at him as a wry smile crouched at the corners of his mouth. "You're staring," he said as he wiggled his fingers in front of Van's face.

"Sorry," he said. What an idiot! He'd been looking at Zach like a lovesick teenager, imagining some cheesy scene out of a bad romance novel for the two of them to frolic around in.

What the hell was the matter with him? He didn't do that. At least not anymore.

Still, he couldn't help the way Zach made him feel. He'd fought it. Hard.

Whatever it was, though, seemed stronger than he apparently was, but perhaps not stronger than Zach.

Maybe he'd made too much of the time they'd been spending together. Sure, a few days had passed since they saw each other at tea, and though they'd had some fun, he had to keep in mind that by Saturday, this would all be over.

Zach would go home.

"No need to apologize," Zach said after a few moments of silence. He rubbed his thumb tentatively across Van's mouth. He pursed his lips and gave the finger a soft kiss. "It's nice. I've never had anyone look at me like that before. It makes me kinda sad."

"How so?" he asked as the wind blowing off the ocean turned colder. Even the waves crashed onto the shore with more force. A storm formed on the horizon.

Zach's heavy sigh drew Van's attention back to him. The weight he'd discarded earlier as he drilled Van in the dunes in front of their spectators seemed to once again drape across his slumping shoulders. "I'm not looking forward to going home," he admitted as he turned his eyes back to the water's edge, where the waves churned upon the shore. "Back to the real world and the mess I left behind."

Although he didn't really want to know the answer, he asked the question anyway. "Do you think you and Ben will get back together?"

Zach shrugged. "I doubt it. He's moved on, and so have I. And it's pretty sad too. He and I could've been good together. We started out that way. I guess we just couldn't sustain it."

"What if he realizes he's made a mistake?" Van asked. "What if when you go back home, you find Ben on his knees begging you to take him back?"

Zach snorted. "That's not something Ben would do," Zach told him. "And even if he did, which I seriously doubt, I've changed from the person he knew. Going back to Ben would be like going back in time. Undoing the progress I've made."

Zach moved his eyes from the roiling ocean back to him. As their gazes met, almost giddy happiness shone from Zach's big brown eyes, but in the frown that squatted upon his lips sat regret. The contradiction unnerved him, especially since Zach looked at him as those emotions warred across his face.

What about him caused Zach to look at him that way?

"You know," he told Van. "I have to keep reminding myself that this is only temporary."

"What? The progress you've made?"

Zach snickered. It sounded different, almost distant. "No. *This*. You and me."

"Oh," he replied as his gut wrenched. It appeared he'd made more out of their time together than he should have. He had been a diversion from Zach's life. Nothing more. How big of a dumbass was he? It was common knowledge that Townies and tourists could never be more than tricks.

Hearts broke when that rule was forgotten, and his heart, which had started to beat again a few hours before, turned sluggish.

He rose off Zach's lap and dusted the sand from his legs and feet as the wind started to whip around them. He needed to get the hell out of there and as far away from Zach as possible. He'd already allowed himself to feel for someone again, when he knew better. If he continued down this path, he would be the one who suffered.

Not Zach.

"Besides," Zach continued. "You're a porn star. Your life's a lot different from mine."

"What the hell does *that* mean?" he snapped. Although he didn't want to argue and he *really* didn't want to discuss his job with Zach, this was what he needed. He needed something to wedge him from Zach, and what better topic than the fact he took it up the ass regularly for money?

"I'm just saying your life's not about responsibility and the day-to-day angst that everyone else deals with." Zach's eyes turned cool. The innocence Van had previously seen in them was gone, replaced by someone he'd never met. This Zach looked mean and spiteful and itching for a fight. "You live in P-town! You get to live the party scene year round with hot guys doing you both on and off screen." Zach stared off into the ocean once again, his eyes taking on a faraway look. "What a life!"

Where the hell was this bullshit coming from? He'd thought they'd been connecting on so many levels. Zach had even been okay with those fans taking his picture at the underwear party. He'd said Hart was their fantasy, but Van was his reality. That one exchange had told him what he'd always wanted to hear from someone.

But now Zach had apparently changed his mind. Or maybe it had been an act all along.

"Man, what a life!" Zach repeated in a more biting tone.

"You don't know one damn thing about my life!" he exclaimed through clenched teeth.

"Sure, I do," Zach responded. "You've told me about your death-defying adventures. How you live without a plan and go where life takes you. No real direction or purpose. That's not exactly the life of a responsible adult."

"Fuck you, Zach. Who the hell do you think you are judging me?" He rose from the blanket. He then shoved his feet into his sandy flip-flops and searched for his sunglasses. How the hell had he done this again? How could he have misjudged someone so clearly intent on hurting him?

"I'm not judging you at all," Zach explained. "You have your reasons for doing porn, whatever they might be. I guess I just haven't quite figured out *why* you do it. Besides the fact that you're a hot fuck."

If Zach wasn't careful, he'd wind up with a broken nose and some loose teeth. He typically wasn't a violent man, but when pushed too far, he'd been known to bloody someone up. "I can't believe what a complete asshole you really are."

Zach didn't move. He just sat there looking out into the ocean. His face and his eyes locked on to the stormy horizon. "I'm sorry," he said, although no remorse played across his face. "I'm just trying to have a discussion. To figure out why someone like you who obviously isn't stupid or strung out on drugs chooses to sell his body to the highest bidder."

"I'll tell you why," he responded after digging his sunglasses out of the sand where they'd fallen after the last time he and Zach had retired to the dunes for some outdoor action. "It's to keep heartless fuckers like you as far away from me as possible."

"How's that working out for you?" Zach asked, finally looking at him once again. The man he'd spent the past two days with had disappeared. Had he ever really been there?

"Like a charm," he finally spat out as he turned around and headed away from Zach.

What a fool he'd been! He had actually entertained the idea of quitting porn and Hart Throb for Zach. For the relationship he thought they might have. Did he really think his luck had changed because of Zach? That he'd actually found someone who saw what he was worth? Someone willing to accept everything about him?

Who the fuck had he been kidding?

Zach was just like all the others.

Nothing would ever change for him. It was time to say good-bye to Van Pierce and simply accept the fact that he would be Hart Throb forever.

At that moment, the storm that had swirled around him finally broke. The heavens opened up, drenching him in a downpour that masked the tears that fell from his eyes.

Chapter Twenty-Three

THE crashing thunder and pelting rain against his bedroom window forced Zach out of his fitful sleep. All night long, he'd been plagued by dreams of Van from their lighthearted meeting at FK Leather to their argument yesterday evening on the beach. Each scene played out in mocking fashion, tormenting him with the images of Van smiling at him as they talked, kissed, or had sex and replacing those memories with the horror in Van's face when he turned cold and abrasive.

What choice did he have? He had to do it. That was what he kept telling himself as he brought the pillow that Van had slept on the past two nights to his nose. Van's scent still lingered on it, and he inhaled deeply.

He'd grown too attached to Van in too short a time span. There was no way anything could come from their relationship. They were acting like two kids with the whole world in front of them instead of two adults with a whole world between them. Not only did they live almost two thousand miles away from each other, but they had completely different tracks in life.

An aspiring author and a porn star just didn't mesh together for the long term, and he had started considering the possibility of a relationship more enduring than a few days with Van.

Continuing down that path would serve neither of them any good. He just seemed incapable of stopping the momentum Van created whenever they were together.

That was why he had to end it the way he did. If he'd done it any other way, left even the tiniest opening in the door between them, he would have walked back through it somehow, some way. It was better for Van to hate him, to never want to see him again.

That was the only way Zach was sure it would be over.

As he held the pillow close, squeezing it as if it were Van and sniffing the fabric while pretending it was Van's pits or his crotch, he remembered how it had started with the small things like when they met and Zach imagined sweeping Van off his feet and taking him in his arms. Fantasizing about unusually squishy and romantic acts wasn't like him at all, and it only grew worse the more time he spent with Van.

He'd grown too comfortable with Van far too quickly, telling Van stories about his sexcapades in Provincetown that he'd promised never to share with anyone. The amount of information equated with being lifelong friends rather than two strangers who had just met.

At Suzy Wroughtinkrotch's show, he became insanely jealous and possessive, which led to the most passionate kiss he'd ever had with anyone. It was like having life breathed into him for the first time, and he hadn't wanted the moment to end.

Even when he learned that Van was a porn star, he didn't stop to really consider what that meant. He was too taken with the man Van appeared to be to even mull over how a relationship with someone in Van's line of work would affect him.

He'd just let the initial concern slide in favor of gazing into the gorgeous blue of Van's eyes, licking the perfect teeth and soft lips, and running his hands over the smooth tanned skin. When they touched and when they had sex, nothing else existed. As much as he filled Van with his cock, Van filled Zach's soul and heart with his presence, making everything else seem secondary.

But it couldn't remain that way.

Zach had to see the situation for what it was, and romance had to give way to reality and reason.

They simply had no future together, and he longed to have a future with *some*one *some*day.

Even though he'd just had his heart broken by Ben, he still valued relationships and the commitments associated with them. He'd just been going about them the wrong way. Over the last few days, he'd come to realize that he tried to change himself to be what everyone else needed, which all started with his dad.

That wasn't how relationships worked. A couple could only thrive when each person in the relationship complemented the other and shared goals and interests that made them stronger, not created points of contention.

His entire existence had been up for debate by whoever squawked the loudest about his shortcomings. He'd been living for others for so long that he simply stopped living for himself.

It took coming here to Provincetown to realize that.

Here, people like Gary, Quinn, Tara, and Van lived according to their own rules and definitions. That was the kind of life he wanted to lead, and he wanted a man who could live that with him.

No matter how much he desired Van or how much Van made him want to be a better man, Van couldn't be that guy. He lived life more casually than Zach did, and while he did enjoy his liaisons here in Provincetown, he didn't want his life to be about constant tricking.

He wanted a man to be only his, not shared with the world over Internet and video, and Van truly enjoyed starring in his films. Although they never really talked about it, he had discerned as much when Van told him he wouldn't apologize for what he did or even hide it. It really hit home when they had sex in front of all those guys on the beach.

Van loved being in the sexual spotlight. It was what he enjoyed, and no matter how much Zach might be expanding his horizons, he'd never become what Van ultimately needed, someone who didn't care that Van had sex with other men or someone who didn't get jealous at the thought of other men's hands on the body of someone he truly cared for.

That was beyond Zach's capabilities.

Van shouldn't have to be punished for that. He admired that Van treasured his life as it was. It was part of what made him so special to Zach in the first place.

He couldn't ask Van to change to be with him. That was unfair to Van just as it had been unfair for Zach when his father, or Ben, or anyone else expected him to change for their own needs.

He cared too much for Van to put him in that kind of predicament.

The best thing for both of them was to go their separate ways now. If they didn't part at that moment, he'd be the one who suffered.

Not Van.

And though he didn't really want to, he also needed to wash his bedsheets and take a shower. Van's smell lingered on everything it touched. He couldn't sleep another night in a bed that reminded him of what he had given up or walk around smelling like the man he had no choice but to set free.

So he climbed out of bed and began the process of erasing Van Pierce from his life.

DESPITE, or perhaps because of, his inner turmoil, Zach managed to pound out another four thousand words of his manuscript during the next several hours. It had been a hard story to write, basically chronicling his time spent with Van and how it made him feel, how he grew because of meeting him, and how he had to let him go.

But as he sat in front of the keyboard trying to figure out what happened next, Zach had absolutely no clue. He couldn't write the next chapter because he hadn't lived it yet. When he tried to imagine where his life would take him now, he only saw a dark, infinite road, which made him feel terribly alone and a bit afraid.

Had he done the right thing? Or had he made a mess out of something that could have been great?

Thunder boomed outside, rattling the patio door the rain rapped against and pounding so loudly it sounded as if someone were knocking. When the taps increased in speed, out of sync with the rainfall, Zach looked up from his computer. Gary stood outside underneath an umbrella, getting completely soaked.

Zach rushed to the door and opened it. The driving rain blew inside as Gary made a dash for the dry interior.

"Good Lord, Zachary," Gary complained as he shivered. "I was knocking for a good minute and calling your name. I thought for sure you were ignoring me, and all I wanted was to see if you were interested in coming over for dinner."

"Sorry about that," he said. Under normal circumstances, he'd welcome an invitation to dine with Gary and Quinn, but today he needed to be left alone. "I was just engrossed in my writing."

"I could see that," Gary replied as he closed the umbrella and deposited it in the kitchen sink. "How's it going?"

"Pretty good," Zach admitted. He realized he sounded miserable instead of ecstatic about what he'd written. Gary's arched eyebrows told Zach that Gary had picked up on his despondency and planned to do something about it.

"Well, for a man who claims to be making good progress in his writing, one of the things he came to P-town to do, you sure as hell don't sound happy about it." Without being asked to sit, Gary sat his damp self down on the couch next to where Zach had been working and stared at him. He obviously expected Zach to come clean.

He had no intention of indulging Gary. The last thing he needed was Gary's advice muddying up the decision he'd already made.

"Just a bit of writer's block," he told Gary, which wasn't a complete lie. Instead of taking a seat next to Gary, he crossed over to the front door, hoping Gary would get the hint and leave.

"Uh-huh," Gary replied as he sat back and made himself comfortable. He either didn't get the hint or refused to take it. After getting to know him these past few days, he decided it was the latter. "Now why don't you come sit down and tell me all about it?" Gary added with a pat to the couch. "Momma Travers has all the time in the world especially with God apparently planning to flood the Earth and all."

He exhaled loudly, hoping Gary interpreted it as his complete unwillingness to divulge anything.

"You can sigh and complain all you want, but I'm not leaving here 'til you spill your guts and tell me what's got you in this horrendous mood." This time Gary patted the couch more forcefully. He obviously wanted Zach to read the gesture as "Sit the fuck down and start talking."

He had two options. He could either grab Gary by the neck and toss him into the rain or do as Gary commanded. After seriously weighing the benefits of the first, he eventually walked over and dropped onto the couch next to his friend.

"Goodness," Gary commented. "Even the way you sit down is maudlin. Tell me what's going on."

After a few moments of silence, Zach finally did just that. He told Gary everything about his time with Van and ended with what happened on the beach yesterday. When he stopped speaking, Gary stared at him rather dumbfounded.

What was that look for?

"Well?" he asked, poking Gary in his arm. "Don't just sit there. You wanted to know, and I told you. You've *got* to say something now."

"I have to admit that I'm quite speechless, Zachary. From what you've told me, you've been an unspeakable ass. I never would've expected that sort of behavior from you."

"Jeez," he complained as he recoiled from Gary's stern gaze. "Don't sugarcoat it or anything."

"If you want a spoonful of sugar to help the medicine go down, call Julie fucking Andrews. I'll give it to you raw and uncensored. Just the way you gave it to Van."

"Fine," he told Gary. If his tone had been any sharper, Gary would have been sliced to ribbons. He didn't need Gary to act like his parent. He had two of those already, and he didn't speak to either of them. "I had no choice but to do what I did. It was better for both of us."

"That's bullshit and you know it," Gary pointed out. His powder-blue eyes took on a hard edge. Zach was impressed. He didn't think Gary had a mean bone in his body, and right now he looked ready to throw down with the best of them. "You did what was best for *you*. No one else. Don't try and convince me that you had no choice. We all have choices, and we do what we decide to do. Saying that you have no choice is a cowardly cop-out. You're much better than that."

"Maybe I'm not," he admitted. He sure didn't feel good about himself right now.

"Zachary, Zachary, Zachary," Gary said as he scooted closer and wrapped his arm around his shoulders. The gesture was sweet and reassuring, and Zach leaned into the offered comfort as Gary's angry eyes returned to their calm powder blue. "I've seen firsthand the kind of person you are. You forget. I'm the one who first welcomed you here to our little patch of paradise. I knew from the moment I laid eyes on your adorable face that you were one of the good guys. Sure, you were a little tentative and a lot lost and heartbroken, but a coward? Not on your life! Do you even realize the strength of character it took to fly across the country to some place you'd never been before after what that awful Ben did to you? Can you not see the strength it took to take on this place by yourself the way you've done? I've seen the insecure, timid man you were when you arrived change into a man who opens himself up to new possibilities. Sure, you became a manslut there for a while, but hey, it happens to the best of us. But what you did to Van wasn't right. And you know it as well as I do."

"Maybe," he relented with a little laugh. He remembered how Van had called him out on answering "maybe" to a question Van asked him. He'd pegged Zach as the type of man not able to admit when someone else was right.

"What's that laugh for?"

"Just something Van told me."

Gary nodded and stroked his hair. Although he guessed only about five to ten years separated them in age, Gary had at least double the maturity Zach possessed. That made Gary older and wiser, which also made it too darn easy for Zach to allow Gary to comfort him as a parent would. Even though he hated it. Well, maybe *hated* was the wrong word, but it sure irritated the shit out of him.

"I want to tell you something," Gary said after a few moments. "I've never see Van as happy as when I saw him with you. Not even when he was seeing that dipshit Jason. Van's a good guy, who's been through a lot of crap over the years. Most of which he doesn't know how to handle because he wears his heart on his sleeve and expects everyone else to do the same. When Jason did those horrible things to him, well, that was the last straw. He couldn't take being hurt like that again, being shoved aside as if he didn't matter. That's why he does porn, you know? Being Hart keeps Van safe."

"And it makes him happy. You can't deny that."

"Perhaps a little," Gary admitted with a nod. "There's no denying that boy's got a healthy sexual appetite. But I've got a sneaking suspicion he doesn't want to do porn forever. Especially if he had a reason not to."

He didn't like the turn the conversation was taking. Sure, what he did to Van might have been harsh and wrong, but it didn't change the fact that it had to be done. Whether Van would eventually stop doing porn or not didn't exactly fix everything. Besides the fact that Van shouldn't have to choose between some guy he just met and what he loved to do, Van and he were just fundamentally different. And they lived thousands of miles apart.

"Gary, I know you mean well. I really do," he said as he pulled himself free from Gary's embrace. "But none of what you've said changes my mind about what I did. You might think it cowardly. That's fine. I can't change that. But you *are* right about one thing. I did what was best for me."

"And *why* was that the best thing for you?" Gary asked. He tried to answer, but Gary held up his hand for Zach to wait. Evidently, he hadn't finished speaking. "Why was it best for you to be so cruel to someone you seemed to enjoy being around and who obviously enjoyed being with you?" Gary dropped his hand to his lap and gazed into Zach's eyes. "I want you to be honest. Not for me but for yourself."

"I already told you," he answered in frustration.

"You've told me you were too different. You've *told* me that you live in Texas, and he lives here. You've *told* me that he's more carefree in his choices than you are. All of which are complete bullshit, by the way, but you have yet to tell me the real reason. And I want to know what that is."

"What more could there possibly be?" he asked. Everything Gary had just listed sounded like perfectly logical reasons *not* to get involved with someone. His time here in Provincetown was meant to clear up the fog Ben's dumping him had left, not add a completely new and more complicated layer courtesy of Van.

"You tell me," Gary pointed out. "You were on a date with this man for over *forty-eight hours*."

He grumbled and rose from the couch. "How many times do I have to tell you it *wasn't* a date?"

Gary stood up and walked over to him. He placed his hands lovingly on each side of Zach's face. "And how many times do *I* have to tell *you* that it was?"

He pulled his head free of Gary's touch and walked to the kitchen to retrieve the umbrella. He handed it to Gary before escorting him to the front door. "I can't do this anymore, Gary," he said. "I've made up my mind. Van and I were supposed to be a trick. Neither one of us were looking for anything more. We pretty much covered that at the Pied and later at dinner. We made each other horny. End of discussion. That's where we should've stopped."

"But you didn't," Gary pointed out as he put his hand on the patio door to leave. "That's what happens when love takes over."

He had no comeback for that. Without another word, Gary left his condo and disappeared in the deluge outside.

He didn't *love* Van. That made absolutely no sense. They hadn't known each other long enough for that, and he definitely didn't believe it possible to fall in love with someone so quickly.

Love took time to form. It wasn't something that just happened like in the musicals he loved, when two people saw each other across a crowded room or in their case an empty leather shop. That wasn't only ridiculous, but it was childish and naïve to believe otherwise.

Wasn't it?

Zach turned around and looked at his computer, sitting where he'd left it when inspiration struck. He rushed over to the couch to write how he saw his story would end.

Chapter
Twenty-Four

AFTER two days of constant writing, with only the occasional potty break and the food Gary stopped by to shove down his throat, Zach had finished his manuscript, a story based upon him and Van. He'd titled it *A Reason to Love*, and after 70,000 words and 245 pages, the time had come.

He had to find Van.

This was his last full day in Provincetown. He couldn't leave for Texas tomorrow morning without apologizing for being an insufferable idiot and telling Van exactly why he'd acted like such an ass.

The reason was quite simple.

He had fallen in love with Van.

That had been apparent as he wrote the final chapters of the book. The main characters, Zane and Vic, were far from an ordinary couple. Zane was a bumbling, awkward mess incapable of maintaining a relationship, and Vic was a smooth-talking escort using sex to suppress the painful breakups of his past. A relationship between two such disparate characters seemed impossible until he told the story of their love.

From their humble beginnings in a porn store to their final date on the beach, Zane and Vic had forged a connection that transcended their very different lifestyles. Which had been fine because it was temporary. Zane didn't live in San Francisco. He'd only gone there to escape a cheating ex-boyfriend. But through the course of their story, Zane started to imagine a life with Vic that extended past his stay in San Francisco.

But how could that be?

Not only did they live in different states, but Vic made a living by selling his body to the highest bidder. There could be no future with those strikes against them. Zane couldn't ask Vic to give up his life for him, and Zane couldn't cope with the fact that the man he'd fallen in love with was an escort.

So Zane did what he had to do. He broke Vic's heart. He made Vic feel as if he was worthless and that his profession made him incapable of love.

After writing that scene, Zach couldn't stop crying. He'd realized he'd written Zane as a complete idiot. Instead of trying to work things out with Vic, he cut and ran. What a fucking bastard!

But then something miraculous happened. Zach's muse seized control of his fingers and told him how the story must end. Zane needed to find Vic. He had to convince Vic that Zane deserved another chance. That the two of them could be great together no matter what their problems were. Because no matter what, Zane loved Vic.

After that, the story told itself. And it also told Zach why he'd acted like such a dick on the beach.

The possibility of leaving Van behind or not having him return those feelings terrified him so much that he struck out in fear, hurting Van before Van had the chance to hurt him.

He'd not only been a fool but a coward as well. Just like Gary said. And just like Zane had been.

But he planned on fixing that. Immediately. Just like Zane.

He saved the manuscript to his flash drive and then ejected the device from the computer. After tucking the storage stick into the pocket of his shorts, he scanned the coffee table for the keys to the condo. Not finding them in the living room, he dashed through the kitchen and then to the dining room table.

They were nowhere to be found. Then he remembered placing the keys in his backpack when he and Van went to the beach. He hadn't left the condo since he got back from Herring Cove, which meant the keys must still be there.

After he emptied the contents of the bag onto the living room floor, he shifted through sunscreen, lube, condoms, and grains of sand only to discover that the keys weren't there.

"Fuck!" he yelled. What did he do with those damn keys?

"You look like you could use a hand," a voice behind him said.

Zach turned around. Gary and Quinn stood in the open patio door with smiles plastered on their faces.

"I hope we're not intruding," Quinn told him. "But now that the rain's finally stopped, we were going to head out for a bit. Also thought we'd check up on you. Maybe see if you were interested in grabbing something to eat on your last official day in P-town."

Zach waved them in as he tossed the backpack onto the couch. "No, you're not intruding, and nothing to eat for me. But if you can help me find the keys to the condo, I'd appreciate it."

"The keys?" Gary asked, staring at him in concern. "To the condo?"

Zach nodded as he tossed the cushions off the couch. What was with Gary's perplexed expression? Had Gary never encountered anyone who'd lost a set of keys before? "I have to find Van. As soon as possible," he told them as if that somehow explained how the keys were misplaced.

"Slow down, Zachary," Gary advised as he and Quinn surveyed the small disaster Zach had created during his quest for the lost keys. "Why do you need to find Van?"

"I have to tell him something."

Quinn came over to him and rested his hands on Zach's shoulders. His grip was gentle yet firm. It reminded Zach of the way his father used to get him to focus when he was a child, too hell-bent on his current course of action to listen to his father's reasoning. If Gary had taken on the role of his Provincetown mother, it seemed only fitting that Quinn assume the role of his Provincetown father. "Zach, I'm not one who normally interferes in my friends' affairs, but I consider both you and Van good friends of mine. If you're going to hurt him again, in any way, I'd really rather you just left him alone."

He turned away from Quinn's unyielding gaze to Gary, who nodded in silent approval of Quinn's request. He was going to have to explain himself before either of them allowed him to leave.

"I'm not going to hurt Van," he told them both. "I need to apologize."

He had been expecting Quinn to release his grip, but Quinn didn't. Instead, he tightened his hold. "That's very sweet of you," he offered, but his face remained serious. "But write him a note or something. Give it to me or Gary, and we'll take your apology to him."

"I'd rather apologize in person," he said, trying to breathe calm into his anger. Quinn had crossed a serious boundary by continuing to restrain him. He stared down at Quinn's hands and then locked onto Quinn's eyes. He didn't enjoy being restrained or told what to do, and he hoped the severity in his eyes expressed his extreme displeasure.

"And I'd rather you didn't."

Just as he was about to shrug Quinn's hands off his shoulders and start something they would both regret, Gary interfered, stepping between the two of them and gently removing Quinn's hands from Zach and placing them around himself.

"Now, boys," Gary said as he eyed both Zach and Quinn. "I love you both dearly, but wouldn't you agree we've had enough drama these past few days to last a lifetime?"

Quinn nodded. "You're right, hon." He gave Gary a kiss, which appeared to release much of the bluster from his sails. "I just don't want Van to be hurt again."

"I'm not going to hurt him," he told Quinn. "I want to apologize. And tell him that I love him."

Gary screamed in delight and leaped out of Quinn's arms and into Zach's. "Oh, Zachary! You big, redheaded fool! It's about damn time you saw what everyone else did."

He smiled at Quinn as he returned Gary's hug. "I'm a bit slow sometimes."

"Slow?" Gary asked. "If you were any slower, you'd be moving back through time."

"Thanks a lot," he told Gary with a roll of his eyes. "Way to make me feel good about myself."

"Oh, honey, that's what Van's for. I'm here to keep you on your toes."

"Are you okay with this?" he asked Quinn. "I want *us* to be okay."

Quinn beamed. "Okay? I'm thrilled!" he said as he shook Zach's hand. "And you and I are just fine."

"Great," Zach said as he once again looked around the condo. "I just need to find those damn keys, so I can go find Van."

"Check your pocket," Gary told him with a wink.

What the hell was Gary talking about? He'd already checked his— The keys dangled out of the pocket of his shorts. Would he always be this much of an idiot?

"You've got to be fucking kidding me," he stated as he stared into Gary and Quinn's laughing eyes.

"Now go get him," Quinn said with a smile.

Gary only nodded in reply. He looked too choked up to do anything else.

Zach led them out of his condo and after locking it shut, he bounded down the walkway and toward the man he'd loved more in a few days than he'd ever loved anyone in his life.

ALTHOUGH Zach had never been to Van's apartment, Van had told him he'd lived above Monty's, Provincetown's famous Christmas store. He'd passed by the holiday shop a couple of times on his journeys up and down Commercial, but he'd never gone into the store itself. He wasn't one of those people who enjoyed Christmas shopping when it wasn't the season for it. Ornament or gift shopping before Thanksgiving irritated him.

Today, however, there was no other place he'd rather be, which was why it only took Zach about fifteen minutes to walk from his condo toward the east end on Commercial and climb the outside flight of steps from Monty's up to the third floor.

Now that he was here, though, he found it impossible to muster up the necessary courage to knock on the door.

His resolve and his feelings hadn't changed. He loved Van, and he wanted to be with him, but after the way he'd treated Van on the beach and the days that had passed since then, he wasn't certain what type of reception he would receive.

It only dawned on him now that Van might not even talk to him. He'd been too wrapped up in what he discovered about himself to stop and consider what Van had been going through.

What would he do if Van refused to see him? Would he force his way inside? What if Van had someone else with him? Someone he'd tricked with the night before? How would Zach respond to that?

If he had his way, he'd kick the shit out of the guy and toss him headfirst over the railing and into the alley. What right did he have to do that, though? Just because he'd finally realized he'd fallen in love with Van didn't mean Van had been waiting for him to grasp what people like Gary and Quinn had already figured out.

He had to prepare himself for the worst.

After inhaling deeply several times, he finally knocked on the door and waited.

When there was no response, he repeated the process. This time louder.

"Van," he called out as he banged on the door. "It's Zach. Please come to the door."

"What the fuck are you doing here?" a voice behind Zach asked. When he turned around, he saw Van's best friend Nino coming up the steps with a hot young jock draped over him.

"I need to talk to Van."

Nino chuffed in disgust as he walked past Zach without looking him in the eye. Nino looked pissed off and ready to fight. Zach was game. He'd knock Nino around a few times if it meant he'd find out where Van was. A pretty-boy model didn't frighten him all that much.

Nino fished the keys out of his pocket and opened the door to the apartment he shared with Van. After asking his boy toy to wait inside, Nino closed the door behind him and then turned to glare at Zach.

"Do you know when he'll be home?" he asked Nino, hoping they could avoid a tussle.

"Look," Nino said as he stepped up to Zach and got in his face. "I don't know who the fuck you think you are coming over here after what you've done. You're either fucking stupid or have the biggest set of balls I've ever seen. Whatever it is, you need to turn your pasty ass back around and get the fuck out of my sight."

Zach made no attempt to move. He returned Nino's glare. He wasn't intimidated. While he understood and even respected Nino's attempts at protecting his best friend, he wasn't about to let Nino or anyone stand in his way. "Do you know when Van will be home?" he asked again.

Nino sneered at him. "You must be stupid, then. 'Cause you're not listening to what I'm saying."

"I'm listening. I just don't care." He took another step toward Nino, closing the space between them to mere centimeters. "All I care about is finding Van."

Nino didn't back away, nor did he shift his gaze from Zach's steady glare. They locked gazes like two alphas about to settle an issue of dominance. "And all I care about is protecting Van," Nino challenged by poking his finger in his chest. "From you."

Zach hated being poked in his chest. His father used to do that to him whenever he tried to make a point he felt Zach was too obtuse to understand. He understood then just as he did now. Nino meant to teach him a lesson by fist or lecture, and how it played out was completely up to Zach.

He could fight Nino if he wanted. He could do his best to bloody up Nino's perfect features and beat the information he wanted out of him, but how effective would that really be? Trading blows might help them relieve the tension, but that would be about all it would accomplish.

When it came right down to it, no matter how much he resented Nino's interference, Nino was simply being Van's friend.

Zach was the asshole here.

Closing his eyes, he broke the stare with Nino and took three steps back. He then turned sideways and rested his palms against the railing with chipped white paint. As he stood there quietly, his shoulders slumped, and gazing down into the frenetic energy that was Commercial Street, he sensed Nino's anger sputter.

Nino had obviously been ready to throw down, and Zach's prompt surrender confused him. Nino didn't know whether to pursue the fight or let it pass. After a few moments of silence and a glance over his shoulder at Nino, who now stood with his arms crossed over his chest and a smug look plastered across his face, Zach could tell that his retreat had accomplished what he meant it to.

Nino had calmed down enough to at least listen.

"I'm sorry," he whispered. "I never meant to hurt Van."

Nino responded only with silence. His face remained unchanged and his posture tense. He'd obviously not let the hostility completely go, preferring to hold on to it in case he needed to finish what they had started.

Zach turned around to face him, but this time not as an opponent. He only wanted to be able to speak with Van, and the only way to do that was to convince Nino that he deserved at least one last chance to make things better.

"And I know that I did hurt him. The things I said were wrong. And horribly cruel. I know you hate me for it. Van probably does too, and I fucking deserve it. And much more. It's just. Well, I don't really know how to put it in words," he told Nino as he turned back around and gazed once again down on Commercial Street and the steady stream of people flowing up and down the pavement. "I just got caught up in everything, I guess. That's what happens in P-town, right? You're supposed to lose yourself here. Make all your troubles go away. And they did. But it wasn't P-town or the tricks that really made them disappear. It was meeting Van, the perfectly tanned man." A smile danced across his lips as Zach recalled their first meeting.

"When I first saw him," he told Nino as he turned to face him once again, "I went stupid. I'd never seen such a beautiful man in my life before, but as I got to know him, he was even more striking than I could imagine. And I'm not talking about his looks. I'm talking about the person I got to know. The Van who lives inside. Getting to know that guy, the guy who hides behind all the pain he's lived through, well, this might sound weird, but it made me happy. And I can't explain why. At least not in a way that would make sense, but it was like I'd found myself, and it all happened so easily. I've known people my entire life that I don't know as well as I'd gotten to know Van in two days. I just forgot all the shit that made me come here in the first place. It was like none of it mattered anymore. My pain just vanished. Gone and forgotten."

Zach sighed deeply, once again looking away from Nino and staring down at the faded wooden slats they stood upon. "But then, I started thinking about Saturday. And how all this was coming to an end. And how different Van and I were. And all that pain came back. But it was a different pain. It hurt more because I hadn't lost something I once thought mattered, but because I was going to lose something I hadn't really even had yet. Something that could never be mine for a whole bunch of reasons. It made me bitter and resentful, so I struck out at Van. Said things I never should have said to someone that I've fallen in love with."

Nino crossed over to where he stood and raised his fist. Zach flinched, expecting a jab to the nose, but he was surprised when Nino's fist unclenched. Instead, Nino rested his open hand on Zach's shoulder. "You're a complete fuckup," he told Zach. "Not worthy of the greatest guy I know."

Zach nodded in agreement.

"But no one is," Nino added. "You, though, just might be good enough."

He looked up into Nino's smiling eyes. "Really?"

Nino shrugged. "I said *might*. Whether you are or not, well, that's not my call. That's up to Van."

"Will you tell me where I can find him?" Zach pleaded. He grasped Nino's forearms, not in anger but in desperation.

Nino sighed before giving in with a roll of his eyes. "He's at the Sandpiper."

The Sandpiper was an exclusive guesthouse next to the Boatslip. If he ran, he could be there in five minutes. He turned around to bolt down the steps, but this time Nino grabbed him by the forearm and prevented him from leaving.

"He's there to work," Nino told him. His stare was even and serious.

Zach understood. Nino was warning him what type of situation he'd be running to. He was about to dash onto a porn set where he might find Van getting fucked by a hot guy. Or two. And if he loved Van like he just claimed to, how was he going to handle seeing the man he loved writhing naked and sweaty underneath another man?

He didn't have the answer. Above anything else, even above breaking his own heart by watching a stranger touch flesh that was supposed to be his to touch or kiss lips that belonged only to his lips, he had to get to Van.

Nothing else mattered when love takes over. Just like Gary had said.

Chapter Twenty-Five

ZACH made a mad dash down Commercial Street. He just had to get to Van before the shoot started. Van had to know how he felt, how sorry he was, and how much Zach loved him. He needed Van to know that Hart Throb couldn't come between them because it wasn't Hart who Zach had fallen in love with.

It was Van.

Sure, it was going to be difficult for Zach to deal with Van's job. The idea of Van having sex with other men troubled him, but in some strange way, the person having sex on film wasn't Van. It was Hart.

That, however, might not last long.

After everything he'd done and the things he said, Van and Hart were in danger of becoming the same person for the first time. If that happened, the loving and carefree Van might be forever lost to the blunted and unfeeling Hart.

He couldn't allow that to happen, so he bounded up the front steps of the Sandpiper Beach House and pounded relentlessly on the front door until a short, pudgy, balding man with an angry red face swung open the door.

"What the fuck, man?" he screamed as he stepped onto the porch. "We're trying to work here."

Ignoring him, Zach sidestepped the furry-looking tomato of a man and rushed inside. "Van!" he called out as he ran to the foot of the stairs to the right and yelled up the staircase. "Van, I need to talk to you. Please, come down."

"The only thing you need is to get your pale ass out of here," fumed the little man at the front door.

When Zach turned around, he noticed a mountain of a man, with perhaps the longest flaccid penis he'd ever seen in real life, standing naked next to Mr. Tomato Head. The newcomer's cock practically dangled past his knees, and for someone who stood well over six feet, that was quite the accomplishment. Not only did the man have a freakishly lengthy cock, he also had muscles in places Zach had never seen them before. He had no idea that someone's wrist could look like a flexed bicep. He didn't find the look sexy at all. It was more gross than anything else.

Still, the naked man's presence greatly intimidated Zach. He looked as if he could flip Zach over and fuck Zach through his shorts if the smaller man gave the word.

"I'm not looking for trouble," he said as he kept an eye on the man's cock. If it made an unexpected move toward him, Zach planned to scream like a little girl until Van came to save him from being spit-roasted by the guy's skewer. "I'm looking for Van."

"For Pierce?" the big man asked. A cheesy grin spread across his face. "He's a great guy. I love him."

"Oh, shut the fuck up, Ram," the smaller guy said. "You're so stupid you love everyone."

"Not everyone, Tripp," Ram pouted. "You're too mean to love."

He left the squabbling duo in the entryway and proceeded into the expansive living area with white walls and mostly white décor. An open door led out to the patio where a gorgeous view of the bay awaited. To the left of the door sat a tripod and a camera and two other men running cable lines from a monitor that sat on a pedestal before a fold-up chair.

The camera pointed to one of the white love seats where a quart-sized jar of lube sat on the floor next to rubber drop cloths and an assortment of discarded condom wrappers. It looked as though a scene had just ended.

He was too late.

Van had become Hart before he had a chance to say what needed to be said.

"Hey," Tripp railed as he rounded the corner and tugged on Zach's arm. "Get the fuck out of here. This isn't some public peep show. It's a place of business."

"I just wanted to see Van," he mumbled under his breath. "Before...." But Zach couldn't finish his thought.

"I don't give a good hot damn what you want. You fanboys have to learn to not barge onto my sets. If you want to see Hart, buy his DVDs. You'll get an eyeful for only $49.99!"

Rage he'd never experienced bubbled up from within. He grabbed Tripp by his shirt and then lifted him off the floor. Zach pinned him against the wall without tripping or bungling the move. Evidently being more confident made him capable of unprecedented grace. "Stop calling him that! His name is Van, and I'm not some random porn enthusiast here to have my ass signed by Hart Throb. And I don't want to see your low-budget skin flick. I want to see Van. And I'm not leaving until I do."

"Low-budget skin flick?" the man screamed. He was obviously more offended by Zach's comment than by Zach dangling him from the ground. "What the fuck are you talking about? Nasty Boy Studios produces quality fuck films guaranteed to get you off or you get your money back."

He dropped the man, causing him to fall into a heap on the wooden floor. Someone who spouted off the company mantra in the face of getting his ass kicked proved too pathetic to deal with. If he wanted Van, he'd have to find him on his own. He turned around to do just that when he ran right into the naked behemoth known as Ram.

The force of the collision caused Zach to bounce backward, fall over Tripp, and land on his ass next to where he dropped the loudmouthed little man. So much for his newfound grace. When he glanced up from where he fell, Ram's enormous cock snaked its way toward him. Above it hovered Ram's large, unamused face.

"I'm not a fan of Tripp either, but he's still the boss," Ram said as he stood over Zach. "And you've gotta go."

Although he couldn't be certain, Zach got the distinct impression from the man's grin and his twitching cock that Ram wanted to fuck him senseless. And there was no way a cock that big was getting anywhere near his back door or his mouth. He'd either be split in two or have to completely unhinge his jaw to accommodate its length and girth.

Ram reached down and yanked Zach up by his collar before escorting him to the door. "Now, you be a good boy and leave," he told Zach after patting him on his ass. "And if you wait 'til I'm done, I'll throw you a bone later."

"What's going on here?" a voice behind them asked as Ram opened the door and was about to toss him out.

He didn't need to see him to know that Van had come down the stairs at last.

Ram turned around with Zach dangling in his hands like a naughty puppy that had pissed on the floor. "Just a fan of yours that I'm tossing back outside," Ram told Van, who was dressed in only a white bathrobe. Judging from his damp hair, Zach could tell Van had just emerged from a shower.

He apparently had to clean up after work. Zach tried not to focus on that.

"Van," he pleaded as Ram tried to shake him quiet, "I need to talk to you."

Van crossed his arms and sighed. "Ram, put him down."

"But…," Ram stammered as he looked from Zach to Van. "Tripp wants him out."

"Leave Tripp to me," Van told him as Ram gently set Zach onto the floor once again.

"Thanks," Zach muttered to Van as he walked over to the foot of the stairs. He made sure to keep himself out of Ram's extensive reach.

Just then Tripp scrambled into the entryway, his face redder than a baboon's ass. "I want him thrown out of here. Now!" he demanded.

"Give me fifteen minutes," Van told Tripp while only staring at Zach. "This won't take long."

"You've wasted enough of my time, Pierce. This shoot's moving on. With or without you."

Van glanced over at Tripp and smiled without an apparent trace of joy in his eyes or on his face. Was he too late? Had Hart taken over completely now?

"You can either let me deal with this now, and we can get back to the shoot in about ten to fifteen. Or you can continue to argue with me and delay it even longer. Whatever you want is fine with me. I can argue all motherfucking day. With you. Or Zach."

Both Tripp and Ram turned to stare at Zach.

"So this is Zach?" Tripp asked while Ram growled low like an angry dog. Apparently, they'd both heard what he had done to Van, and even the heartless Tripp seemed disgusted by him.

"Let's go," Tripp told Ram as he led the larger man back to the living room. "Once Pierce's done here, we won't have anything further to worry about."

When Tripp and Ram were out of sight, Zach opened his mouth to speak, but Van held up his hand and quieted him. "Not here," Van told him. "Follow me."

Van then turned around and proceeded up the steps without another word. Although he'd never seen a Hart Throb film or encountered Van in Hart Throb mode, by the tone of his voice and the difference in personality, he wasn't dealing with Van, the man he fell in love with. The man he followed up the stairs was Hart Throb.

VAN led him into a bedroom on the second floor. The four-poster bed and upscale furniture made the room look expensive, but the mounted cameras and sound equipment taking up most of the floor space turned a spectacular-looking room into something cheap and tawdry.

The lube-splattered rubber play sheets atop the bed ramped up the sleaze factor by at least ten.

He glanced about the room in a state of confounded silence, while Hart, not Van, stood silently staring at him. He regarded Zach with no emotion whatsoever. The way one might look at a stranger or an acquaintance met years before. The joyful sparkle with which Van once looked at Zach had been snuffed out.

He had only himself to blame for that.

"So what's this all about?" Van asked, evidently trying to hide the fact that he was a tad annoyed. "In case you haven't noticed, I've got business to get back to."

Zach nodded. No doubt about it. This was Hart, not Van. "I've noticed." He gestured toward Van's bathrobe. "You're dressed and ready to go."

"For the second time," Van added.

He attempted to fake a smile, but it died immediately on his lips. Instead, he gulped, trying to force down the rising sob that threatened to unleash his misery. He'd already accepted that having sex with other men was a part of Van's job. It was something he couldn't change any more than he could change where they lived or how hopelessly in love he'd fallen with Van. He'd come here with no intention of making Van choose between him and his job, but after meeting Ram, a man whose cock looked like a baby anaconda, he was having difficulty accepting the reality of it all. "I see" was all he could muster.

"Okay, then," Van said as he crossed back to the door. "If we're done here, I need to get back to work."

"Please, don't," he pleaded before Van could open the closed bedroom door.

"'Please don't' what?"

"Don't be cold and distant. Not now." He paused, and then said, "Please bring Van back. I want to talk to him. Not Hart."

Van turned around and glared at him. "Hart *is* me. He's *always* been me. At least the part of me that I've used to stay safe. Hart's the only one to truly do that, so excuse me if I'm not the man you want me to be right now. I tried just being Van for you. All that got me was the cold and distant asshole you were on the beach."

"I shouldn't have done that," he told Van. "That's why I'm here. To apologize."

"I have no interest in an apology, Zach. I would, however, like to get on with my work."

"But I really need to speak my piece before I head back to Texas tomorrow. To apologize for being such an asshole."

"There's nothing to apologize for," Van said plainly. The chilly indifference seemed to drift away almost immediately. In its place settled a polite cordiality that he found disconcerting. Was Van somehow breaking through? "You only spoke the truth on the beach," he said with a sigh. "I really shouldn't have taken it so personally."

Van crossed over to the bed and sat on its edge. He patted the rubber sheets, asking Zach to join him in a manner similar to when Van had wanted Zach to sit next to him at Suzy Wroughtinkrotch's show or on the barstool at the Pied. Van was back, but the steely exterior that was Hart remained. He could handle Hart rejecting him. Because that wasn't Van. Not the real Van. He would fight Hart Throb tooth and nail for the man he loved. But if Van rejected him, what could he do about that? "I should really be apologizing to you. I'm sorry for ruining the good time we were having together."

What was happening? He'd been ready to make amends, to crawl back on his hands and knees if he needed, but Van really didn't seem to care anymore. When Van first saw him, he'd been unmistakably pissed off, but that anger was entirely gone. That wasn't a good sign.

"I don't understand," he finally managed.

Van smiled in response, and his perfect, white teeth once again magically appeared. Zach still longed to dive for each exquisite pearl. "What's so difficult to understand, silly? You were right. We were just temporary. A distraction from each other's lives. Me from my shoots and the craziness that is being Hart Throb. And you from your breakup with Ben."

Van reached over and held his hand. His touch was still warm and inviting, causing Zach to shudder. "You were right to say what you did. You probably could've done it a bit nicer," Van chuckled. "But sometimes ripping the Band-Aid off is the best way to go. I can be a big baby about that sometimes. Usually, though, I tend to see that it's all for the best after it's been done."

"I'm so confused," Zach admitted. "I thought we might've had something real between us."

Van punched him playfully in his shoulder. "Stop teasing!" he warned. "How could we have anything real between us? I live here in P-town, a thousand miles from Texas. I don't do the regular world well like you or everybody else. I'm really quite happy with my party-boy, tricking existence. Just like you said. I know you're not exactly happy. Yet. But you will be. Once you get home and you maybe get some closure with that douche bag Ben, I think you'll be able to find what makes you happy. Maybe even that special guy who makes you want to be the better man you've talked about."

The room spun around Zach. If he passed out, he hoped he landed on the floor instead of on top of the slimy used sheets. Had he been so wrong after all? He'd believed he'd found someone special in Van. After all, Zach wanted to be a better man for *him*. That was why he'd been able to accept himself instead of be embarrassed about all his flaws. He came to embrace that he was a screw-up, and that it was okay to be that way because it was who he was.

He'd even come to understand how love between two people should be. It was about acceptance of the other person, not about changing each other to fit what the other needed. That was why he'd come to the decision that Van's career choice didn't matter. They would find a way to work through it, and as long as he had Van, he'd have what he needed to overcome anything.

Now, it seemed he really had nothing all along.

"Hopefully, we can keep in touch," Van said as he rose from the bed. "Maybe if you come back to P-town, we can hook up again. I'm not the only one who's a good fuck, you know?"

Van winked and kissed him tenderly on the cheek, and for a moment, the Van he'd fallen for stepped forward. His soft lips communicated something quite different than the words Van spoke. But the light that once resided in the steely-blue that had entranced him was completely gone.

Only a sad, lonely boy remained.

Although it might make him even more of a dumbass and a screw-up, he had to do what he came here to do. He wrapped his arms around Van, drawing him close and devouring Van with his senses.

He'd missed Van's touch, his taste, and most significantly his smell. He inhaled deeply at the crook of Van's neck, taking in the distinct scent that was Van's body. The ruggedly musky aroma, even hidden by the slight odor of soap, comforted him. There, in his arms, he was safe and at home. That sensation along with the weight of Van's body as it rested against him caused Zach to grow instantly hard. But more than the sexual arousal, his heart longed once again for the mate it had found in Van.

He wanted to lose himself completely in Van's body, to inhale and ingest everything there was about Van so that neither of them could tell where one ended and the other began.

Just as they had done on their forty-eight-hour non-date.

"I don't have time for a quickie," Van told him with a laugh as he released himself from Zach's embrace. "I'm a busy boy."

"I was an ass to you, and I was wrong," he said as he once again pulled Van back into his arms. He wasn't going to let Van get away that easily. The time for playing it safe had passed. The timid and cautious Zach had to give way to the Zach who went after what he wanted, and damn the consequences.

And he wanted nothing more than Van.

"What we had wasn't temporary," he told Van. "We were on the verge of something great. Something bigger than the both of us. Sure, it wasn't something either of us was looking for, but we found it. Or it found us. Whatever." He held on to Van tightly, resting his forehead on Van's, and kissed lips that slightly trembled beneath his touch. "I don't care about your porn job. I mean, I care, but it's not a deal breaker. I don't care about how far apart we live. That doesn't matter. It's all just bullshit that we can overcome. Quite easily. I love you, Van Pierce. And I'll do whatever it takes to be with you."

Van pushed away from his kiss and embrace. His eyes were wide and mystified. "Have you lost your mind?"

"I haven't lost my mind," Zach replied. "I've lost my heart. To you."

"You don't love me, Zach. You love the idea of me. Just like my fans love Hart Throb. I became something you needed while you were here, and for a while there, I might have thought we had a shot at something, but that day on the beach, I knew we needed some wedge to come between us. It was time to end whatever was happening because it wasn't going to end well for either of us. Those things you said on the beach, whether they were true or not, were mean. And sure, you don't need to apologize for them. I've already told you that. But if you're able to say those things to someone, that means you *don't* love that person. Because that's not the way someone should love. At least, that's not the way I want to be loved. I'm not for you, Zach, and you're not for me."

Van walked away from him and crossed to the bedroom door. He paused before turning around. "I think we should just say good-bye, Zach, and be done with it. I can't have you thinking we belong together. Confusing what you might think you want with what actually is."

He opened the door and stood before it, not making any move to cross the boundary. He evidently meant for Zach to be the one who left.

What was he supposed to do now? He'd finally taken action, to be the man he'd always wanted to be. Instead of Van rushing into his arms and accepting the man he'd helped Zach become, Van rejected him. Van didn't want what he offered.

All Van wanted was for him to leave him alone. For good.

"Van, I...."

"Just go, Zach," Van told him. "This sudden newfound 'love' you have for me isn't real. It's only been brought on by your guilt for what you've said. I'm not sure what else it might be, but I know what it's not." He gestured to the open door. "You've got a plane to catch tomorrow and some packing to do. I've got a shoot to finish."

Nausea rolled through his body. Van really had no interest in pursuing anything further with him. Whether they had a chance at something real before this or not, he'd killed it on Herring Cove, amid the sand and sea grass.

He had no other choice but to accept that fact and move on.

After crossing the length of the room, he paused before the open door and Van, who didn't look him in the eye. What they had might be over, but he still wanted to thank Van for everything, for giving him the greatest gift anyone had ever given him.

Helping Zach find himself.

"I want to give you something," he told Van after retrieving the flash drive from his pocket and placing it in Van's hand. "I finished my book, and I wanted you to have a copy. Maybe you'll read it. Maybe you won't. But you inspired me to write it. I just wanted you to know that. And to thank you for everything." He reached out to caress Van's face one final time but stopped himself before his hand made contact with his flesh. If he touched Van, he might break down right there.

Neither he nor Van wanted that. So he withdrew his hand from the empty space between them and shoved it back in the pocket of his shorts.

"You're a remarkable man, Van Pierce. I was lucky to have known you."

He then left the bedroom, walked down the stairs, and out the front door. The never-ending river of people coursing down Commercial Street carried him back to his condo, and even though he was surrounded by the same vibrant throng that had so revitalized him a few days before, in the midst of their radiant happiness, the lost and lonely feeling he had brought with him from Texas once again found him in Provincetown.

ZANE clutched Vic in his arms, using his words and his embrace to evidently convince him that he was sorry for what he had said on the beach. Vic didn't believe it. How could he? Zane had said terrible things to him. He'd made Vic feel like a common whore, when Zane had been the only person in recent years who never once made him feel that way.

He'd believed they had something special. That he had finally found a reason to love. Zane had destroyed that.

"Please forgive me," Zane begged as he clutched at Vic's shoulders. "I was awful to you. So damn awful. I don't deserve you or your forgiveness, but that's what I'm asking you. Can you do that? Can you forgive me and give us another chance?"

"I can't," Vic replied without hesitation. He released himself from Zane's desperate embrace and stepped away. He'd already done far more for Zane than he'd wanted. He'd fallen in love with the clumsy buffoon and gotten his heart broken. "It was fun while it lasted, but it had to end sometime. We're two different people, and this isn't some movie where everything works out in the end. This is reality, and in real life not everyone stays together."

"But we can," Zane pleaded. His brown eyes appeared completely convinced of his words. If only they hadn't been equally as convincing when he'd broken Vic's heart. "I love you, Vic Stone. The two of us can work through anything. I know it."

"Not this," he told Zane. "Not us."

"Why not?"

"Because this isn't a gay version of Pretty Woman, *Zane. You don't get to march up my fire escape at the end of the movie, apologize for being the biggest dick of the century, and then carry me off into the*

sunset. *In the real world, actions have consequences. You promised you'd never hurt me, and that's just what you did. There's no coming back from that. Not in my movie."*

"This isn't your movie," Zane replied. "It's ours." He once again wrapped his arms around Vic's waist, pulling their bodies closer together. Whenever Zane's strong, muscled body rested against his, Vic lost all sense of rational thought. Why couldn't Zane just leave him be? Why did he have to insist that they had a future together? There were no happy endings for an escort and a high school English teacher. At least none that weren't paid for in advance with cash.

"Stop it," he said. He attempted to break out of the comforting warmth that was Zane's embrace. Zane refused to let him go. He clawed his hands up and down Vic's back, evidently searching for some magical handhold that would allow them to stay that way forever.

Was that really what Zane wanted? To be with him forever?

"Why are you doing this?" Vic asked. "Why after everything you told me on the beach?"

"Because I was scared," Zane replied. "I didn't think I could handle being in love with an escort, but the truth is, I don't care what you do. I thought I did, which is why I said those things, but that was my fear talking. It turns out I'm more afraid of not having you. Of not holding you every night. Of not getting to spend every waking moment gazing into your beautiful blue eyes. You're what I care about. You mean more to me than anything else in the world. More than the distance between us or some stupid job. Those are the things in life that are temporary. Not the people we fall in love with. They are permanent. They stay with us forever. And that's what I want. A forever with you. I can't let fear dictate my life anymore. Sure, it kept me safe. But I don't need fear to keep me safe. Being with you will do that for me."

"Zane, please...," he started, but Zane wouldn't let him finish.

"You've changed me. My life, in fact. You've given me purpose and a direction. A reason not just to love but to live like I've never lived before. Yes, the old me came back. The one who doubts everything. He made me question us. But those doubts were never about you. They were about me."

Vic remained unconvinced. Doubts didn't vanish like some unwanted ghost. They hung around, haunting the relationship until their mere presence sent both parties running in fear. No matter how sweet the words were or how much he wanted to believe in them, he had to be smart. Think with his head. Not his heart. "Since they're about you," Vic finally replied, "they have nothing to do with me."

He went slack in Zane's arms, no longer struggling to be free. He simply let his body communicate the fact that he was done. Zane evidently sensed the change. He released Vic and took three tentative steps back. "But..."

"No buts, Zane. I'm glad you changed. I truly am. I want nothing but the best for you. But that isn't me."

"It is you," Zane said. He stepped forward again. His moment of hesitation had apparently ended. He obviously wasn't going to give up on Vic. Or on them. That was quite evident from the determined look etched across Zane's features. "You can reject me today if you want. That's fine. I'll leave. But I'll be back tomorrow. And the next day. And the day after that. I won't stop, Vic. You're a part of me, and I won't rest until you make me complete again. You have my word on that."

Zane's words were spoken with such conviction that Vic wanted to believe them. But could he? Was he willing to trust that they could both abandon their fears and be happy together?

With a sigh, Van closed the document reader on his computer. He'd begun reading Zach's novel after he left the Sandpiper, and now he didn't need to read anymore. He possessed the answers to his questions. What he had to do now was what needed to be done. He just couldn't do it alone. This was going to require the help of a few good friends.

Chapter Twenty-Six

EVEN though it was his last tea, Zach had no desire to be there. He'd wanted to stay alone in the condo and sulk after Van had rejected him and told him they had no future together, but Gary and Quinn refused to let him stay and wallow. They claimed that he had to go to tea, to capture the last bit of magic Provincetown had to offer before he left it all behind.

He had been too tired to argue.

He secretly hoped that the exhilaration of the crowd might prove infectious and drag him out of his funk, but as he stood among the shirtless men who drank to excess and scouted the deck for the final fuck of their vacations, loneliness seized his soul.

Yes, he stood among them, but he remained alone. He was once briefly like them. Now, he couldn't be more different from each and every one of the men who smiled wantonly at each other. They lived for immediate gratification. They either didn't care or didn't think about their existence after the here and now. Their lives away from Provincetown lingered in the wings to embrace them and welcome them home.

Each and every one of these men had something waiting for them somewhere else. They had a significant other who would depart with them once their vacation ended. Friends and family who had been left behind anxiously awaited their return, to hear the stories of their time on the Cape and the adventures each one of them had.

Zach didn't have that.

All that waited for him back in Texas was a failed relationship and forgotten possessions he needed to reclaim at the apartment he once shared with Ben.

His hasty jaunt to Provincetown had been to escape pain, and for a while he had accomplished that goal. He'd found lifelong friends he planned on visiting as often as possible. He had some crazy stories to tell about things he'd done that he never thought he'd do in a million years, and he met a man who left a lasting mark on his heart and his soul.

But somewhere amid the windswept dunes, the starry nights and sunny days, and the eclectic cast of characters, the pain he fled caught up to him and crushed him with its weight.

He'd never known love before Van. At least not true love. It took someone like Van, who lived life on his own terms and who didn't give a flying fuck what others thought about him or his choices, to teach Zach he hadn't been living. It took someone like Van who wore his heart on his sleeve to coax Zach's heart from underneath the layers of caution where it hid.

When all was said and done, it was a porn star, who bared all for the cameras, who helped the author, who hid beneath a mountain of layers, to find his lost voice and rediscover what his heart was meant for.

Van gave him the reason to love he'd unknowingly been searching for his entire life.

But now he had to leave all that behind, and the prospect of doing so left him hollow.

"Enough with the sourpuss," Gary told him as he handed him a Planter's Punch. Behind Gary, Quinn and Tara looked at him with eyes far more hopeful than he felt. Why did his friends look so chipper when he felt so much like shit? What were they up to? "Drink up and be merry."

"I can't be merry," he announced. "But drinking is something I can definitely do." He then knocked back the glass and downed the drink in one gulp. The alcohol burned his throat as it went down, and a soothing warmth spread throughout his body. If he couldn't be happy, he could at least get drunk.

"I guess that's a start," Gary said with roll of his eyes. "But I'll be damned if I let you get plastered and miss such a momentous event."

"Momentous?" Zach asked. "What's so momentous about this?"

Quinn and Tara stared intently at Gary. If they had a club, they'd obviously thump him over the head. Something was most definitely up.

"It's your last tea," Gary told him as he waved Quinn and Tara's reproachful looks away. It was a lie, and that confused him. Why was Gary lying about tea? What was really going on here? "It's a significant event for you, my dearest Zachary. When you first got here, you were a newborn babe, looking to find your way in the world. You had absolutely zero fashion sense and no clue how to have fun. That's not *you* anymore," he announced as he spun Zach around. "Just look at you. You dress flawlessly now. Thank God. No more baggy, mismatched clothes. You've also learned to grab life by the balls. And grab you have. From so many men that I've lost count. You've grown so much under my tutelage that you've even fallen in love."

"And got my heart broken," he added. None of this explained why Gary was lying to him. Or what Tara and Quinn obviously wanted Gary to keep mum about.

"True," Gary admitted. "But you're missing the entire point here. You've become the man you wanted to be. At least the one you told us about. You came here looking for answers and for your voice to write your book. You found both, and in finding both, you found something wonderful in another person. It might not have worked out the way you intended it, but some things don't. That's life. You now know what you want, and you have the means to find it. Don't let the bad cover that back up. Sure, it may sting like a bitch right now, but so did your breakup with Ben. Yet you still found Van, and you put your heart on the line. Something you had no intention of doing. When the time's right, you'll do so again. But this time, you'll not only be wiser because of everything you've been through here, but you'll also know what it takes to make it last."

He wanted to tell Gary to shut up, but the wisdom of his words spoke volumes. He couldn't backtrack now, not when he'd come so far. He'd written his book because he'd now lived instead of standing by on the sidelines and observing. He didn't let others take the reins and direct his actions as he'd done with his father or any other man he let in his stable. He swung the horses down the path on his own.

No matter how badly he wished things had worked out with Van, they hadn't. He might have screwed the pooch on that one, but that didn't mean he had to sacrifice everything else to it. He didn't need to be that clumsy of a fool.

He owed it to himself and what he had with Van to make the rest of his life as great as it could be. His happiness had to reside in himself, not in another person or in what could have been.

It was a lesson Zach needed to be reminded of again.

"Thank you," he told Gary and then kissed him on the cheek. "You've been a wonderful friend."

Gary basked in the compliment. "I know. I'm wonderful at everything I do."

"And humble," Quinn added as he drew Gary into his arms.

"You love me, Bobby Quinn, and you know it."

Quinn kissed Gary tenderly. "More and more every day."

"That's what I want," he told them. "To find a love like yours."

"What you find, Zachary, will be even better. Because it'll be yours."

Gary was right. Yet again. His happily-ever-after would burn brighter than anything else he'd ever seen or experienced. All he had to do now was find it.

Just then, the music from the dance floor stopped, and feedback surged through the speakers. Zach and everyone around them flinched while plugging their ears with their fingers. When the teeth-shattering noise ended, a familiar voice took its place.

"Can I have your attention, please?"

Zach and everyone else at tea turned their attention to a small platform set up in front of the railing around the pool. The raised area, which typically spotlighted oiled-up go-go boys, had been decorated with red-and-black streamers set up before a makeshift red curtain that hid the small area behind. Zach had noticed the stage earlier but didn't give it a second thought. He'd seen the dancer areas decked out with stripper poles and even an improvised outdoor shower, so when he saw what resembled a small theater, he simply figured it to be yet another elaborate presentation of man meat on display.

But now, the hairy tomato named Tripp, who was also Van's director, stood on the stage, and a knot formed in the pit of Zach's stomach. Tripp didn't have to say any more. Zach understood what was going on.

They were promoting Van's latest release from Nasty Boy Studios, and he had no intention of sticking around for that.

As Tripp launched into a speech about the premiere movies released by his studio, he turned around to escape, but the crowd had pressed tightly together, making passage impossible.

"I need to get out of here," he said, his voice panicked. He couldn't be there to hear this, especially if Van took the stage as Hart Throb. While he might have embraced his newfound strength of character and more positive outlook on life, he had no desire to watch the man he still loved endorse a movie where other men fucked him senseless.

"This place is jam-packed," Tara told him as she strained against the boys pushing her forward. "There's nowhere to go."

"I can't stay," he said as he tried to wedge himself forward.

"Zach, just stop," Quinn told him with a slight pat on the back. "There's no way any of us are getting out of here."

"Bobby Quinn's right, Zachary. Just look around you. We're packed in tighter than a bottom getting double-penetrated by two horse-hung tops."

Zach surveyed his surroundings. His friends were right. The hundreds of men who filled the entire length of the deck and the dance floor a few minutes before now all crowded around the small stage, where Tripp stood addressing the assembled horde.

Not a spare inch of space existed that would allow him to slip through to the exit more than a hundred feet away.

"For those of you who don't already know," Tripp said as his voice came back into focus for Zach, "we've been here in Provincetown filming the latest and greatest release from Nasty Boy Studios."

The crowd erupted in applause, and each clap made Zach's heart plunge farther down into his stomach.

"We went looking for a place even hotter and hornier than San Francisco or Fire Island, and I think we found what we'd been looking for here in Provincetown."

This time, the men hollered in approval. Every man, including Zach, had firsthand experience of the debauchery enjoyed on the Cape.

"We wanted to make a film that would give you masturbating motherfuckers carpal tunnel. We set out to make a movie that would require you to keep a cold pack close by to ice your junk because your cocks would be so hard it hurt. After all, there's no better way to spend your days in Provincetown than with a dick in your mouth or up your ass. Or however you prefer to enjoy a nice piece of meat. And that's just what we've done for all you guys who like to watch guys fuck other guys."

The crowd roared in unison, stamping their feet on the wooden deck so vigorously Zach thought for certain they'd all crash down onto the beach below.

"Slow, steady breaths," Gary advised behind him. He wrapped his arms lovingly around Zach and kissed the nape of his neck. "Sometimes the things we dread the most turn out to be the best things for us in the end."

What the hell did that mean? How was this going to be good for him? Gary obviously knew more than he was letting on.

"Now, you've been asking for weeks what the name of this new film would be. You've been clogging our web site with questions, trying to ferret out information like the curious little fuckers you are. Well, we're here today to answer those questions."

Tripp paused onstage for effect as the thundering crowd slowly grew quiet in anticipation. He then walked over to a string that hung to the right of the stage and wrapped his hairy, little hands around it. "The name of our upcoming release is…." he paused again and pulled the string and a banner uncoiled from the right of the curtain and spread out to the left with the name of the film printed on it. "*The Holes I Wanted.* A movie filled with the bottoms you've all dreamed of drilling and the tops you've wanted to plug your holes!"

The crowd whooped and pounded their fists in the air, their sexual frenzy stirred up by Tripp's tantalizing words.

"Now, before we go any further, I have to ask you a question. Would you like to meet the hot tops, who'll be busting their nuts for your pleasure?"

"Yes!" the crowd screamed in unison, to which Tripp nodded, pretending to be stupid for asking such an obvious question.

"Well, here they are," he said as the curtain opened, and five hot men dressed in skimpy swimsuits that barely contained their bulges paraded about onstage. The men around him squealed in delight as Tripp called out their names. "Brick Hard, Tom Cougar, Rod Major, Buck Wylde, and Ram Steele.

"Now, what about the stars of our show? The bottoms who take it all hard and nasty just the way you like it? Would you like to meet them?" When the crowd screamed even louder, Tripp closed the curtain, and this time when he opened it again, four hot guys dressed in even skimpier swimsuits than their top costars pranced onstage.

Zach didn't hear the names of these men because he could only focus on the fact that Van wasn't up there. He craned his neck left and right, straining to see around the raised hands and screaming men all around him.

"Where's Van?" he asked. Gary, Quinn, and Tara shrugged, but all three of them were smiling. Something was most definitely up.

"I'm not sure," Tara replied, obviously lying through her teeth. "He should be up there. He *is* in the movie."

"I know that," Zach told her, trying not to sound annoyed. "Then why isn't he up there? The three of you look guilty for some reason. What do you know?"

"Why would we know anything?" Gary asked. His sparkling eyes betrayed him. He obviously held some secret. "Van's the biggest star the studio has right now. He's probably going to make a grand entrance."

Zach didn't like the answer, but Gary could be right. He'd been right about so much so far. It made sense that Hart Throb would be the last one to take the stage. From what he'd learned, Hart had become their biggest seller, so it made sense he got special treatment.

Still, for a brief moment, he had a glimmer of hope that the reason Van wasn't onstage was because he was right now looking for Zach, to tell him that he'd been wrong. That he loved him too.

"But wait a minute," Tripp said from onstage. He walked back and forth, counting the actors as they posed for the cameras by flexing their muscles or pulling down their suits to let their asses or hairy crotches peek out from the fabric. "There's someone missing. Isn't there?"

At that moment, everyone started repeating two words. "Hart. Throb. Hart. Throb."

Their voices chanted in unison, as if they were invoking some spell that once cast would bring the one they wanted, the one they all longed for, onto the platform before them.

"You're right," Tripp called back as the curtain once again fell shut. "We're missing the brightest star at Nasty Boy Studios. Hart Throb."

When the curtain opened again, Van stood on stage, dressed not in a tight, barely there swimsuit, but in a white muscle shirt and skintight jeans. The crowd either didn't notice or they didn't care that Van hadn't been dressed up like his costars.

In fact, he looked so different from everyone else. Just why was that?

Instead of parading around, Van just stood there, center stage, staring out into the mob and scanning the face of every man in the crowd.

"And our surprises aren't done yet," Tripp announced as he crossed over to stand next to Van. "We planned on making *The Holes I Wanted* a classic, a film that would be talked about for years to come, and we've done that not only with the hot guys and the fabulous locations of our shoots, but by what we are going to reveal to you today. For the first time ever. And this revelation is guaranteed to make this film an instant collector's item." Tripp stared out into the quiet crowd. "Would you like to know what that surprise is?"

Once again, the gathered men answered in a resounding yes. Zach even found himself echoing their desire to know.

Without another word, he handed the microphone over to Van.

When Van held the mic in his hands, he proceeded to the edge of the stage as every single person on the deck grew impatiently quiet.

"First of all," Van said, "I want to thank everyone for your support of my career. You've been the best fans a guy could've ever hoped for." The crowd yelled their appreciation, with a few guys screaming out that they loved Hart, before quickly becoming silent again. "And when I signed on to do this film and even suggested we shoot it here in P-town, I'd hoped to make the hottest, nastiest film for each and every one of you guys. To show how much I love you all. And I think I've succeeded in making this video one you're not likely to forget anytime soon."

A cacophonous roar exploded around Zach as more people applauded and professed their love for Hart.

"Because you see, *The Holes I Wanted* will be the last film of Hart Throb's career."

A low murmur spread throughout the crowd, as each man turned to the one next to him wondering if they'd all heard correctly. After a few moments, the murmur grew to a buzz of discontent, as guys started shouting out questions like "Why?" or "Is this some publicity stunt?"

Van answered them all with a simple shake of his head as he continued to scan the crowd until Van found Zach.

All Zach could do was stare back in silent amazement when Van's steel-blue gaze locked on to his. In Van's stare, the wonder and awe with which Van had previously looked upon him returned. In response to the smile that drew itself across Van's lips, his heart fluttered to life once again.

He hadn't lost Van to Hart Throb. Hart had been abandoned for Van Pierce.

"You see, something happened to me over the last few days," Van told the crowd while he still only stared at Zach. "I met a guy. He literally tripped his way into my life, and when I first saw him, he was wearing the most god-awful clothes I'd ever seen anyone wear. But there was something about him. Something that drew me to him. Something that made me want to date, when I'd given up on dating so long ago."

Van pointed at Zach, and the crowd before him slowly parted until a path opened up that led from Zach to the stage.

"It's time for you to move now," Gary whispered to him from behind. "This is what we brought you here for." He then gave Zach a push that set Zach stumbling forward and across the deck to where Van waited onstage.

"I knew it was a mistake," Van said, once again speaking into the microphone. "There was no way someone like me who lives here in Provincetown should *ever* get involved with a man from Texas who had absolutely no fucking clue who Hart Throb was."

When he reached the end of the stage, Van held out his hand and helped Zach hop onto the platform without incident or embarrassing blunder. Zach had never made such a graceful trek before, and he owed his newfound grace to the man who now held his hand in front of hundreds of adoring fans.

"But I couldn't help myself," Van continued as he turned sideways to stare into Zach's eyes. "We've hit a snag or two the past few days. Both of us stubborn as mules. And even when this sexy, redheaded beast came to my shoot this afternoon, telling me how he felt and that he didn't care about Hart Throb. That all he cared about was me. I still didn't embrace what he so willingly and so selflessly offered."

Van pulled him closer before resting his forehead on Zach's with only the microphone between them. "You see, Zach," Van said, still talking into the mic but only addressing him. "I'm not used to being pursued as Van. I have guys climbing over themselves to get at Hart, but when it comes to who I truly am, no man has ever really wanted Van Pierce. But you did."

"And I still do," Zach whispered softly into the microphone. His words were met with a unified "aw" from the crowd before them.

"But I didn't believe it. I didn't think you could *truly* want me. For who I am. Until I read your book. I'd never known someone to bare his soul as you did. To be brave enough to put in writing and present to the world what he wanted. And what I got from reading your book is that you want me."

He nodded. "I've never wanted anyone more," he told Van. "I love you."

"And I love you too."

Van then tossed the microphone into the crowd, and when their lips once again pressed together, the roar of those around them completely disappeared, for Zach's future no longer existed in some faraway imagined place.

Zach held his future in his arms.

Chapter Twenty-Seven

ZACH had never been happier than he was at that moment. Not only was he naked in bed with the man he loved, not only had Van professed his love for Zach in front of everyone at tea and announced that he'd be retiring Hart Throb, but he once again smelled like Van from head to toe.

They'd spent the remainder of the evening making up for the last few days they lost. They made love on the floor in the living room, on top of the dining room table, against the kitchen sink, on the private back-patio deck, and just now finished up on the bed that they would share for the rest of their time together.

Whenever he took deep breaths, which he'd been doing every few minutes, he could smell Van's stink on his beard, and when he licked his lips, he could taste every single place on Van's body where his mouth had roamed—against his soft lips, over his hard cock, and between his beautiful ass cheeks.

He doubted he smelled like himself at all, and that was the way he liked it.

Now, though, as Van snuggled into his embrace, his head resting on Zach's right shoulder and his left leg draped over Zach's waist, he dreaded the approaching dawn, which was only a few hours away.

The coming light meant he'd have to leave Van behind. He'd have to return to Houston while Van remained here. Their separation, however, would only be temporary.

They had managed to discuss their future in between their marathon lovemaking.

Zach planned on collecting the rest of his things and quitting his job. It was time to pursue his dream of being an author full time, and once his campus found someone to replace him, he'd return to Provincetown permanently. Not just to be with Van, who was a big reason for the move, but to also be with the friends he'd made and to reclaim the life he'd managed to cobble together in just a few days on the Cape.

Zach hoped he'd only be gone a few months. Six at the most.

While he closed out his life in Texas, Van had plans to start anew here. He had some money saved up from his porn gigs, enough to last him a few months while he got some training in hotel services. Sebastian and Jonas, the innkeepers at the Carpe Diem, the bed-and-breakfast where Zach had tried to stay when he first planned his trip, apparently jumped at the chance to hire Van.

They wanted to share some of the burdens of their business so they could enjoy themselves more. Their gracious offer had been a tad self-serving. They planned on advertising that former porn star Hart Throb now worked for their bed-and-breakfast and banked on Hart's popularity to bring in even more guests to their establishment.

Even knowing that they'd fly back and forth as often as possible until they were together full time, he didn't want to imagine spending one moment without Van in his arms or Van's smell on his body.

"Can I take one of your shirts with me tomorrow?" he asked before he kissed the top of Van's head. "I want to be able to smell you any time I want."

"Sure," Van replied as he gazed up at him. Van's blue eyes looked wet, which meant he regretted the impending departure as much as Zach did. "As long as I can have one of yours."

"Naturally," he told Van. "You liked the green one the best right?"

"Nope," Van replied as he crawled on top of him and rested his head on Zach's pale chest. "I want the one I first met you in."

"The blousy blue-and-white one? I thought everyone hated the way I looked in my old clothes."

Van shook his head. "I never hated the way you looked," he admitted. "I think I fell in love with you the first time I saw you. Shitty clothes, fucked-up hair, and all!"

He couldn't help the cheesy grin that pranced across his face. If he looked like a grinning idiot, he didn't care. "Okay, then. It's yours."

"Yay!" Van cheered before he gnawed on Zach's sore right nipple.

"Ouch!" he called out. "That one's sensitive now."

"I know," Van confessed with his trademark wide grin. "That's why I'm doing it." He then proceeded to clamp back down and chew.

"You little stinker!" he laughed as he rolled over on top of Van. He held Van's head between his hands and rained kisses upon his forehead, cheeks, and nose. "I'm gonna have to torture you with kisses now."

"That's not torture," Van told him as he squeezed Zach's ass. "That's what I like."

He halted the deluge of kisses and hovered over Van's lips. "I know what else you like," he said as he parted Van's legs with his right hand and rested in between them.

After wrapping his limbs around Zach's midsection, Van wiggled his ass against Zach's cock. "Yes, you do."

Zach then brought his lips once again onto Van's, and their tongues danced wildly in each other's mouths. Never had he craved someone's body as much as he desired Van's. He just couldn't get enough of him, and he wanted one final joining of their bodies before they spent the next few weeks or months away from each other.

He'd reached across the bed to grab the almost empty box of condoms when Van stopped him. "No," he said. "Not that. Not this time."

Although he tried not to look disappointed, Zach withdrew his hand and allowed his fingers to rake through Van's hair. They'd just had a whole lot of sex in a few hours. Van was probably tired and far too sore to go another round. "Okay," he said. "Let's sleep, then."

"Are you crazy?" Van said as he squeezed his legs like a vise around Zach. "There's no way I'm wasting a moment with you unconscious."

Now Zach was really confused. "I don't understand, then."

"I want you inside me again," Van told him. "I need you inside me. But this time, without anything coming between your skin and mine."

"Without a condom?" he asked.

When Van nodded, he didn't know how to proceed. He found the idea hot, and he wanted nothing more than to slip his bare cock inside Van. He'd just never done that before. He'd always been careful with the men he slept with, even in long-term relationships like he had with Ben.

And he'd been right to do so. Ben had probably been cheating on him. If he hadn't been using condoms, there was no telling what he might have picked up by now. But as he looked down into Van's eyes, the eyes of a man he wanted to give himself completely to, the need for caution floated away.

He and Van were together forever, and just as he would do nothing that would ever endanger Van's life, Van would do nothing to place his in jeopardy.

"I tested negative last month," Van told him. "And I've never barebacked with anyone before. Like I already told you. I know this is a big thing to ask, and if you don't want to, I completely understand. I just thought that—"

But before Van could continue, Zach pressed his index finger against his lips. "My last checkup was three weeks ago. I was negative too. And I always use condoms."

"Like I said, I'm fine with it," Van said as he stretched out his arm for the box.

He reached out and grabbed Van's hands and laced their fingers together. "That's why I'm glad that my first time without them will be with you." He reached over to the bedside table and grabbed the bottle of lube. After generously squirting its contents into his left hand, he coated his cock and then rubbed the remaining liquid onto Van's twitching bud, already dripping with sweat and lubricant from their previous encounters.

He grabbed the base of his cock and then pointed it at the entrance to Van's body, the place that would truly unite them as one for the first time, and he stared down into Van's hungry eyes.

"I love you, Van."

Van grabbed his hand to help him bring Zach's hard cock against his ass. "And I love you."

Then, together, they both inserted Zach inside Van.

He let out a loud gasp as Van's smooth insides wrapped around his unsheathed cock and pulled him farther inside. Van also cried out, raising his hips upward as he worked every inch of Zach inside him until Zach lay firmly entrenched within.

For a few moments, he didn't move. He wanted to cherish the feeling of being inside Van unencumbered. The heat of Van's insides radiated all around him, traveling up Zach's cock and coursing throughout Zach's body. Every part of him touched every part of Van, and he didn't want the moment to end.

"Oh my God, this feels great!" Van whispered before he kissed Zach's lips and cheeks. "I can feel you everywhere. Deep inside me. Your cock throbbing. Your balls against me. Your arms around me. Your breath on my skin." He slipped his tongue inside Zach's mouth as he rocked his hips up and down on Zach's dick. "All I need is one final thing of yours inside me. Your cum."

He growled as he thrust inside Van, but he didn't pick up the pace that Van so eagerly wanted. With glacial slowness, he slid himself in and out of Van, sending shivers of pleasure creeping down their already sweat-drenched bodies.

"I need to be filled by you," Van urged as he tried to buck harder against him, but Zach slid his hands down to Van's waist and slowed the frenzy that had taken control of his hips. He used his hands to guide Van, to force him to rock to a slow, steady beat that still mirrored the primal lust that held them both in its grasp.

"Please," Van pleaded. His eyes begged for Zach to fuck him faster and harder, but Zach maintained the steady motion as he trailed one finger down the length of Van's side until he reached underneath to tease Van's buttcrack with not only his cock but with the finger that coursed through the wetness that their bodies used to glide together.

As he teased Van with the finger, Van moaned in pleasure, finally giving himself over to the fact that Zach held complete dominion over his body, and that Van had no choice but to go along for the ride. With Van's surrender, Van opened up, and Zach fell deeper and deeper into Van's body, completely until he was encompassed by Van's internal embrace.

"I could stay inside you like this forever," he told Van.

"I'm counting on it," Van replied.

The leisurely pace of their union that Zach enforced upon them opened up a chasm of anticipation filled by their moans and grunts and the smell of sex and sweat in the air. Zach raised Van's arms above his head and dove into each sweaty pit, coating himself with the musk Zach now craved in order to survive.

Van shuddered as Zach's tongue swirled within his hairy armpit while Zach slowly advanced and withdrew his cock from the shuddering molten lake that had become Van's ass. Their entire world shrank down to the need that rested deep within Van's ass and the burning passion that charted a path in Zach's groin.

They become entranced and ensnared, unable to see or think. Only able to feel Zach's cockhead as it slid past Van's puckering flesh, digging inside with animalistic need as their heartbeats pulsed around their lovemaking, beating faster and faster the longer they coupled.

Zach slowly began to pick up the pace as his rigid cock drove between Van's clenching cheeks. The pressing of their flesh, the mingling of their pubic hairs, and their slick bodies increased the yearning for needed release.

With his balls churning, Zach let escape a low moan that signaled the final act, and Van quickly read the sign. He too picked up the tempo, driving his hips upward to meet Zach's now pounding thrusts. He furiously yanked on his cock, obviously lost in the pleasure of Zach's cock massaging the bundle of nerves inside Van's body.

After a few jerking motions, Van exploded all over himself. Long jets of cum splashed across his chest and abs as Van's ass clenched down upon Zach's cock. The throbbing flesh surrounding Zach's cock brought him quickly to the edge.

"Are you ready?" Zach grunted as Van wrapped his arms around Zach's neck to bring him closer.

"Yes, baby," Van told him. "Come inside me. Give it to me. Give me all of it."

"Fuck!" Zach screamed as his cock went off inside Van, blasting his insides with the love they'd both brought forth.

When the trembling in Zach's body finally subsided, he collapsed on top of Van, breathing deeply the scent of the man he loved and the only man he'd ever shared so intimate an encounter with.

"That was awesome," Van panted. "We need to do that more often."

"We will," he told Van. "That was only the beginning."

"That sounds like a challenge."

He kissed Van's lips. "It is. Think you can handle it?"

"Are you kidding me?" Van asked before he leaned into Zach's kiss and drew Zach's tongue between his lips. "Challenge accepted."

JACOB Z. FLORES lives a double life. During the day, he is a respected college English professor and midlevel administrator. At night and during his summer vacation, he loosens the tie and tosses aside the trendy sports coat to write man-on-man fiction, where the hard-ass assessor of freshmen-level composition turns his attention to the firm posteriors and other rigid appendages of the characters in his fictional world.

Summers in Provincetown, Massachusetts, provide Jacob with inspiration for his fiction. The abundance of barely clothed man flesh and daily debauchery stimulates his personal muse. When he isn't stroking the keyboard, Jacob spends time with his husband, Bruce, their three children, and two dogs, who represent a bright blue blip in an otherwise predominantly red swath in south Texas.

You can follow Jacob's musings on his blog at http://jacobzflores.com or become a part of his social media network by visiting

http://www.facebook.com/jacob.flores2

or http://twitter.com/#!/JacobZFlores.

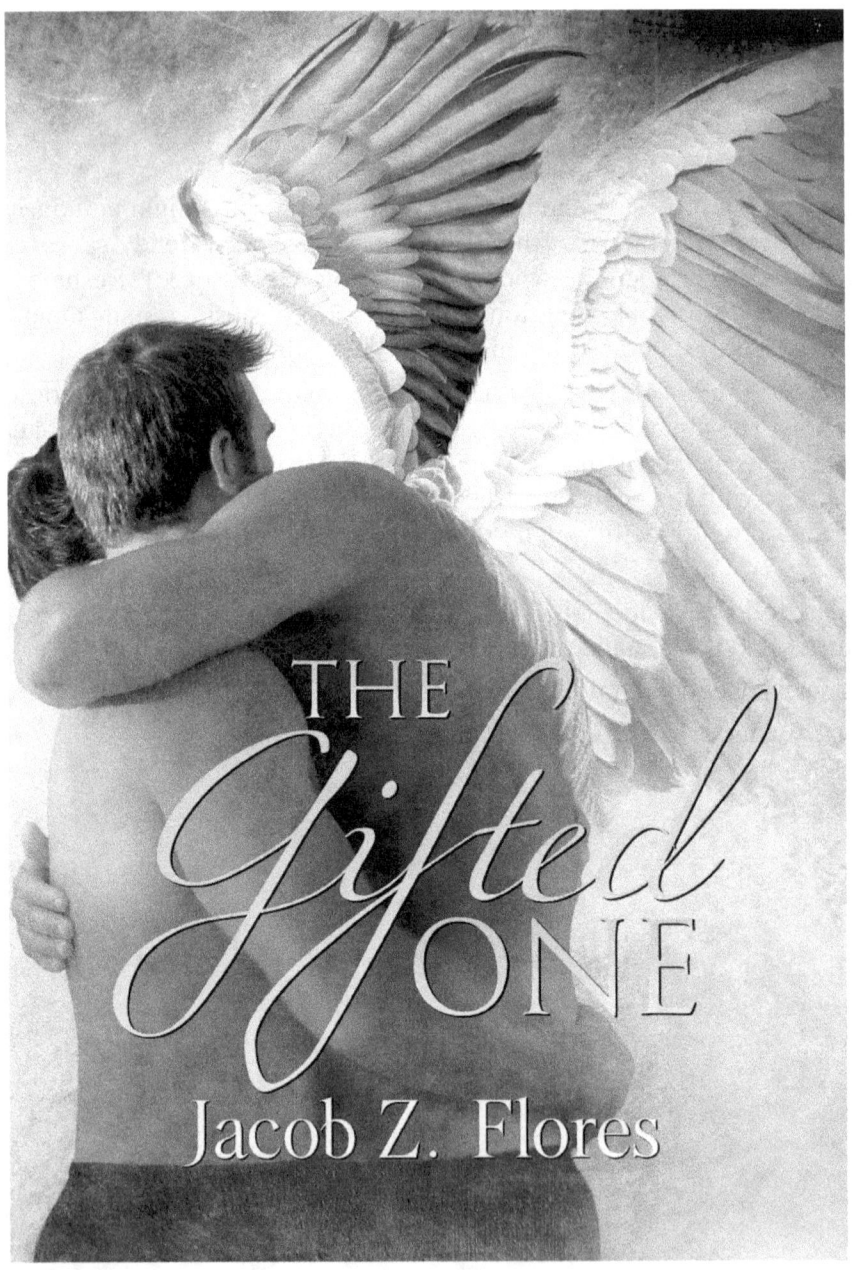

THE
Gifted
ONE

Jacob Z. Flores

http://www.dreamspinnerpress.com

Romance from DREAMSPINNER PRESS

www.ingramcontent.com/pod-product-compliance
Lightning Source LLC
Chambersburg PA
CBHW051627260626
47170CB00004B/1074